Michael

FROM GRACE

KRIS NORRIS

NORRIS BOOKS

OTHER BOOKS BY KRIS NORRIS

SINGLES

CENTERFOLD

KEEPING FAITH

IRON WILL

MY SOUL TO KEEP

RICOCHET

ROPE'S END

SERIES

'TIL DEATH

1 - DEADLY VISION

2 - DEADLY OBSESSION

3 - DEADLY DECEPTION

BROTHERHOOD PROTECTORS ~ Elle James

1 - MIDNIGHT RANGER

2 – CARVED IN ICE

3 - GOING IN BLIND

COLLATERAL DAMAGE

1 - FORCE OF NATURE

DARK PROPHECY

MICHAEL

FROM GRACE

KRIS NORRIS

Michael

Edited by Chris Allen-Riley and Jessica Bimberg

Cover Art by Kris Norris

Published by Kris Norris

Released in print ~ June, 2017

To those who keep getting back up. Because even if you fall flat on your face, you're still technically moving forward.

And to Kyle, Jared and Sydney for always believing in me, whether it be in work or in play.

CHAPTER ONE

What am I doing?

Michael groaned inwardly as he stood at the edge of the pond, staring at the shore across from him. Sunlight danced along the calm surface, reflecting the sinking orb on the distant horizon. Frogs called to each other in the tangle of reeds at the edge of the water, the low sound adding to the surreal atmosphere of the glen. A light breeze rustled the feathers on his wings, tousling his hair across his face, and for a moment, his reasons for visiting the faery realm didn't seem so crazy.

A door creaked open behind him, followed by the pad of footsteps across the stone path. The noises around Michael paused, almost as if the surrounding land was taking a long, slow breath before picking up, again, the constant chatter not as peaceful as it had been seconds before. A sigh lit the air, followed by a disgruntled huff.

"Tell me, Michael. How long are you going to stand there, avoiding him?"

Michael sighed under his breath before glancing

over his shoulder. Gabriel leaned against a tree, his silhouette illuminated by the warm light of his brother's cottage. The angel's shadow stretched out in front of him, the edges joining with the darkness on the soft grass. His grace shimmered around him—not quite as luminous as it'd once been. More of a muted fluorescence than the blinding light Michael knew surrounded him. A testament to the combined energy of Gabriel and his mate Kei—a fire mage whose magic had been woven through his brother's grace when the sorcerer had inadvertently saved Gabriel from falling. Though Michael guessed Gabriel hadn't minded the way the event had turned out—Kei and Gabriel. Together.

Michael looked back at the setting sun, watching the different shades of orange and yellow chase each other across the sky. He'd spent more than a few nights watching the sphere dip below the horizon—enjoying the simple pleasures he'd allowed to slip away. Vowing to make the most of his second chance.

Pain and anger churned in his gut. He'd nearly died at the hands of Abaddon. If it hadn't been for Gabriel, Kei and Greyson, Michael never would have survived. A chuckle sounded inside his head. Lucifer. His brother had been the one to free Michael from Abaddon's cage. Had healed him when Gabriel had been unable, and that one act had opened a channel between them. Not that Michael couldn't block the other man. He just didn't seem to have the energy most days. Penance for not being strong enough. For allowing his complacency to cloud his judgment. Blind him from seeing what had been festering around him for years.

He drew a deep breath. "I think Kei's love of fire has melted your brain, brother. You're talking nonsense."

Gabriel snorted. "Still in denial, I see."

Michael huffed as the other angel moved in beside him, the man's gaze taking in the colors staining the clouds. "There's nothing to deny. I was just watching the sun set. Something I've taken for granted for far too long."

"No, you were trying to catch a glimpse of Greyson as he headed out for his nightly patrol."

It was no secret that Greyson checked the various portals dotted along the perimeter each day, a fact that had made watching the fae dangerously easy.

Michael shrugged off the comment. "The portals have been warded, even against us. If Greyson hadn't given me a means of bypassing them, I wouldn't be here. Which means he doesn't need to perform nightly checks."

"We both know Greyson sees it differently. Ever since Uriel popped in for an uninvited visit, he's been obsessively vigilant about security."

Michael nodded, despite the jab of guilt. Just another way he'd failed as God's Warrior. He'd allowed Uriel to destroy parts of the faery realm. Kill some of Greyson's people. And Michael knew it was a burden he'd never truly shed. "That's not his cross to bear."

Gabriel arched a brow. "Nor is it yours."

Michael huffed, staring at the water, again, when the door behind them opened and closed. Another shadowed silhouette moved across the ground. Michael didn't need to turn to know Kei had joined them. His brother's mate was rarely far away, especially with them still learning how to share their power.

Kei gave Michael a pat on his shoulder before stopping

in front of Gabriel. He leaned into the other angel's chest as Gabriel wrapped one arm around his upper torso. "What is it with you angel types and all the guilt?"

Michael glanced at the mage. "I'm merely shouldering what is ultimately mine. If I hadn't allowed Abbadon to imprison me—"

"The guy was crazy. No one's responsible for his decisions, but him. And I doubt either of you would have believed your own brothers would rise against you."

"Regardless…" Michael glanced away. Arguing with Kei and Gabriel was about as effective as arguing with Greyson. Stubborn didn't begin to describe their joint personalities.

He raised his chin. "So, why allow Greyson to continue his obsession?"

Kei laughed. "He's about as reasonable as you are. But you're only lying to yourself if you think he's this vigilant because he's afraid something might get past his wards."

"Then, why make the nightly rounds?"

Kei's lips lifted into an amused smile. "Maybe because he's got ulterior motives for following such a strict, dare I say, predictable schedule."

Michael ignored the insinuation. "I'm sure having an archangel lay waste to your homeland changes your priorities."

"Please. I've known Grey for decades. Trust me. Not much gets to him. Which brings me back to my hypothesis that he's not scouring the borderlands for the good of his people."

"Why else would he spend all that time alone?"

Gabriel rolled his eyes. "Probably because he's hoping he won't be alone for long."

Michael released a weary breath, allowing his head to bow to his chest as his shoulders drooped. "Gabriel…"

"Why are you making this so difficult? I saw the way Greyson looked at you. Not to mention the fact he finds a way to bring you up in damn near every conversation. And while I know the reasons for his people giving Kei and me a home here are pure, he doesn't visit us as often as he does because he lacks for companionship. He's hoping my brother will drop by."

Michael glanced at him. "Did he tell you that?"

Kei groaned, pulling free of Gabriel's embrace to fully face Michael. "He didn't have to. The guy's an open book. But what I find puzzling is why you come here then hide your presence from him."

"It's…complicated."

Gabriel nudged him. "What's so complicated? He likes you, you like him…"

"I'm an archangel."

Gabriel laughed. "As am I."

"You're…different."

"Why?" Gabriel's gaze slid to Kei. "Because I have a mate? Or because I'm not as pure as I used to be?"

"I didn't mean…" Michael raked a hand through his hair as his wings fluttered with impatience. This wasn't going the way he'd hoped, not that talking about Greyson was ever a direction Michael enjoyed going. The fae clouded Michael's judgment. Made him consider paths he'd never imagined he'd choose. Made him dream of a life he couldn't have.

He crossed his arms over his chest, hoping to change the subject. "What you and Kei have…it's a bond very few of us will ever find. It makes you special."

"I'm not special, brother. I just listened to my heart instead of all the reasons I shouldn't let my mate in."

"I'm a warrior."

Kei shrugged. "So's Grey."

Michael threw up his hands, stomping away before spinning. "He's a prince. Heir to the throne. His father is practically a god."

"And yours is." Gabriel gave him a small smile. "The only difference between us, Michael, is that I wasn't afraid to make myself vulnerable. To admit that there's someone else who means more to me than...me."

"Don't you mean your job? Your faith?"

"It doesn't have to be like that. I still serve Father as I did before. I'm just not a slave to that faith. I see the bigger picture, and so can you."

"I'm God's Warrior. I can't put my own happiness, my needs, above those of His children."

"If Father didn't want us to fall in love, we wouldn't have fated mates lurking around, waiting for us to find them."

Michael glanced across the pond as a man appeared on the far side. The fae paused, lifting his head to the sky before letting it fall to his chest as he trudged off. Even this far away, Michael knew it was Greyson. He felt the other man's soul beckoning to him like a beacon. Heard the echoed beat of Grey's heart thrum in his head. Michael's wings twitched, again, and he had to fist his hands at his side to stop from simply taking to the sky—closing the distance between them.

Gabriel cupped his shoulder. "Greyson's a good man. A worthy man."

"He's not a man, and I'm afraid I'm the one who

isn't worthy. If you and Kei hadn't intervened...I'd be dead."

"And if Kei hadn't accidentally summoned me, so would I."

"I don't think it was an accident."

"The point is, we all played a part. You saved us equally, I assure you."

Michael shook his head. "All I did was look like a fool."

"Michael—"

"I had to have Lucifer heal me. He broke the cage's warding. *Lucifer*. And he didn't even ask for anything in return. Do you know how that gnaws at me?"

Gabriel released a weary breath. "Lucifer isn't our enemy. He's our brother. While I realize his past isn't exemplary, he's still family. And if I've learned anything from my time in this realm, it's that family matters. Greyson would never hold that against you. In fact, it was his idea to summon the man, which leads me to think he doesn't have any issues with Lucifer being your brother." Gabriel squared his shoulders, drawing himself up. "As I recall, Lucifer healed Kei, as well. And I'm thankful for it."

"That's different. Kei nearly died summoning Lucifer. He owed your mate."

"Now, you're just grasping at excuses. This has nothing to do with Lucifer or Father and everything to do with the fact you're scared."

"Of course, I'm scared. If Abaddon can get to me, if my own brothers can cast me out—"

"You're an archangel. There's always going to be someone who has a grievance with you."

"Then you know why I can't ask Greyson to give himself to me. Not when I know there are more than a few entities who'd love to use my feelings against me. He'd be a target."

"And you think Kei isn't? Need I remind you that Greyson chose to accompany us. To face Abaddon. He doesn't scare easily." Gabriel motioned to where Greyson had reappeared across the water. "Whether he wants to take the risk is his choice."

"Not if he never knows how I feel." Michael held up his hand, once again, fighting the urge to take to the sky and join the other man on the opposite side of the water. "It's better this way. Without me...he'll be free to find someone who can give him what he needs."

"All he needs is for you to let him in. To love him despite the odds. The risks. It's all any of us can ask for. And often more than we deserve."

"He'll find someone else. Someone far more worthy than I."

Gabriel grabbed his wrist when Michael turned to leave. "Faeries aren't that different from us, Michael. He only has one true soul, as well."

"Then, it's best I leave so he can find it."

"Michael—"

Michael ignored Gabriel's call as he took off, heading for the portal back to his world. To where there was order. Peace. The sharp pain through his chest didn't mean anything, least of all that he cared for the fae.

CHAPTER TWO

"I know you're there, Michael."

Greyson poked at the bonfire he'd built next to the shoreline, watching as the flames flickered higher into the darkness. A bluish hue colored the fire where it kissed the wood, gradually shifting into a deep orange. Heat waves rose into the air, distorting the outlines of the trees in the background. The scent of cottonwood filled the glen, the heady fragrance easing some of the tension bunching his muscles.

He clenched his jaw, wondering how long it'd be before the archangel finally removed his glamour and materialized behind him. Or if his mate would choose to vanish—fly away without even acknowledging his presence.

Mate.

Christ, when had Greyson accepted the fact Michael, archangel and God's Warrior, was his true soul? That the sudden racing of Greyson's heart, the unrelenting urge to wrap his fingers around the other man's hair and taste his perfectly sculpted lips, meant anything more than uncontrolled lust? That Grey was worthy of someone so...pure?

The word settled uncomfortably in his gut. He was a playboy at best, and one good deed didn't erase a lifetime of ditching his responsibilities. Of allowing his sister to become one of Abaddon's victims. If he'd been the kind of man his people had needed, if he'd taken anything remotely serious, he knew in his heart she'd still be alive.

A soft fluttering noise sounded behind, followed by a rustle of wind across his back. The air thickened, the telltale strum of energy prickling Greyson's skin as Michael's glamour slowly diminished until Grey felt the angel's grace envelope him.

Grey inhaled, closing his eyes against the rush of power that rippled through the air. It swirled across his skin, bathing it in a yellowish glow before slowly fading. While he'd experienced his fair share of powerful beings, including his father and Kei's mate, Gabriel, nothing compared to the pure energy of Michael's grace.

Hushed footsteps padded the soft grass behind him, stopping a few feet away. "How did you know I was there?"

Greyson shrugged. He didn't need his inherent abilities as a prince of the faery realm to know Michael already knew the answer. Or that it was the truth that scared the angel more than anything else. "Please, angels aren't bad with glamours, but faeries pretty much invented them."

"I'm no ordinary angel. Only a few of my brothers should be able to sense my presence."

Greyson fisted his hands in order to stop from

spinning around—from grabbing Michael and shaking some sense into him. "We both know I'm not your brother."

He turned, wanting to see Michael's reaction when he finally stated what he'd felt since the first time he'd met the angelic man. "I'm the other possibility you don't want to admit exists."

Michael's lips twitched, his expression faltering as he stared at Greyson. The angel closed his eyes, drawing several long, slow breaths, before finally gazing at him again, only there was no mistaking the sadness in Michael's eyes. The restless shift of his feet as he stood there, his feathers rustling in the breeze, the iridescent pearl color reflecting the different shades of orange from the flickering flames of the bonfire. Indecision creased the lines around his mouth before he sighed and turned, walking a few paces away.

The angel's shoulders slumped as his head bowed toward his chest. "Greyson."

"Stop. Just...stop."

Michael tensed, his wings snapping with what looked like impatience before he spun, all semblance of indecision gone. He drew himself up, making Greyson's stomach clench and roll. This was the man Grey had fallen for. The archangel of lore whose courage and honor were legendary. The man who'd fought to save the world, even though he'd had to shove aside his personal feelings for his brother Lucifer to do it. Though Grey wondered if Michael saw himself the way Grey did. Majestic. Unwavering. Pure.

Christ, just staring at the way his grace shimmered like an exploding star around him made Grey want to stay in the man's presence and never leave. Forever feel the warmth of Michael's power. His love.

Greyson shook away the sentimental thoughts. Despite Michael's stance, there was no mistaking the look on the other man's face. The one that said he'd never willingly admit what Grey was to him. That he'd rather suffer alone than give himself to someone who obviously wasn't worthy of an archangel's soul.

Michael frowned, tilting his head to the side as if he thought Grey was crazy. "Is that what you think? That I see you as unworthy of my soul?"

Grey's heart skipped, then raced, making it hard to breathe. "Did you just read my thoughts?"

Michael glanced away, but there was no mistaking the flash of guilt Grey had seen in his eyes.

Greyson crossed his arms over his chest. "Still going to deny what we both know? Feel?"

Michael's gaze snapped to his. "There's nothing to deny. We're...friends, if I'm capable of having such a thing."

"Friends? That's your explanation? So can all your friends sense you when you're hiding behind your glamour? Can you read their thoughts, too?" He shook his head. "It's one thing to hide behind duty and honor, and another to lie to me to my face. All you have to do is tell me this..." he waved his hand back and forth, "...thing between us is one-sided. That you don't care, and I'll walk away. But don't stand there and pretend that what I'm experiencing isn't real. I think I deserve better than that."

The muscle in Michael's temple jumped as the angel clenched his jaw. "I never said it wasn't real."

"You're just not interested. Not affected the way I am."

Michael pursed his lips, the fine lines around his mouth tightening. "It's…complicated."

"Why? Because I'm not an angel?"

Michael furrowed his brow. "Why would that matter?"

"How the hell should I know? But there's got to be a reason you're shunning me, unless we're back to the simple explanation of you not being interested."

"Nothing with you is simple."

"That's not an answer." Greyson arched a brow. "Is it because I'm not female? I thought with Gabe and Kei being mates that wasn't a thing, but—"

"I'm free to love however I see fit."

"So it's just…me."

Michael groaned, carding his hand through his hair—poking it up in every direction. "Why are you pushing this?"

"You know why." Greyson threw up his hands when Michael merely stared at him. "You think I like this? That I enjoy being drawn to someone who probably won't ever return my feelings? Who is so bound by duty that he'll most likely never say what I need to hear?"

"I'm God's Warrior. I have…obligations."

"And I'm heir to the throne. True, Oberon will hopefully choose to rule for another five hundred years or so, but that doesn't negate the fact you're not the only one whose heritage affects their life."

"Then you understand why I have to remain distant."

"What I understand is that you're scared and hiding behind your legacy so you don't have to face the truth." Grey sighed. Arguing with an archangel was like arguing with his father. Stubborn didn't begin to describe them.

Grey drew a calming breath. The last thing he needed

was to get angry. In the end, Michael had to choose to be with him. Grey couldn't force the man any more than he could push aside the unrelenting voice in his head that demanded he lay his claim. Recite the ancient binding rite and join their souls. A union only death could sever.

Crickets chirped around them as Grey relaxed his shoulders, stuffing his hands in his pockets in an effort to stop himself from closing the distance and running his fingers along Michael's arms until he'd reached the angel's shoulders. Not that Grey would be able to stop there. He'd been longing to sink his hands in the other man's hair—wrap the golden strands around his fingers—finally discover if the locks were as soft as they looked.

"Greyson."

Grey cursed under his breath, focusing on Michael's face. "I'm trying, so cut me some slack." He rolled his shoulders a bit. "Just tell me this—if you're so damn determined to remain distant, why come here at all? And before you answer, you should know that I sense it when you travel through one of my wards."

Michael arched his brow. "You sense it when people pass through your wards?"

"I said *you*. That I sense *you*. Like I'm always telling Kei...words have meaning. And in this case, I was very specific, but that's not an answer." He took a step closer. "Why visit when you have no intentions of seeing this go any further? Do you enjoy taunting me?"

"I'd never knowingly hurt you. You know that."

"Do I? Because from where I'm standing you're a big blank slate. And try as I may, I can't figure you out. You come to my realm, then hide from me. You say what we have is complicated, yet you never say why." Grey shook his head. "You can't have it both ways, Michael."

His lips quirked a moment before the color rose on his cheeks. "Believe me, if I could stay away, I would. But..." He slammed his fists against his thighs, fluttering his wings in the process. "I care. More than I know I should. But if I cross that line—take you as my lover..."

Grey sighed as Michael closed his eyes, his mouth pursed into a slight grimace. While a part of Grey wanted to shake some sense into the other man, another understood the angel's turmoil. Felt his pain as if it were his own.

He closed the distance between them, palming Michael's chest. The angel's tunic bunched beneath his grip, the soft fabric gathering between his fingers. Michael's eyelids flew open, his gaze clashing with Grey's.

Grey took a moment to study the guy. To memorize the deep blue of Michael's eyes, the hint of pink in his lips. How the skin over his nose creased as he furrowed his brow. The flash of arousal that colored his cheeks.

Michael gripped Grey's wrists, holding his hands tight against his chest. Grey waited for the other man to shove him away, but Michael merely stood there, his heart pounding beneath Grey's touch, his harsh breath sounding around them.

Grey gave him an easy smile when Michael's hold tightened. "Surely, you've taken lovers before."

The muscle in his jaw tensed. "I have, but..." He averted his gaze. "You're different."

Grey's stomach clenched, and he knew those two words might be the closest Michael ever got to admitting they were mates. That there was so much more than mere attraction between them.

He forced himself to shrug, despite the frantic beating of his heart. "I don't have to be different."

Michael slid his focus back to Grey's face. "What do you mean?"

"What if it didn't have to be about anything more than one night?"

Michael frowned. "One night?"

"Are you going to repeat everything I say?"

"Only when you're not making any sense because we both know neither of us would settle for one night."

"Are you offering more?"

His jaw muscle jumped again. "It's not that I don't want to. It's just—"

"Complicated."

He muttered under his breath. "You make it sound as if I want to hurt you. Deny us, both."

"All I'm asking for is one night." He eased free of Michael's hold then took a single step back. "I'll make this simple. Gabe mentioned that every angel has a sanctuary on Earth. A place no one else knows about. If you accept my offer, and grant me one night with you, all you have to do is picture that sanctuary, and I'll meet you there tomorrow night. Sunset."

Michael frowned.

Grey smiled. "Trust me. I'll know where to go."

"How did you know I was questioning that?"

"Same way I'll know the location of your sanctuary." He held up one hand. "I won't say it. Won't claim to be anything other than what you need me to be." He backed away. "One night, Michael, then I'll never ask again. Think about it."

He turned, striding purposefully away from the pond. He didn't need to glance over his shoulder to know Michael had taken to the air. Grey felt it. Felt the other man pass through his ward as he used the closest portal, not that leaving the faery realm would sever their connection. An echoed strum of Michael's heartbeat sounded in Grey's head, the firm press of Michael's chest still a ghosted memory on his palms.

Grey hung his head. What had he been thinking? Michael was right. Greyson would never be satisfied with only one night. But under the circumstances, he'd take whatever he could get. Even if it meant he'd spend the next millennium alone.

CHAPTER THREE

This is a colossal mistake.

Michael mentally told his inner voice to shut up as he paced the length of the room, once again warring with the reasons he'd journeyed to the small cabin not far from where Abaddon had nearly killed him. And the cruel irony that his sanctuary was so close to where he'd almost been responsible for starting the apocalypse hadn't been lost on him.

"Christ, Michael, you're always so dramatic. Stop talking to yourself and stop agonizing over the past. We kicked Abaddon's ass. That's what you need to focus on."

Michael muttered under his breath. Now wasn't the time to have Lucifer mumbling in his head.

Lucifer chuckled. *"What's wrong, big brother? Afraid I'll be too much of a cockblock for you? That is why you're in your 'special place,' right? Expecting a certain fae to drop by. Call me crazy, but that I didn't see coming. I always pictured you as more of a pure human kind of guy. Faeries…hate to break it to you, bro, but I've heard they can be assholes."*

"Fuck off."

Another laugh. *"Damn, he must be pretty special for you to break out the potty mouth. And, for the record, I don't have any problems in that area. You're the one who hasn't gotten laid for the past century. Or has it been two?"*

"I mean it, Lucifer, bugger off. I'm not in the mood today. Any day."

"Yet, you rarely block me. Can't help but wonder why that is."

"Lucifer."

"Fine. But I want all the juicy details, later."

His presence faded, and Michael made a point of erecting a mental barrier, just in case the other angel decided to drop back in. The last thing he needed was for Greyson to think he was crazy. Michael already thought that enough for both of them. Especially when Lucifer had a point. It'd been centuries since Michael had sought out any form of intimate contact, and even those encounters had been sporadic. Mostly curiosity mixed with lust. He'd always chalked it up to gaining a better understanding of humanity. Of embracing the hint of it that lived inside of him. But not this time.

This was different. A burning need that refused to be smothered regardless of how hard he tried. How often he told himself Grey wasn't his mate. That the fae wasn't about to appear at Michael's doorstep because he felt the same unrelenting desire that Michael did.

He turned and stared at the door, not that Greyson needed a door to enter. The faery was definitely capable of simply materializing inside the walls, especially since Michael had removed the cabin's warding. He chuckled. Something told him the Prince of the Fae had more than a few tricks up his sleeve and would have found a way in regardless. Kei had mentioned how gifted Greyson was with spells, and Michael didn't doubt that fact. He just wasn't convinced the guy would show up.

Michael carded a hand through his hair, ignoring the way the strands just fell across his face again. Who was he kidding? He hadn't told Greyson where to meet him, but had played along with the faery's game—pictured the small cabin in his mind all day. The chances of the other man actually finding his way to Michael's door...

His inner voice snickered this time, daring Michael to deny the truth. Pretend that Greyson wasn't his true one. That their increased connection was merely a byproduct of their two species. Of course, if Greyson found him... denying they were mates would be the least of his problems, not when he'd be faced with spending the night with the one man he knew he couldn't have.

A loud knock drew Michael from his thoughts, the hollow sound making his stomach clench. No one had ever knocked on his door in the thousands of years he'd used the cabin as his refuge. Anticipation warred with uncertainty as he strode toward the entrance, his footsteps ringing through the uneasy silence. He didn't miss the way his hand trembled ever so slightly as he gripped the handle. He drew a deep breath before yanking the door aside.

Greyson stood on the porch, looking far too much at ease for the situation. He blinked as the door bounced against the wall, a high-pitched squeak hanging in the air. He arched his brow as his pink lips quirked into a smile, the lines around those brilliant hazel eyes creasing as the man gazed at Michael. "Call me crazy, but I thought you'd have a few thousand wards protecting this place. Funny how I don't sense any."

Michael stared at the man, watching the way his mouth moved as he spoke before giving himself a mental shake. "Greyson."

The other man laughed. "Were you expecting someone else?" He crossed his arms over his chest. "Or, perhaps, no one at all."

"I…" He shook his head. "I removed the warding. Just in case."

"You weren't convinced I'd get your message." He raised his hands, palms up. "Relax. I already promised I wouldn't ask for more than a night. Don't start freaking out on me, already. I only just got here."

Michael leaned against the frame. "I'm an archangel. I don't 'freak out.'"

"Would you prefer the term, panic?"

"I'm not panicking, either. I'm just…" He groaned inwardly at Greyson's knowing smile. "You're not helping matters, any."

"If it makes you feel less stressed, we can just pretend I got lucky. Though I have to say, the location…not where I thought you'd be."

"Trust me, the irony isn't lost on me. Just another reminder of all that's happened."

Greyson frowned slightly then smiled again as he motioned to the sliver of space between Michael and the entry. "Are you going to let me in, or do I have to stand out here on the porch all night?"

"Again, not helping." He moved aside, waving the other man in. "And I didn't expect you to knock. I thought with your expertise, you'd simply appear in the middle of the room. Kei swears you have a penchant for springing up when you're least expected."

"Anytime is least expected with Kei and Gabe. They always seem to be in the middle of pinning each other to a wall." He stopped in the center of the room, spinning as he scanned the surroundings. "And for the record, yes…I could have just popped inside, but I chose not to."

Michael arched his brow. "Any particular reason why?"

"I wanted to be invited in. Give you one last chance to back out."

There was no mistaking the grim tone of Greyson's voice or the way his posturing changed, as if he were bracing for Michael's rejection. But how could he when just standing there, staring at the fae, kicked up Michael's heart rate until he was sure the other man could see it thrashing inside his chest.

The scent of earth and leaves drifted between them, the spicy aroma spiking Michael's shaft against his pants. If he got any more aroused, he'd be hard pressed to close the short distance between them without having to adjust himself first.

Grey's gaze dropped to Michael's groin, then back to his face. He made a point of looking around the room again, before drawing his brows together. "So this is your sanctuary. It's very…uncluttered."

"I don't really need much. Chairs. A bed, though I don't always sleep. I use this place more for meditation. An escape."

"It's not the lack of furniture, but more that it seems void of anything personal." Grey focused on Michael's face. "I thought you'd have a few items that meant something to you. Memories, I suppose."

"I don't need things for that." He pursed his lips. "Do you?"

Grey snorted. "Please, faeries are like packrats. At least when it comes to spell books and scrolls and the like. I have an entire wall of tomes my father has handed down to me, and that barely touches the surface of the collection he has. I guess, I'm just used to places that look more lived in."

"I don't live here."

"Right." He pointed at the ceiling. "Upstairs."

Michael chuckled. "You make it sound so odd."

"You live in Heaven. And you're an archangel. Trust me, that's unusual."

"Not many people can claim to be heir to the throne of the Fae. Thinking you're just as unique."

Grey's cocky grin faded, a hint of color rising on his cheeks. "Not tonight." He took a step toward Michael. "Tonight, I'm just Greyson. And you're Michael. We're not a prince or a warrior. We're just...us. That is why you came here, right?" He took another step, quickly closing the distance between them. "One night. No labels. No expectations. No promises, just...you and me. Together."

Heat flushed Michael's skin, just the thought of finally touching Greyson the way he'd envisioned since that fateful day in the desert fading his remaining doubts until they'd vanished much like Lucifer's voice inside his head. He took a jerky step forward, clenching his hands into fists as he stopped with his chest mere inches from Greyson's. The other man's rapid breathing sounded around him, the increased rhythm making Michael smile. Knowing the faery was as affected by him as he was by

Greyson calmed the restless feeling inside him, and for the first time in months, he felt at peace.

He lifted his hand, tracing his thumb along Grey's jaw. "Are you certain? Even knowing this is all we'll share?"

The vein in Greyson's temple pulsed, a flash of sadness shining in his eyes before his mouth lifted into a forced smile. "The alternative is living out the rest of my life always wondering. Regretting, so yeah. I'll take what I can get. Just do me a favor?"

"What's that?"

"Make it a night to remember for the next thousand years."

Pain shot through Michael's heart at the broken quality of Greyson's plea, but he pushed it aside. This way was their best option. Surely Grey would come to understand that with time. And the fae would move on. Find a mate worthy of devotion. Grey frowned, as if he'd heard Michael's thoughts.

Michael locked his hand behind Greyson's head, weaving his fingers through the dark strands. He still couldn't tell if the man's hair was a deep brown or black, not that it mattered. Just the feel of the silky mass set his damn skin on fire.

He leaned in close, his lips brushing Grey's. "Wish granted."

He closed the last breath of distance, molding his mouth to Greyson's. The faery tensed, then relaxed, wrapping one arm around Michael's back while the other gained a similar hold on his hair. Nails scratched across his scalp, the tiny vibrations sending a cascade of goosebumps along his flesh. His wings trembled in response, and he had a sudden urge to have Greyson trace the length of them.

A chuckle sounded in his head, only it wasn't Lucifer this time. Michael recognized the gravelly tone of Grey's voice, even without hearing him speak. The fae mumbled something that resembled, "I told you so," a moment before the hand on Michael's back moved up his spine, landing on the edge of one wing. Grey's fingers spread out along Michael's feathers, the pads outlining each one.

Michael inhaled as he broke the kiss, resting his forehead on Greyson's. "Do you have any idea what that does to me?"

The other man grinned against Michael's lips. "If I said yes, you might think I'm capable of reading your mind. And we wouldn't want that." He pressed a soft kiss on Michael's mouth. "So why don't you tell me?"

"No one's ever touched me like that."

Grey snorted. "Your wings take up a lot of space. I can't imagine they haven't come into some form of play with your previous lovers."

He pulled back enough to catch Greyson's gaze. "They've never been exposed before."

"What do you mean?" Confusion swam across Greyson's face. "Are you implying that you've never been intimate without hiding your true self behind your glamour?"

"Why do you find that so hard to believe?"

"Because they're a huge part of who and what you are? I'd just have thought that taking a lover was the one time you would have let yourself be free."

Michael shrugged. "Being in my true form makes me vulnerable. That's not something I take lightly."

The smile faded from Greyson's mouth, a moment before he seemed to swallow with effort. He moistened his lips with his tongue, breaking contact as he stepped back. Fear prickled along Michael's spine, and he wondered if he'd just unknowingly ruined his one chance at loving Grey.

Greyson shook his head. "You haven't ruined anything, I just..." He exhaled slowly, lifting his shirt over his head then tossing it on the floor. He took what looked like a fortifying breath then closed his eyes. The air around him shimmered, crackling with a pure, blue light before sending a flash through the room. Michael shielded his eyes until the glare receded, his gaze landing on the fae.

Michael inhaled, holding that breath as he watched a pair of translucent wings flutter behind the other man. Unlike his, Greyson's were nearly invisible, with only lines of blue and green contrasting the pearl-like surface. They radiated outwards, looking like living vines breathing in the air behind the fae. But the swirls didn't only cover the man's wings. They continued across Greyson's body, the delicate pattern crisscrossing the length of his ribs before disappearing beneath his pants.

Michael took an involuntary step forward, drawn to the exquisite beauty of the man. "You have wings? Markings? But... All this time, I've never seen them. Never sensed them. Even Kei hasn't mentioned it."

The fae shrugged. "It's not something many people know about me. I'm the first male heir to be born with wings in millennia. Sort of a throwback, if you will. My father always warned me not to divulge this part of me to just anyone. That it was special. Hell if I really know why, but... It stuck with me, so I mostly keep them hidden. Not sure even Kei has seen me…" he waved at his body, "…in this form. The wings. The markings."

"But why?"

"Same reason you hide your wings. This makes me feel…exposed. My people might be more tolerant than most, but different is still different, especially if you're Oberon's son. And I've witnessed what happens to creatures who show their true selves to the world. It rarely ends well."

"Kei would never hurt you."

"Guess I wasn't willing to risk it."

"So why now? You could have kept the glamour. Obviously, you were correct before. Your skills in that department far exceed mine."

Greyson lifted his chin, looking every inch the warrior and prince Gabriel had spoken of. "If I'm only going to get one night with you, then I want it to be with me. The real me, not the shell I hide behind. If you're strong enough to share that side of you, then so am I. Unless this makes you uncomfortable."

Michael's throat thickened at the other man's words, his chest squeezing off any hope of breath. He closed the distance between them, cupping Greyson's chin in his hand. "You're stunning. And I'm honored that I get all of you. But…did you really come all this way just to talk?"

CHAPTER FOUR

Greyson moaned as Michael slanted his mouth over his, the angel's hand sliding back to tangle in Grey's hair again. The firm grip soothed the raw feeling inside his chest, and he responded in kind, anchoring one hand on Michael's wing, the other around his waist. Smooth skin slid beneath his palm, followed by the flex of muscles against his fingers.

He'd never truly appreciated how strong Michael was, his body always hidden beneath his tunic. But the man had forgone his usual garb and had donned nothing but a pair of worn jeans. Jeans that fucking looked painted on. Greyson had damn near drooled on the spot when Michael had appeared in the doorway, chest bare, his heavily muscled torso rippling with every movement. Knowing Grey would finally get the chance to feel every inch of the other man...

He exhaled when Michael broke the kiss, once again resting his forehead on Grey's. The intimate gesture made his stomach flutter, the sensation matched only by the frantic pounding of his heart. His pulse sounded in his head, Michael's echoed strum reminding Greyson of just how invested he truly was. And how he'd have to make this one night last a lifetime.

Michael sighed, his breath cooling Greyson's suddenly warm skin. "If this is going to be too hard on you—"

"Did I say that?" He eased away enough to look the other man in the eyes.

"You didn't have to."

Greyson bit back his immediate response. He'd known coming in Michael wasn't going to admit they were mates. And he'd already made peace with the fact he'd only get this one chance. Either he accepted what Michael was able to give him, or spend the rest of his life wondering. Forever wishing he'd had the courage to make one lasting memory.

Greyson took a deep breath. He needed to clear his mind or risk having Michael read his damn thoughts before he could block them. He managed an easy grin, once again thumbing the edge of the angel's wing. "I'm fine. And I'm pretty damn sure you could never be too *hard* for me. Though if you want to put that theory to the test…"

He skimmed his hands across Michael's ribs to his chest, savoring the strong beat of the other man's heart. It matched the rhythm inside his head, easing any remaining doubts. At least, he'd always feel that connection. Know his mate was all right, even if he couldn't be with him. It wasn't the kind of pairing he'd wish on anyone, but seeing as he'd never expected to find his true soul, he'd take whatever comfort he could find.

He quirked his lips as he made lazy patterns across the

angel's torso with his fingertips. "Damn, you're impressive. Wasn't expecting you to be dressed this way."

Michael arched a brow. "You seem to dislike my tunic."

"It hides everything."

"I'm a warrior. That's kind of the point. It's like armor."

"Fashion challenged armor. But these jeans..." He whistled. "Not sure I want to know how you got them on, but I'm going to enjoy every second of taking them off you." He thumbed the button. "They will come off, right? They aren't actually painted on?"

"Are all faeries this annoying?"

Grey laughed. "Only the ones worth getting to know. And for the record, angels aren't any better. You, my friend, have been the cause of a lot of hair pulling."

Michael smiled, tugging on the strands still wrapped around his fingers before allowing them to fall to his side. "If you want me to pull your hair, all you have to do is ask."

"Soon. But first..." Grey flicked open the button then grabbed the zipper. "I was about to help you get more comfortable."

"I thought you'd use your magic. Save us some time."

"Normally, I would. But..." He sighed. "If I'm only going to get one shot at this, I'd like to make it last as long as possible."

Michael's gaze softened. "The sun doesn't rise for another twelve hours or so. I plan on using every minute, which means we'll have time for more than *one shot*."

"Have you stopped to consider I enjoy unwrapping my presents?"

The intensity returned to Michael's expression, the

brilliant blue of his eyes darkening. "Have you stopped to consider it's taking an enormous amount of self-control not to pin you to that wall and fuck you senseless?"

Grey's breath caught. He'd never heard the archangel swear before. A devious smile lifted Greyson's lips. "And here I thought you were too pure to talk like that."

A deep blush stained Michael's cheeks a moment before the air thickened around him, rushing forward with a dizzying whoosh. Greyson blinked, inhaling roughly as his back and wings hit the far wall, his body trapped in place by Michael's chest. Ragged gasps sounded around him, the fresh scent of cottonwood infusing his senses. He inhaled, knowing that the aroma would be forever etched in his mind.

Michael's mouth brushed his jaw, followed by a gentle lick across the shell of his ear. "Trust me. Pure is the last word I'd use to describe anything associated with you. Now either touch me the way that's playing through both our heads or submit to me."

Greyson grinned. "Fine." He muttered the spell under his breath, hissing out that breath when their clothes vanished, the hot press of skin on skin making his stomach flip-flop. His cock pressed against Michael's abdomen, and Grey knew there'd be a smear of fluid on the other man's flesh. He huffed. "Happy now?"

"Insanely." Michael chuckled. "Don't worry. This is only the start. I promise, I'll make this small concession up to you." One hand trailed along his ribs as the man eased back a bit. His gaze dropped to follow the line of his fingers. "The patterns..." He hummed. "I doubt I'd ever grow tired of tracing them across your skin."

Greyson tensed as Michael's words sank in. The angel

was going to kill him. He swallowed the hint of disappointment. Just another slip from his mate, not that Michael would comment on it. He'd made it quite clear this was a one-night only deal.

Grey arched a brow. "I thought you were in a hurry?"

"So did I, but now that I have you where I want you... That need pales in comparison to the one that wants to taste you. Watch you unravel in my hands. My mouth. See if your wings are as sensitive as mine." He leaned in, his other hand teasing the edge of one wing. "I'm betting they are."

Greyson snagged his lower lip, biting back a moan as Michael dragged his fingers down to the tip then back. Shivers raced along his spine, and he focused on the rough press of the wood wall behind him to keep from finishing on the spot.

Michael's breath washed over his damp flesh. "I get the feeling you've never had a lover touch you like this before."

Grey clenched his teeth and squeezed his eyes shut. If he looked at Michael, he'd lose it despite his concentration.

"Greyson."

He forced his eyelids apart, finding the strength to hold Michael's gaze.

The angel flicked the edge of one wing. "Well?"

Greyson cursed under his breath, his cock throbbing with need. "You already know the answer."

"Maybe I want to hear you say it?"

"I wanted to undress you, but..." He grinned at Michael's frown, knowing he was helpless to deny the man anything. "No. I've never had anyone touch my wings. Ever. But don't think that you're always going to get your way. I'm as dominant as you are."

Those perfectly sculpted lips of his lifted into a knowing smile. "You can explore to your heart's content —" He nipped at Grey's bottom lip, mimicking the hold he'd had moments before with his own teeth. "As soon as I get a taste."

Michael captured Greyson's protest with a brutal press of his mouth, drawing the kiss out until Grey's lungs burned. He gasped in a ragged breath when the angel finally released him, moving to the muscle threading into his shoulder. Michael mouthed his skin, leaving a trail of moisture behind as he slowly inched his way down Greyson's torso, pausing long enough to tease his nipples. The small buds hardened against Michael's lips, the sensitive tips accentuating the ache in his groin.

The other man didn't seem to notice the way Greyson anchored one hand in Michael's hair, the other fisting against the wall. Grey dug his nails into his palm, hoping the slight hurt would stop him from shooting his release across Michael's chest long before the man so much as touched him.

A raspy chuckle sounded in his head. Fuck, it was irritating having his mate hear his thoughts without being able to acknowledge it. Not when he feared the angel might bolt—leave Greyson standing there, cock weeping against his skin, his heart damn near busting through his chest. It didn't matter how hard it would be to walk away tomorrow, he'd get his one night. Catalogue each moment until he could replay every second of their time together. Time that would have to last forever.

Michael nipped at Greyson's abdomen, jolting him

back to the present. He glanced down, regretting the decision when his gaze clashed with Michael's just as the man poked out his tongue and swept it the length of Grey's cock.

Greyson's head clunked against the wall, the hand on Michael's wing tightening. "Damn."

Michael smiled against Grey's skin, sucking the tip of his shaft into his mouth before easing free. "You taste just how I thought you would. Pure. Fresh. Makes me want to have you empty into my mouth."

"No." Greyson hissed out a breath when Michael took his entire shaft into his mouth. "I want to be the one to taste you."

Michael made a second pass before letting Grey's cock spring free. "Next time." He tsked at Grey's irritated huff. "Don't worry. You'll get your turn, but the first time is mine." He locked his gaze on Grey's. "Now behave and give me what I want."

Greyson clenched his jaw, holding back another moan as Michael started up a rhythm Grey knew was designed to take him over. There wasn't any gentle buildup. No easing him into the sensations. Michael devoured him. Conquered. Plunging up and down Grey's length as if it were a damn mission from above.

Grey managed to pry his hand off the wall and grab Michael's other wing, using both to anchor himself as the angel moved between his legs, the white-hot pressure damn near taking Grey to his knees. He'd never had a lover this intense, and he knew he wouldn't be able to hold off much longer. Deny Michael his release for more than a couple minutes.

He panted out a few rough breaths, tugging on the angel's wings. "If you don't stop, this is going to be over too damn fast."

Michael made a few more passes before easing Grey's shaft free. "Nothing will be over except my burning need to taste you. And I have a feeling that won't be close to being quenched." He tilted his head to the side, looking genuinely confused. "I promised you the night. I don't intend to spend much of it sleeping, so this..." He waved at them. "It's only the beginning. Think of it as taking the edge off so I can muster just a hint of control."

"You don't fight fair."

"You didn't ask me to."

Then he was moving, sliding his lips around Greyson's cock and taking him deep again. Each downward stroke sent another shiver along his spine, coiling heat in his sac. Greyson fought the burning sensation swirling in his groin, wanting to give in, but desperate to make the moment last. To draw out every second of Michael's mouth and hands on his body. To etch each encounter into his memory.

Michael hummed, the tiny vibrations breaking Greyson's control. He banged his head against the wall again, grabbing a handful of feathers as he moaned in defeat. He punched his hips forward, meeting every downward stroke of Michael's mouth.

Michael released him for a second, fisting his hand along Grey's length. "Don't you hold back on me. I want to hear you scream my name. I want the damn walls to shake."

He took Grey deep again, this time swallowing with

Grey's cock lodged in the man's throat. Grey released a strangled gasp, knowing he couldn't hold back any longer.

He moved one hand to Michael's hair, tangling it in the mass of blond locks as he thrust into the angel's mouth, all semblance of control a distant memory. Michael moaned around Grey's shaft, dipping his finger inside his mouth alongside Greyson's cock before tracing that hand back until he grazed Grey's ass. The angel paused, teasing the opening before sliding it inside. Pleasure shot through Greyson's core, stealing the last of his resolve.

He bowed his head, giving in to the rush of heat down his shaft. "Fuck, yes. Michael!"

His voice resonated through the small space, Michael's name hanging in the air. Grey's release surged along his length, pausing for one more pass of the other man's mouth before shooting forward. Michael grunted, pumping Grey through five more pulses before finally easing up. Black dots rimmed Grey's vision, his pulse echoing inside his head.

He closed his eyes, struggling to calm his breathing as his heart rate slowly returned to normal. His arms fell to his sides as a low chuckle sounded next to his ear, the soft brush of lips across his jaw bringing him back. He blinked, Michael's face wavering into focus.

The other man grinned, looking more than pleased with himself as he thumbed Grey's jaw. "I could watch you give yourself to me over and over. And now that we've taken the edge off, I can slow it down, just a bit. Though I'm afraid this first time won't be gentle, you..." He rested his forehead on Grey's. "What you do to me."

Greyson smoothed his hands up Michael's chest,

spearing them through the man's hair and anchoring them together. "Don't recall saying you had to be gentle. So stop worrying about what you think I want, and give me what I need."

CHAPTER FIVE

And all I need is you.

The words resonated through Michael's head as surely as if Greyson had spoken them aloud. Michael could even detect the hint of sadness in the man's tone that had made its way into a few of the fae's sentences tonight, testament to the underlying truth they were both choosing to ignore.

Mates.

There was no arguing the fact, now. No convincing himself Greyson was merely a distraction. Michael felt the man's emotions as a ghosted reflection of his own. Heard the fae's inner thoughts as an endless loop inside his head. Since the prince had walked through Michael's door, he'd been consumed with images and memories he knew weren't his. Connected in a way he'd never really thought possible. A way only his true one could manifest.

He drew a deep breath. He could try to block the man. Erect a similar mental barrier as the one shielding these moments from Lucifer. Distance himself in every way possible. Though Michael wasn't convinced it would work to the same degree. His defenses were geared toward other angels. Humans. Against a magical being as powerful as the Prince of the Fae... Just his luck all he'd accomplish would be to give the other man a puzzle to figure out. And he had little doubt that Greyson could pick any lock Michael put in the fae's path.

He groaned inwardly. Any inability to block Greyson stemmed from them being mates, not because the man was a gifted faery. Prince or not, Michael was equally as strong—except where his mate was concerned. Hiding thoughts and feelings from his chosen one was nearly impossible. More of an exercise in frustration than anything else.

A thought swirled to life in his head, and he frowned as he gazed at the other man. "How were you able to hide your true self from me?"

Greyson furrowed his brow, looking thoroughly confused. "I just came in your mouth, your cock is making a groove in my stomach, and you want to know why my glamour fooled you? That's seriously what's on your mind right now?"

"You shouldn't have been able to hide like that. Not from me."

Greyson's eyes widened, his breath hitching with an audible gasp. He eased his fingers free of Michael's hair, palming them on Michael's chest. "I told you. Faeries pretty much invented glamour."

"Perhaps. But those tricks should have limitations, just like mine do. And seeing as we're..."

Greyson huffed when Michael caught himself, allowing the sentence to just fade into his increased breath.

The fae broke eye contact, muttering something Michael couldn't make out before meeting Michael's gaze again. "If I answer your question, there's no crying foul and skipping off. You promised me one night. I'm holding you to that."

Michael nodded, silently wishing he'd never let his thoughts drift in this direction. If he'd just focused on Grey's request, he'd be balls deep inside the other man instead of rooted to the spot as he waited for Greyson to voice what neither of them had dared to say aloud.

Greyson clenched his jaw, taking what looked like a fortifying breath before relaxing against the wall. "Despite our origins, faeries and angels aren't that different. We share similar abilities, though, obviously, the source of our gifts varies greatly. You have your grace, whereas I draw my power from the life force all around us. You're immortal in a sense, where faeries simply live extremely long lives. But we both mate for life. Regardless of whether that mate shares our genetic makeup or not. But unlike angels, faeries aren't fully bound until they recite the ancient binding ritual. Until those words are uttered..." He shrugged. "We're able to shield ourselves to a certain degree, even from our true soul."

The full extent of Greyson's words hit hard, leaving a sick feeling churning through Michael's stomach.

He leaned in, making Greyson push against his chest to keep from fully pinning the other man to the wall. "Are you saying you can deny the mating? Pick a different person to share your life with?"

Greyson's chin quivered before the man physically drew himself up. "In theory, yes. But do you have any idea how hard it is to be with your mate and not recite the ritual? It's like a relentless hammering inside my head. I hear horns and flutes, and the words play over and over and over until it's all I can do not to shout them out." He seemed to swallow with effort. "But I promised you this didn't have to be about anything other than what you were willing to give. And I intend to keep that promise. So unless you want me to chant the phrases sounding inside my head right now, I suggest you focus on giving me something else to scream about." He reclaimed his hold on Michael's hair. "And for the record, there will never be anyone else for me. So, either fuck me and hold true to our deal, or admit what we are, and I'll claim you as mine."

Michael's affirmation weighed heavy on his tongue, threatening to pop free of its own accord as he stood there, staring into Greyson's hazel eyes. But as much as he wanted to belong to Grey—to spend the next millennium loving the one man who made Michael feel like the honorable warrior of lore—he couldn't get that single word to make it past his lips. Couldn't risk it when he wasn't convinced he'd be able to keep Greyson safe. Not after his disappointing encounter with Abaddon. And Greyson meant more to Michael than his own life. To fail the other man... He'd never survive the loss.

Instead, he ground his mouth against Grey's, pushing out every other thought but the feel of Grey's tongue against his as the man fought for control. Nails scraped across Michael's scalp, the rough caress spiking his need to the point he thought he might shoot his release across Greyson's stomach.

Greyson pulled back, holding Michael's head firmly in his hands. "No way. Your first release is going to be inside me. If you want to paint my skin next time..." He shrugged one shoulder. "I could probably be swayed in that direction. But right now..." He tugged on the strands, jerking Michael's head up. "I need you. Hard. Deep. Demanding."

"Lube." The word rasped between them, the single syllable morphing into a grunt when Greyson nipped at Michael's jaw.

"Faery, which means I have a spell for damn near everything."

Greyson mumbled some ancient dialect a moment before a cool sensation covered Michael's shaft. The intimate touch only increased the raw feeling inside him, warning him to claim the other man before he ran out of control.

Greyson released Michael's hair, shifting his hands until they cupped both of Michael's wings. "Control is overrated. So stop worrying about anything else but fucking me."

Michael growled against the man's mouth as he kissed him again, this time pushing him hard against the wall. While he'd had every intention of moving over to the bed, the unrelenting need burning beneath his skin just couldn't wait for him to cross the room. Instead, he scooped up Grey's thigh, locking one heel behind his back as he wedged himself between the man's legs, trapping Greyson's cock against his stomach. The man's shaft had already recovered, the hard length weeping more fluid across Michael's flesh.

He glanced down, half considering sucking the other man off again, when Greyson tugged on his wings.

Michael lifted his gaze, instantly pinned by the desire ragging in Greyson's eyes.

Michael nodded, lodging the head of his cock at Grey's ass, smiling at the slippery glide of lube on the fae's skin. Apparently, Greyson had prepared both of them with his spell. Michael tilted his hips, pushing just the tip inside Greyson's channel. The fae moaned Michael's name, allowing his head to fall against Michael's shoulder.

The intimate gesture tightened his chest, and he responded by easing Greyson's cheeks apart as he slowly pushed against the snug opening. Intense pressure built along his length, stealing his breath until Grey's muscles relaxed, and Michael slipped inside.

Greyson lifted his head only to let it fall again as Michael inched his way in, finally stopping when his sac connected with Grey's skin. The fae moaned against Michael's shoulder, ending with a firm bite to his to his nape.

Michael's hands flexed against Greyson's flesh as his mouth caressed the man's ear. "Fuck, Grey. So tight."

"Move, please, Michael. I'm dying here."

"Not quite, but…"

He eased out, feeling every inch of Greyson's body close around him before he paused, just the head of his shaft still lodged within the other man. He savored the tight clasp then pushed back in, once again locking himself inside the fae.

Grey grunted, doing his best to angle his hips—take Michael even deeper. The motion squeezed his crown, igniting the coiling sensation already gathering along his spine. He firmed his grip, trying to hold his lover still as he withdrew then thrust back in, banging Grey against the wall.

Grey's head snapped up, his eyes drifting closed as Michael repeated the motion, once again knocking Grey against the wall. "Damn. So fucking good. Do it again. Harder."

"I don't want to hurt you."

"Do I seem fragile to you?" He hissed out a breath when Michael's next stroke rammed him into the wall. "Yes. Just like that."

Michael sighed in defeat, wanting the rough coupling as much as Greyson seemed to need it. Michael pistoned his hips, setting up a steady rhythm he knew would send him over long before he wanted their encounter to end.

Grey scratched a line along his wings. "This is only our first time. Trust me, you can have my ass again just as soon as I get a chance to claim yours. And you can draw it out next time."

Michael thought about telling the man to get out of his head, but the words died on his tongue when Greyson squeezed around his length, dimming Michael's vision at the edges.

He nipped at Grey's bottom lip. "You did that on purpose."

"You complaining?"

Another deep thrust. "No. Now, hold on, I can't..."

His words faded into a moan as his climax surged forward, taking the last of his control with it. Michael lowered his head to Grey's shoulder, then let go, pounding into the man at a frenzied pace. Grey shouted his affirmation, screaming Michael's name when he shifted his other hand to the fae's wing, using the edge as another anchor point. Smooth, skin-like tissue rippled beneath his fingers, the swirling colors giving the illusion of moving vines.

Michael lost himself in the beauty of Greyson's form. In the flex of his muscles, the throaty pleas he mumbled with every breath. How the markings on his body seemed to darken, turning nearly black before the man stiffened, his shaft jerking against Michael's abdomen as the other man emptied across his skin.

The heady scent of Greyson's release was all it took to push Michael into his. He grunted through several more strokes before locking his cock deep as it pulsed inside Grey's ass, draining him of his seed as he slumped against Greyson's body, his muscles spent.

Grey's arms cinched around his back, his fingers absently flicking Michael's feathers as he seemed focused on simply drawing air in then blowing it out. Michael grinned against Grey's cheek, losing himself in the steady rise and fall of Grey's chest against his until the man sighed, finally lifting his head from Michael's shoulder.

Michael closed his eyes. He'd done it. He'd actually crossed the line and taken Greyson as his lover. And God help him, but he couldn't even muster the strength to care that he'd most likely just made the biggest mistake of his life. He'd known from the start the other man would haunt his dreams. Now that he'd actually gotten a taste of how it could be between them—he wasn't sure if he'd be able to walk away when the sun finally brightened the horizon. If he could continue to hide behind honor and duty.

Greyson dropped a kiss on his jaw, nuzzling his neck until Michael opened his eyes and met the fae's gaze.

Glassy eyes stared back at him, but Michael didn't sense regret emanating from the man. In fact, Greyson looked like a man with a purpose, and Michael had a gnawing feeling he was the subject of Grey's next conquest.

The fae's lips kicked up into a sexy grin. "Damn straight you're my next mission. You promised me I'd get my turn, and that starts now."

"And here I thought you'd wait until I'd at least pulled out."

"Do I look like a fool? You're an archangel, which means you like being in control. So my best course of action is to pounce while you're still recovering. Less chance of you turning the tables on me."

Michael chuckled. "I hold true to my word. Let's just get cleaned up and you can do whatever you want to me."

Greyson arched a bow. "Anything?"

"Why does that one word seem to hold a different meaning for you?" He sighed as his cock slipped free. Damn, but he already missed the pressure. The heat. The intimate connection.

Grey cupped his chin, grazing his thumb along Michael's cheek. "Standing right here. Nothing's lost."

"Must you invade my thoughts?"

"You're practically screaming them at me. I can only shield you for so long."

"Bastard."

"Have I told you I love it when you talk dirty to me? Makes the purity I sense in you so much hotter."

"As I said. I'm far from pure where you're concerned." Michael nodded toward a small door off to the right. "Shower?"

"I could just mutter another spell."

"And miss the chance to have one of us drop the soap?"

Greyson's lips quirked a moment before the air rippled around them and Michael found their positions reversed. The fae pressed him against the wall, his mouth hovering an inch from his face. "Mark my words. It's my turn to claim you. And I won't consider the job done until you're so full of me, you won't know whether to beg me to finish or make it last all night."

CHAPTER SIX

Greyson stood there, Michael's body pressed against his, the man's breath cooling his sweat-damp skin, and all he could do was stare at the pure perfection trapped within his arms. The brilliant blue of the angel's eyes, the slight shadow of stubble on his jaw. The way the man's wings lightly caressed Grey's torso, the feathers brushing across the colored patterns swirled on his flesh. He hadn't anticipated how important Michael's acceptance of his true form would be. Knowing his mate seemed as taken with his unique traits as Greyson was with Michael's had strengthened their connection to the point it was all Grey could do not to let the words looping in his head form on his tongue. Bind them together in a way only death would undo. Though, at the moment, Grey wasn't convinced even mortality would free him.

Michael narrowed his eyes, tilting his head as if listening to an internal voice. Greyson did his best to block his thoughts, but simply crushing the urge to recite the ritual took all his control. He bowed his head and closed his eyes as he leaned against Michael, taking a few deep breaths as he gathered his composure.

A soft tsk sounded close to him followed by the press of Michael's mouth on Greyson's forehead. "Greyson. Look at me."

Grey clenched his jaw, vowing he wouldn't let a single word pass his lips as he forced himself to meet Michael's gaze. But the stern expression he'd expected was conspicuously absent, nothing but searing compassion in the angel's eyes.

Michael quirked one side of his mouth into a small smile. "I'm yours. While that might not last for as long as we both want, it's far from over. So tell me what you need to quiet the voices inside your head and, if it's within my power, I'll give it to you."

Your love.

The answer resonated through Greyson's mind, but he managed to erect a barrier before it echoed inside Michael's. Instead, he slanted his lips over his mate's, soothing some of the raw ache with the feel of the angel's tongue on his. The steady give and take of the kiss. The haunting sounds eased, nothing but the mournful tone of a flute fading into silence.

He drew a deep breath as they parted, instantly surrounded by the scent of male musk with a hint of cottonwood. The combined aroma infused his senses, and he knew he'd always picture this moment whenever he happened upon either fragrance. A tangible link to the man who'd forever hold his heart and soul.

The flute started playing again, but Grey shoved it aside as he took a step back. He extended his hand to the archangel. "I believe you mentioned a shower?"

The fine lines around Michael's eyes crinkled with suppressed humor. "I thought you were merely going to wave us clean?"

"I could. But I like the idea of touching every inch of you. Of watching the water bead along your skin. Of having it spray against my back while I suck you dry."

Michael's coughed as he seemed to choke on his saliva. "What if I decide that should be my role?"

"Are we really going to have to go a few rounds to see if I can dominate you? Though the idea of wrestling does have its benefits. Unfortunately, you've already promised, and I know firsthand angels hate breaking promises. You might want to remember that before you grant me anything I desire next time."

"Point noted. Shower, it is."

Michael took his hand, weaving their fingers together as he led Greyson across the room and into the small area beyond. It wasn't fancy—just a glass shower lining one wall and the usual amenities positioned against the other. Michael headed for the open space beside the transparent panel, ducking inside long enough to turn the taps. The patter of water against tile filled the space, the soothing sounds easing the tight feeling in Grey's shoulders.

Christ, what had he been thinking? Fucking each other was one thing. It was hot. Primal. Raw. But this— showering with Michael, allowing himself to tend to the angel's needs—that was intimate. A small concession that changed this from a sexual encounter with his mate into something far deeper. Not that he wanted it any other way, but it definitely made pushing aside the need to bond with Michael more difficult.

Grey sucked in a few quick breaths then made his way

to the shower. Michael grinned as he stepped beneath the spray, making enough room for Greyson to join him. Grey moved inside, smiling at the echoing sound of the water. It reminded him of the sacred waterfall back home, the constant clattering easing any doubts. This was where he needed to be. Where he belonged. And he'd make as many memories as he could in the short time they had together.

He reached for the soap, lathering his hands before skimming them along Michael's chest. Damn, but the man was built. Layers of taut bands crisscrossed his torso, a scattering of scars the only imperfections visible. Grey traced the length of a few, wondering how the angel had gotten them when Michael's hands captured his wrists. He raised his gaze, locking his focus on the archangel's face.

Michael arched a brow. "Those are in my past. I'd much rather stay in the present, with you."

Grey moved, pushing Michael against the wall and claiming his lips in a brutal kiss. He ate at the man's mouth, not giving an inch until Michael palmed Grey's wings, drawing his hands to the tips and back. Pleasure arced along his skin, leaving him gasping for breath as he leaned fully against the other man.

Michael nipped at his jaw. "I knew they'd be as sensitive as mine. But the feel... The surface is silky, like your lips. Nothing like my feathers."

"I quite love the feel of your feathers. They're soft, but strong. Like an extension of you. And the pearl shade matches your grace."

"Is that why yours are colored? To mimic your personality? Your magic?"

"I never really gave it much thought. I've spent more time hiding them than anything else."

"Not tonight. Tonight they stay as is because I plan on getting a much closer look at them. Study the way the colors swirl across the length then onto your torso." He hummed. "Makes me want to trace the patterns with my tongue. Lick every inch as it continues along your skin. Damn, but you're beautiful."

"Christ."

"Is that a yes?"

Greyson gripped Michael's shoulders, stopping the man from escaping his embrace. "Did you actually think that would work? That I'd relinquish control with only a few pretty words?" He cursed when Michael grazed his fingers along Grey's wing, again.

Michael chuckled. "You were saying?"

"Granted, that makes me so hard I can't even think straight, but..." He applied more pressure, keeping Michael's back tight against the tiles. "I want to watch you give yourself to me more. You can torment me by teasing my wings on your turn."

"I think the word you're looking for is pleasure."

"Either way, I won't be satisfied until I swallow your next release. Until I'm bottomed out inside you. So be a good angel, and give me what I need." He quirked a brow. "You did promise me anything."

"I have a feeling I'm going to regret saying that."

Greyson grinned, claiming Michael's mouth in another kiss before working his way down the man's torso. He lingered on the angel's chest, taking his time to nip and lave at Michael's nipples. The archangel responded by threading his fingers through Grey's hair, the firm grip drawing a strangled rasp from deep inside Grey's chest. Damn, but he loved the slight bite. The clear message that Michael was only submitting because he wanted to, not because Grey had demanded control. While he'd never seen himself as submissive, where Michael was concerned, Grey was willing to concede that he enjoyed having the other man lead.

Michael tugged the strands. "I heard that."

Greyson ignored the way Michael's gravelly tone curled around him, swaying him to concede. Do anything to please the man. He went to his knees, focusing on the angel's shaft as it hung hard and heavy between the man's legs. A drop of fluid beaded on the tip, the shiny offering drawing him down until he could lick the head clean. Spicy musk burst on his tongue, the taste more than addicting.

He hummed his approval, this time taking the entire crown in his mouth as he sucked at the hard flesh. Michael's fingers flexed against his scalp, the man's thighs tensing against the pressure. Greyson closed his eyes, slowly descending along Michael's length until the head hit the back of his throat. He paused long enough to make Michael moan before easing his way back—ending with a light nip.

Grey looked up Michael's body, meeting the man's gaze along his torso. Intense blue eyes stared down at Grey amidst the dips and planes of Michael's muscles. The vein in his temple jumped as he clenched his jaw, finally allowing his head to fall back against the wall.

And Greyson knew he had him.

The spray of the shower faded into the background as he focused on consuming Michael's cock. On sliding up and down the angel's length, loving the throaty moans that echoed around him as Michael gave himself over to the simple act. Grey kept moving, using his hand when he dipped down to suckle the man's sac, taking each side into his mouth. Michael rasped his name, cursing quietly before slowly thrusting his hips.

Greyson moved back to the man's cock, allowing Michael to set the pace. The angel grunted, the muscles in his abdomen tensing before his head bowed forward, and he let go.

Forceful thrusts claimed Greyson's mouth as Michael chased his release. Grey used one hand to keep the man's shaft sliding between his lips as the other traced a line behind his balls, sinking into Michael's ass. The angel's movements faltered, stalling for a few moments before increasing. All semblance of control vanished as he fucked Grey's mouth, Michael's fingers holding Grey's head firmly in place. Steam billowed around them, nothing but Michael's ragged breathing sounding above the splash of water against the tiles.

"Too good. Damn, Grey, I'm about to lose it. If you want it somewhere else…" He hissed when Grey merely sucked harder. "You win."

Michael's hips jerked, his cock swelling before emptying in a series of spurts across Grey's tongue. He kept pumping until Michael curled over him, bracing his weight on Grey's shoulders. Grey smiled as he eased the man's shaft free, dropping a kiss on his hip. A tremor shook through Michael's body, followed by a low moan.

Grey gained his feet, shouldering into Michael when the man looked as if he might slide onto his ass. A satisfied smile tugged at Grey's lips. Knowing he'd brought his mate to his knees made his chest tighten. And not just anyone—Michael. Archangel and heavenly asskicker.

Michael chuckled, finally managing to meet Greyson's gaze. "Not sure anyone has ever described me quite like that. But then, you are one of a kind."

Greyson leaned in closer, licking a drop of water off of Michael's jaw. "You know, for someone who asked me to stop invading his thoughts, you're all up in mine."

His grin was nothing short of sinful. "That's because you never reciprocated, which is basically an open invitation."

"I'm not sure it works that way but...don't get upset if you hear something you don't like."

His grin widened. "Based on the thoughts you're having, I'm about to love your next move."

Greyson's heart skipped at the man's choice of words, but he recovered, choosing to match Michael's smug smile. "That's cheating. But seeing as you're spying..."

Greyson closed his eyes, allowing his magic to cover them in a bluish light. He pictured the bed in the other room, smiling when he felt the mattress give beneath them. Michael stiffened, glancing around before settling on Grey's face, his brow raised in question.

"I couldn't copy your approach and fuck you against the wall. You'd get the impression I lack creativity."

Grey shuffled enough to position himself between Michael's thighs, his hands on either side of the angel's torso. He took a moment to sweep his gaze over the length of Michael's body. Take in the rippled muscles and smooth skin. It was hued a slight bronze tone, and he wondered if Michael walked around naked up in Heaven.

Michael laughed. "Can you imagine that? Every angel buck nude just to avoid some tan lines?"

Grey shook his head. "Are you saying you're naturally this color?"

A flash of shame shone in Michael's eyes before he made a show of shrugging off the question. "I'm still suntanned from the week I spent in the desert, courtesy of Abaddon. As I recall, I wasn't wearing much until the night of that final battle. I guess Abaddon wanted me to go out fully garbed as a symbol of my failure to the cause. To my faith."

Greyson frowned. "You didn't fail."

"Didn't I? If it weren't for you and Kei, we would have lost."

"As I recall, you, Gabe and Lucifer played equally important roles."

Michael cringed slightly at the mention of Lucifer, though he masked it quickly. "I allowed Abaddon and his followers to obtain my blood. To imprison me. That doesn't equate to a victory in my books."

"Nor does it mean you failed. The battle was won. The book is secure."

"I'm afraid it doesn't quite work that way."

Greyson snorted. "I'm starting to understand what Kei means when he accuses Gabriel of thinking in absolutes. You angel types sure do carry around a lot of guilt, don't you?"

"I'm not the only one who suffers from self-blame. Though I'm not sure why you think you're responsible for your sister's death."

The words hit Grey hard, and he rocked back on his heels, staring down at the man. "How... Did you—"

"No." Michael pushed onto his elbows. "I didn't search your mind. I'd never use our connection like that. Kei told me what happened one night when I was visiting. The guy feels equally responsible. He mentioned that you hadn't been the same, since, and with everything I've learned about you…" He tilted his head to the side, looking strangely vulnerable for the first time since Greyson had met him. "I don't have to read your thoughts to see the burden you're carrying. One I'm all too familiar with."

Greyson closed his eyes, images that were better left forgotten flickering through his mind. Of all the times to bring up Sirena, now was about as bad as it got. He only had one night with Michael, and the last thing he wanted to do was spend it talking about how he let his little sister down. Missed the signs that Abaddon had long since lost his grace. That the bastard was just using those around him to gain the ultimate power.

Fingers raked across his jaw and behind his head, settling in his hair. Greyson opened his eyes, inhaling roughly at the stunning blue that filled his gaze, and he knew he'd never grow tired of staring into those eyes. Of seeing another side of the man humanity viewed as God's greatest weapon.

Michael sighed, drawing Grey's forehead toward him until it rested on his. "It would seem we both have crosses to bear. But I'm willing to bury mine for the night if you are?"

"Pretend?"

Just like they were doing with each other. Pretending they weren't already bound far more than any rite could accomplish.

Michael nodded. "Just for tonight."

Grey tamped down the residual guilt and pain, focusing on the feel of Michael's fingers along his scalp. The fresh scent of cottonwood that seemed to linger on the man's skin. The slight increase in his breathing as their gazes locked again. "Deal. Which means it's still my turn. Lay back. I'm nowhere near done with you."

CHAPTER SEVEN

Michael dragged Greyson's head toward his, claiming the fae's mouth as he took them both to the bed, moaning when Grey's weight settled on top of him. Though he'd taken both male and female lovers over the millennia, he'd rarely given up control, usually preferring to be the one on top. But feeling the strength of Grey's form cover his chased away any doubts, and he knew he needed to submit to his mate as much as Grey needed to dominate him.

Mate.

Michael needed to stop thinking in those terms. True or not, he'd already decided he couldn't risk fully claiming the man. And continually using the term, even just inside his head, was clouding that decision. Daring him to consider a path he'd sworn he'd never venture down. Greyson tensed above him for a moment, and Michael knew the man had heard his thoughts.

To his credit, Greyson didn't react more than breathing a soft sigh as he braced his weight on his elbows, filling

Michael's field of view. The man muttered words in what Michael guessed was the faery's native tongue, more of the blue light coloring his skin. The glow seemed to concentrate in the swirls along his wings and down his sides, making the lines look as if they were moving.

Michael quirked his brow. "Strange how I never noticed your magic seems to emanate from your markings, and not all of your skin."

Grey leaned down, nuzzling Michael's neck as he kissed his way along Michael's jaw. "All masked by my glamour. But with it removed..." He pulled back a bit, grinning when Michael inhaled. "I see my spell worked. Wouldn't want to hurt you."

"I'm an archangel."

"And I'm about to stick my cock up your ass. Even warriors of your magnitude need something to ease the bite. This is about pleasure, not whether or not you can man up." Grey dropped a gentle kiss on Michael's chin. "It would kill a part of me to knowingly hurt you."

Guilt prickled at the edge of Michael's conscience—subtly reminding Michael that he was doing just that to Grey. Consciously denying the man his mate when he knew the toll it took on the fae. Indecision clouded his thoughts, fading sharply when Greyson nudged his ass, the thick head of the man's cock pushing against Michael's flesh.

Greyson lowered until his chest grazed Michael's, the fae's lips brushing his. Grey didn't try to kiss him, just stayed there, Grey's gaze locked on his, the man's breath fluttering the stray strands of hair around Michael's face. The firm thrum of Greyson's heartbeat sounded in Michael's head as the faery slowly thrusted his hips, inching his way inside. There was a moment of extreme pressure before Grey's cock slipped past the tight ring of muscles, slowly burying within his ass.

Michael pressed his head against the bed, closing his eyes as the pinching sensation burned into fiery need. It settled low in his groin, coiling inward as every nerve sparked to life. Pleasure raced along his spine, the ghosted echo of a flute sounding in his head.

Lips caressed his jaw. "Open your eyes."

Michael resisted, knowing if he complied, all the reasons for not acknowledging the bond would fade away.

A soft sigh feathered over his face followed by a huff. "Michael. Open your eyes. Look at me."

Michael braced himself against the inevitable rush of need as he blinked open his eyelids, staring up at the man who would forever hold his heart. But the fear he thought would surface was strangely absent.

Grey shifted as he ran a finger along Michael's cheek, another echo of a distant melody thrumming around them. "I know what you're thinking, but I promise I won't…"

His words drifted into a groan, the music seemingly gathering strength.

Grey clenched his jaw, releasing a slow breath. "Just this once, give me all of you."

Michael moaned as Grey's mouth claimed his, opening for the other man's tongue. The kiss was raw, desperate, and Michael couldn't stop his grace from rising to the surface in a show of pure light. Some of the tension eased from Greyson's muscles as the fae's magic joined Michael's, the blue glow curling through the white in the same swirling pattern that adorned Greyson's skin.

Greyson's forehead connected with his. "Now, I can love you."

He eased back, leaving just the head lodged inside before reclaiming the lost inches, pressing his sac tight to Michael's flesh. Heat billowed up through his core, increasing his breath until the ragged sound filled the room. Greyson never wavered, pinning Michael beneath him, his elbows tucked against Michael's ribs, his fingers lightly caressing Michael's neck. Every thrust shook the bed against the wall, the dull thud adding to the sensuous atmosphere.

Greyson's head tipped back, the cords in his neck straining as he increased his pace, slamming their hips together with each punishing stroke. He scratched at Michael's skin, the added sensation only pushing Michael higher. He managed to skim his hands up Grey's back, anchoring them on the man's wings. Grey's head snapped back down, his gaze nothing short of lethal.

He grunted, letting his head fall forward in seeming defeat. "Damn, when you touch me like that." He released a series of choppy breaths, ending with a growl. "Can't hold off. Too damn good."

Michael grinned at the man as he tightened his hold on Grey. "Then come for me. I promise I'll be right behind you."

Grey shook his head. "Need more time."

"Night's still young. And there's no way you're leaving here without me claiming you again, so...let go."

"Shit."

Grey's voice sounded thick, as if he'd had to force out the single word. He seemed to fight against his need to finish before cursing again, all semblance of control vanishing with the next frenzied stroke. His rhythm faltered, every muscle in his back flexing as he pushed onto his hands, using the position to increase his thrusts.

Pleasure arced through Michael's core, spiking his cock against Grey's abdomen until he thought it'd burst. "Now. Grey, I can't... Yes!"

His climax surged forward, spurting across their flesh in ropey strands of white as Grey continued to ride him, somehow holding off until Michael collapsed beneath him. The fae clenched his jaw, pushing into Michael a few more times before stiffening, Michael's name whispering around them.

Greyson's hips jerked against his, the hot feel of Grey's release soothing something raw inside him. Michael dragged in a few quick breaths, trying to tug Greyson down against him when the other man groaned. Michael blinked, finally focusing on his lover as a tremble shook through the fae. Sweat beaded his brow, a grimace of pain shaping his lips.

The inklings of panic gnawed at the euphoria still coursing through Michael's veins. "Greyson?"

Grey shook his head, mouth clamped shut, the muscles in his arms shaking. Michael managed to push onto one elbow, lifting his other hand to palm Greyson's jaw. More snippets of the strange melody sounded around them, fading in and out with every ragged breath Greyson managed.

"Grey. What's wrong?"

Grey's gaze slid to his, the desperation in the man's expression clearly visible. He grunted through a few more breaths, whimpering in seeming distress. "You...are...my sun." He cursed. "No!"

Greyson tugged against Michael's hold, hissing in seeming frustration. "My...moon. My darkest night. No!"

Michael stilled. "Greyson."

"The flute... The godforsaken flute. I can't..."

The man's chin drooped, the sheer agony of fighting the mating rolling off him in waves. Michael felt his pain, his fear. Heard the echo of the song that was obviously looping inside Greyson's mind.

Michael released his hold, shifting his other hand to Greyson's face. He cupped each side, raising the fae's head until their gazes clashed. He gave Greyson a genuine smile. "It's okay. Let me help you."

He channeled his power, allowing his grace to cover Grey's skin. It swirled along his flesh, mixing with Grey's magic before slowly sinking beneath the surface. A flash of white light filled the room, gradually fading into a soft blue. Greyson gasped, his eyes widening before he collapsed on top of Michael.

Michael gathered the man in his arms, bracing against the tremors that racked through his mate as Greyson drew a series of shaky breaths. Silence grew around them, only the ghosted strum of Grey's heartbeat sounding inside Michael's head. He didn't speak, simply held on, praying he'd given Grey enough of his grace to soothe the pain without actually completing the bond.

He waited, assessing if he'd inadvertently taken the other man as his mate. If he'd crossed the line without a second thought when Greyson stirred within his arms. The man shifted to the side, somehow finding the strength to push onto his elbows. His gaze clashed with Michael's a moment before he sighed.

He broke eye contact, shame hunching his shoulders as he released a weary breath. "Thank you."

Michael palmed his jaw, waiting until Grey looked at him. "If I could give you more, I would. I just…"

Greyson nodded. "It's complicated."

"I know you don't understand—"

"You don't have to explain. I asked for one night and you've given me that." He glanced away again. "I just need a minute."

"The night's not over. But maybe a change of venue. Hungry?"

Greyson chuckled. "Nice deflection. Very smooth. But since you mentioned it, yes…I'm starving."

"Then perhaps you'd mutter a few words and clean us up so I can put something together."

"What? You don't want to take another shower?"

"We both know what will happen if we step inside that shower again. And I can still feel how unsteady you are. Food, first. Then…"

He arched his brow, smiling when Grey rolled his eyes. The faery drew a deep breath, muttering more foreign words. His magic flared around them, the blue glow streaked with white this time. A cool sensation covered Michael's body, the scent of earth and dew heavy in the air.

Greyson pushed onto his heels, then scrambled off the bed, offering Michael his hand. Michael accepted, startling with his pants appeared on his body. He glared at Grey, but the fae merely grinned, adjusting his own clothing.

"If you want me to focus on eating instead of you, you'll have to at least cover part of your body, though like I said before…those jeans, your ass."

"You look equally inviting." Michael made a point of walking over to the small kitchen area. He'd taken the time to stock it with food his guest liked—even if he hadn't been convinced his mate would show up—though he was far from experienced in cooking.

A chair scraped out behind him as Grey took a seat at the table. "Call me crazy, but I didn't realize angels required food. Though, I suppose, Gabe eats all the time."

"It's more for pleasure than need. As for Gabriel—my brother is somewhat unique in that fashion. With his grace woven through Kei..." He shrugged. "He exhibits more human-like traits. A compromise, I suppose, for not falling."

"You make it sound like a bad thing."

"On the contrary, I consider Gabriel more fortunate than most."

Grey arched a brow but didn't comment. He glanced around. "So, everything that's different about Gabe is because of Kei's spell?"

"Not entirely." Michael stacked some vegetables on the counter, glancing at Greyson over his shoulder. "Once an archangel fully bonds with their true soul...they often inherit some of their mate's traits. Eating, for example. Needing to sleep more often, even the way Gabriel's grace blends in color with Kei's fire..." He paused, recalling the swirls of white in Grey's magic before pushing the thought aside. It was merely a byproduct of the healing energy. Taking Grey's pain as best he could. It didn't mean Michael had fully bonded with the fae. Surely, he'd sense the change.

His grace surged slightly, giving his skin a pearl-like shine before Michael reined it in. He really needed to get his mind on what he was doing before he ended up making the entire cabin glow. He met Grey's gaze, ignoring the flash of curiosity in the man's eyes. "It's all part of their connection."

"Wouldn't it just be easier if your fated mates were angels?"

Michael laughed. "I'm afraid Father doesn't see it that way. Though, He insists He isn't the one to choose. That our grace chooses our mates. One it finds worthy." Michael sighed. "Or perhaps it's the other way 'round. A worthy soul chooses us." He turned back to the food, posing the question that had been burning inside him since he'd first met the fae. "I thought faeries only mated with their own kind? That Oberon wanted your bloodline kept pure?"

"That's generally the case. Though sometimes faeries have relationships with humans and the like, I've never heard of a fully bonded pairing outside of the realm."

Michael's stomach dropped at the man's words. While a part of him had been anticipating that answer, hearing Greyson voice his fears out loud cut deep. Even if Michael couldn't fully bond with Grey, it hurt knowing he'd never be welcomed as Grey's mate. Never be viewed as anything other than an outsider. A hand landed on his shoulder, and he glanced back.

Greyson tsked. "Stop. Just because there hasn't been a mating beyond the realm doesn't mean it can't happen. In the end, it comes down to fate. Or maybe faith. I'm not really sure, anymore. And for the record, I really don't care what anyone else thinks." He let his arm drop to his side. "Not that it matters. I'm only here for the night, remember? Nothing more, nothing less."

He inhaled a shaky breath, taking a healthy step back. He motioned to the food. "Are you going to stare at those vegetables all night? And where's the meat? Kei swears Gabe eats more of that than anyone he's ever met."

Michael forced himself to focus on the counter. "Honestly, I'm not much of a cook. And I didn't bring any meat. Kei said you prefer not to eat it." He looked over his shoulder at the fae. "Though, I think the mage might have gotten that part wrong."

Desire colored Greyson's cheeks, fading down his neck and upper chest. He inched closer, allowing his gaze to drop to Michael's groin then back up to his face. "Are you offering?"

"I thought you were hungry?"

"I am, just not for what I thought I was." He closed the distance, taking Michael's mouth in his before releasing him with a slight nip to his bottom lip. "Round three?"

CHAPTER EIGHT

Greyson snuggled against Michael's side, listening to the archangel snuffle in his sleep. For a guy who said he didn't require much, he'd been out cold for two hours. Grey had already gotten up once to use the washroom then again to grab a quick bite, and Michael hadn't so much as stirred.

Grey exhaled a slow breath. Their "round three" had turned into four, then five before they'd both collapsed in a heap of skin and sweat and wings. Grey hadn't realized how huge the man's wings were until they'd taken up half the bed, not that Grey was complaining. There was something dangerously hot about being encased by feathers, especially knowing how sensitive they were. And he knew he could easily spend the next few centuries discovering every way those feathers could excite the man.

A horn blasted inside his head, followed by the haunting lilt of a flute. Words echoed through his mind, threatening to spill free with each passing breath. While Michael's intervention had curbed the urge for a while, the barrier was slowly chipping away. Another few hours, and the damn need would be hammering at Grey again. Demanding he do the one thing he couldn't—claim his mate.

Pain shot through his skull, stealing his breath. He rolled off the bed, grabbing some pants as he headed for the door. Maybe a bit of distance would stem the pounding in his head. Give him a chance to catch his breath before spending the last few hours he had left with Michael. Allow Greyson to indulge one final time.

He opened the door and moved onto the porch. The moon sat large and round in the sky, the fullness of it making Greyson smile. He hadn't ventured to the human realm that often lately, since Kei had been spending most of his time in Grey's world—other than the days he spent with Gabriel up in Heaven. Though, they seemed to prefer the faery realm. Greyson suspected it had to do with the fact Gabe was still gaining full control of his grace. Or maybe Gabe was trying to ease his mate into the reality of being with an archangel. Whatever the reason, they both seemed ridiculously happy.

Sadness tightened Grey's gut, but he pushed it away. He might not have the future ahead of him his friend did, but at least he'd have memories. Moments to replay when the cold reality of the situation burned deep. It was far more than he deserved.

A murmur of voices sounded off to the left and he turned, scouring the nearby forest for any signs of life. But nothing moved in the darkness save for some rustling branches. He frowned, wondering if he should investigate further—ensure Michael's sanctuary wasn't being watched

—when the floor creaked behind him. He went to turn just as arms wrapped around his chest, tugging him into a strong embrace. The scent of cottonwood surrounded him, the flutter of wings making him smile.

Michael nuzzled his neck, nipping at his earlobe. "Trying to escape?"

Grey laughed. "And give up my last few hours? Not likely. I just needed some air."

"Are you unwell?"

"Of course not. Never better. Why?"

Michael sighed, the soft exhalation tickling Grey's neck. "I sense your pain. The music, the words—they're haunting you again, aren't they?"

Grey closed his eyes for a moment, wondering how he could effectively lie to his mate without the man picking up on it. "It's complicated."

"Jackass."

"Oh, more dirty talk. Are you ready for another round?"

Michael released him enough to spin him around. Sadness filled the man's eyes, regret bunching his shoulders. "I never should have asked you to come here. It was selfish. Had I known how hard this would be, how painful—"

"Don't." Grey shook his head, pulling free of the angel's embrace. "Don't stand there and apologize for giving me what I asked for. I was the one who suggested the arrangement, fully aware of what would happen inside my own head."

Michael frowned. "You want more."

Grey threw up his hands in frustration, unsure

whether to kiss the man or shake some sense into him. "Of course, I want more, Michael. You know what you are to me. What we both are to each other, but—" He held up his hand. "I said I wouldn't ask. Wouldn't bring it up. Tonight isn't about rituals or fate. It's not about how we'll spend the next thousand years. I just needed some fresh air. To clear my head. That's all." He waved at the doorway. "Shall we?"

Michael nodded, though his expression clearly conveyed that he didn't believe Greyson's reasoning. But he motioned Grey inside, obviously choosing to let the topic drop. He continued over to a cabinet on the far wall, removing a flask and two glasses.

He turned, arching his brow in question. "You do consume spirits, don't you?"

"I really hope you're referring to wine."

Michael grinned. "Red okay?"

"Anything with alcohol is more than okay." He accepted the glass, taking a tentative sip. "Wow. This is incredible. Where'd you get it?"

Michael's lips quirked. "There are a number of grape orchards in the sacred garden. Zarachiel used to make wine as a hobby. He was quite talented."

Greyson cursed inwardly. "Shit. I didn't mean to upset you—"

"It's fine. Abaddon's crimes weren't your doing."

"That doesn't mean I want to bring up things that hurt you."

"You haven't hurt me. Friends should be remembered. Celebrated."

"Agreed."

He took a long drink, smiling when Michael topped up

his glass. Hell, if he'd known the guy had wine, he'd have drunk half the bottle when he'd first arrived.

Michael chuckled. "Thinking we did just fine without the liquid courage."

"True. But God knows there're more than a few things I'd like to ask you that would be easier if large amounts of alcohol were involved."

"You can ask me anything. I have nothing to hide."

"If that were true, you wouldn't have barriers erected inside that sexy head of yours."

"Barriers?"

Greyson cursed inwardly. The stress of fighting the mating was obviously getting to him. He waved one hand. "Forget it. I… I'm sure we have other, more pleasurable ways to pass the last few hours before sunrise."

Michael palmed Grey's chest when he moved into the angel's personal space. "What barriers?"

"It's nothing. Really."

"Greyson."

"Just something I sensed when you were practically screaming your thoughts at me. It's none of my business. I shouldn't have brought it up."

"Do you think I'm trying to block you?"

"It's not me you're blocking. It's your brother."

Michael stilled, the hand wedged against Grey's chest fisting in response. The angel stared at him, lips slightly parted, a mixture of fear and shame shaping his features before he turned sharply, placing his glass on the table then moving quickly to the other side of the room. His wings snapped, the feathers ruffling. "You sensed that? How?"

"You know how. But I promised not to say the word."

Michael's head bowed to his chest.

Grey put down his glass, making his way to Michael. He studied the man, wondering what move to make next before throwing caution to the wind and wrapping his arms around his mate. The guy tensed, pushing against Grey's hold before relaxing. A desolate sigh drifted between them as Michael leaned against Grey, allowing him to bridge some of his weight.

"Ever since Lucifer healed me..." He let his head connect with Grey's shoulder. "I could force him out, but..."

Grey smiled against the man's head. "But you haven't."

"He saved my life, Greyson. Without asking anything of me in return. Nothing."

"He's your brother."

"That's hardly the point."

"Really? Maybe that's the entire point." Grey released Michael enough to spin the man within his arms. "Just because you and Lucifer have some ugly history doesn't mean you can't be there for each other when the shit hits the fan. You're still family."

"It doesn't work that way. He chose his path."

"Is it really that absolute? Or are you saying that because you don't want to admit there's a part of you that still loves him? That wants to believe there's a way back?" Greyson snagged Michael's elbow when the archangel tried to push free. "Do you know why Sirena died that night?"

Michael froze, giving Grey a small shake of his head.

Greyson pursed his lips. "We'd had another fight. I'd

been spending a lot of time in the human world, drinking. Fooling around. Telling myself I was simply making some memories before duty and responsibility ruled my life. Sirena disagreed. Said I needed to act like the prince I was. I reacted...poorly. Kicked her out of my home. Told her not to come back. She ran into Abaddon on the path back to her place, and..." He broke eye contact. "Family doesn't always agree. That doesn't mean you love them any less."

Michael stared at him, nothing but the whisper of air sounding between them before he twisted, yanking Greyson hard against his chest as his mouth claimed Grey's. Grey surrendered, holding Michael tight as a flash of white consumed them. Grey gasped as his back hit the mattress, the pants he'd donned absent. Michael loomed over him, eyes narrowed, lips pulled tight. His wings stretched out to either side, making him appear every inch the warrior of legend.

Michael's grace slowly receded, dimming into a light blue color before winking out. "I need you. If you'd rather not after learning..."

Greyson frowned. Did the guy really think he'd change his mind because of Lucifer? Because his mate didn't outright hate his kin?

Grey pushed onto his elbows, locking his hand behind Michael's neck. "Like this or on my hands and knees?"

The muscle in Michael's jaw jumped followed by a wide smile. "Hands and knees."

Michael helped Grey spin, smoothing a hand along Grey's spine once he'd positioned himself between Michael's thighs. He started to recite the spell, when Michael stopped him.

"Not this time. I want to prepare you, myself."

Grey glanced over his shoulder as Michael opened a small drawer on the side table and removed a long tube. He popped off the top, grinning at Grey as he covered his fingers in the slick gel. The angel's gaze never wavered as he lowered his hand, circling one finger around Grey's ass.

Grey let his head bow forward, anticipating the first brush of Michael's finger. He held his breath, exhaling when his mate probed his opening, sliding his slick fingers inside Grey's passage.

Michael hummed behind him, dropping a kiss on Grey's shoulder blade. "So tight. What you do to me."

Grey breathed through several passes, each one adding more lube until he thought he'd scream. He looked back, hissing around his clenched teeth when Michael scissored his fingers apart. "I'm ready. Just... Damn, I need more than your fingers."

Michael made a point of thrusting in a few more times before slowly removing his hand. Grey snagged his lip to brace against the loss, moaning when Michael's cock pushed against his ass. He relaxed his muscles, easing his mate's way as the man buried his shaft inside him, not stopping until his sac connected with Grey's flesh.

Michael curled over him, nipping at his shoulder. "You feel so good. So right."

Grey nodded, knowing if he tried to speak he'd end up binding them together. Instead, he focused on the slow glide of Michael's cock. The steady thrust of the man's hips as he drove them both higher, coiling Grey's release tight in his groin. It gathered strength, gnawing at his control with every firm stroke. Michael kept his chest pressed to Grey's back, one hand wrapped around Grey's torso while the other toyed with his wing, adding another depth of sensation.

Michael grunted against Grey's neck, locking his shaft deep. "I can't hold it off. I don't want to finish, but..." He moved his hand to Grey's cock, fisting his fingers around the length of it. "Come for me. Give yourself to me one more time."

The words burned unshed tears behind Grey's eyes. This was it. The last time he'd feel his mate join with him. Revel in the sound Michael made as he emptied inside him, nothing but skin between them. While Grey didn't know what his future held, he was certain it would never compare to this moment. This night.

Michael stiffened behind him, pumping Grey's cock as the angel quickened his pace. Pleasure overshadowed the gnawing sadness, taking Greyson headlong into release. His cock swelled within Michael's grip, covering his stomach and his mate's hand with his seed just as Michael thrust deep, the telltale pulse of the man's shaft marking his climax. Michael rasped Grey's name, a surge of white swirling around them. Grey's magic joined in, blending the light into a muted blue before slowly fading.

Michael collapsed, taking Grey with him as he fell onto his side, tugging Grey into his chest with a possessive curl of his arm. The angel's wing settled over them, an exhausted sigh breezing across Grey's damn skin.

Michael kissed his shoulder, giving him a squeeze. "Rest. We'll clean up later."

Greyson nodded, still fighting the words that formed on his tongue. The melody sounded in his head, the mournful tone impossible to miss, as if fate recognized the inevitable outcome. He fisted his hands, focusing on the bite of pain as he dug his fingernails into his palm. Michael's breathing slowed, the steady rise and fall of the man's chest indicating he'd fallen asleep. Grey waited until he was certain Michael wouldn't wake before gently lifting the man's wing. His feathers tickled Grey's palm as he laid the edge along Michael's side then eased out of the bed, careful not to jostle the mattress.

Michael huffed, burrowing into the bed then settling once more. Grey took one last opportunity to study the man. Memorize every curve, every angle. The way his feathers seemed to shine in the hint of light beyond the window. This was how he'd remember his mate. Safe. Content. His skin still flushed from their lovemaking.

He leaned forward, dropping a gentle kiss on Michael's shoulder. "I'll always belong to you. Even if I can't say all the words."

He backed away from the bed, pulling on his clothes then heading for the door. He opened it slowly, releasing his held breath when it gave without groaning in protest. Just a few more feet, and he'd be gone. Free to use his magic without worrying the pulse of energy would wake his mate.

Grey moved onto the porch, closing the door behind him before turning to gaze across the hills. Yellow smeared the horizon off to the east, the sun still several minutes away from rising above the landmass. He'd always been fond of this time of day. The promise of a new start dawning with the first rays of daybreak. But not today. Today marked the end of his journey to find his true soul. Nothing but a stark reminder that he'd failed the only truly important mission he'd ever been given.

He trudged down the three short steps and across the

open grass toward the woods. He could have easily have flashed home, but his heart wasn't in it. How could he face Kei or Gabriel when all he wanted was to hold the one man he couldn't have?

Shadows loomed around him as he picked his way along a path. He'd give himself a few more moments of solitude before heading somewhere distant. Somewhere he could disappear for a few hours to gather his composure. Erect the necessary barriers to block Michael from sensing him. The archangel had upheld his end of the bargain. Seemed only fair that Greyson give him some semblance of peace. And somehow being connected the way they were didn't seem like a viable way of achieving that.

A twig snapped behind him, stopping him in his tracks. Damn, Michael must have sensed his absence. Followed him. Shit, Grey should have zapped out of the damn human realm the moment he'd cleared the cabin.

Greyson drew a deep breath, preparing himself for the onslaught of emotions as he turned, raising his gaze to the man standing behind him. He froze, the inklings of uncertainty crawling along his spine. "You're not..."

The guy grinned just as a series of darts struck Greyson in the thigh. He reeled backwards, yanking the damn things out as the scenery swam around him. He tried to phase but only succeeded in slamming his face into the moss-covered ground.

Boots appeared beside his head, a rough laugh filling the woods. "Looks like today's your lucky day, Prince. My boss has been searching for you forever. About time you two got acquainted." His breath washed over Grey's face, the stench of smoke and ash filling Grey's senses. "Never would have guessed you were the guy in the prophecy, but then you rarely show your true self, do you? An heir with wings. Who'd have guessed?" He laughed again, the sound fading into black. "That's all about to change. Your time in the spotlight has come."

CHAPTER NINE

Three days.

Three long, godforsaken days since he'd woken to discover Greyson had already left. Since Michael had been able to sense the man's presence, even just as a ghosted heartbeat inside his head. Obviously, his mate hadn't been exaggerating. The fae seemingly had more than enough power to block Michael from even the most basic elements of their connection. And that truth was slowly driving him mad.

He cursed then stood, pacing the length of the pond in the sacred garden. He wasn't Greyson's mate. Couldn't be. The man deserved someone worthy of Greyson's soul, not a damaged archangel in desperate need of redemption. Besides, once word of their pairing got out—and it would —Greyson would be the target of every being who'd ever had a grievance against Michael or his family. And he'd be damned before he allowed the only man he'd ever truly love to be hurt because of him.

"For fuck's sake, Mikey, lighten the Hell up. And while you're

at it, stop lying to yourself. We both know this has nothing to do with who your daddy is and everything to do with the fact you're just plain scared."

Michael let his head tip back as he fisted his hands at his side. "Please, Lucifer. Not now."

"Careful, bro. Someone might hear you talking out loud to no one and wonder if you're losing your mind."

"That's because I am!"

"Easy. No need to shout. I can hear you just fine."

Michael groaned in defeat as he scrubbed a hand down his face. He should force the man out. Erect a permanent barrier. "What do you want?"

"Can't I just chat with my big brother without it being about something? After all, you still haven't shared all the juicy details about your night with the Prince of the Fae."

"And I won't be. So, if that's all you were interested in, you can go."

A sigh sounded inside his mind, the usual smug tone noticeably absent. *"Why are you fighting this?"*

"Why do you care?"

"Look. I know we don't see eye-to-eye on most things, but... Have you stopped to consider that maybe Greyson is the redemption you seem to think you need? That he's the answer to all those questions floating around inside your head?"

"Even if that's true...I can't put him at risk."

"Right, because making him spend the next thousand years pining for his mate is a much kinder fate. Pull your head out of your ass and start seeing this from his perspective. Besides, the guy gave Kei both of those spells, which essentially pulled our collective asses out of the proverbial fire. Thinking he can hold his own."

Michael stilled, Lucifer's words resonating through him. "Why are you doing this?"

"Have you ever spent any quality time in Hell? There's no one here I can have a good, in-depth conversation with. But you—"

"Helping me. Why are you being...nice?"

Lucifer laughed. *"Hey, don't go getting all sentimental on me. I offered one tiny piece of advice. I'll still likely kick your ass the next time we meet. You're the one who's riddled with guilt. I'm perfectly fine with who and what I am."*

"Then what do you want in return?"

Another laugh. *"Nothing. Which is kind of the point. I know that drives you crazy."*

"Damn it, Lucifer."

"Whoa. You keep cussing like that and Dad might get the wrong idea."

"This conversation is over."

"Fine. But I'm not going anywhere, and you seem pretty fucking reluctant to banish me, so...until next time." His presence faded then surged back. *"Now, go talk to Greyson. I'm sure even someone as pure as you can come up with one, tiny, little white lie as an excuse to visit your...friend."*

Michael cursed again. He really needed to stop talking to his brother. Lucifer was starting to make sense, and Michael suspected nothing good would come from that. He groaned. Who was he kidding? Lucifer's opinions weren't changing, Michael's were. And they all revolved around his feelings toward his brother. Ones he wasn't sure were in his best interest.

Michael closed his eyes, once again searching out his connection with Grey only to get the same, empty void he'd been experiencing since the fae had left. Uncertainty surfaced, spurred on by Lucifer's lingering thoughts. His brother was right. Checking up on Greyson was common courtesy. To ensure his *friend* was all right. It didn't have to mean anything more than that.

A distant chuckle echoed in Michael's head then quieted. Just what he needed. A devil on his shoulder. He made his way to the edge of the garden, glancing down at his attire. He was still wearing jeans instead of his tunic, and he wasn't sure if he should show up on Greyson's doorstep dressed in anything other than his usual clothes.

"Stop overthinking this and get your ass down there. Christ, you're high maintenance."

"I believe I asked you to leave."

"Then, stop being a fucking coward and go."

Michael mentally flipped off his brother, erecting the barrier between them then taking to the skies. He soared toward a portal not far from the garden, shivering as he passed through the wards. A ghostly echo of Greyson's voice calling his name resonated inside his mind, quickly fading as Michael emerged on the other side. He stopped and scanned the area, wondering if he'd inadvertently dropped in on Greyson's current position, only to frown when the glade appeared completely deserted. Even the usual background chorus of crickets was conspicuously absent.

The inklings of fear prickled the hairs on the back of his neck. He did his best to rerun the exact words Greyson had used in his sanctuary—determine if the man had said he could hide all trace of their connection or just parts of it—only to curse in frustration. He'd been far too preoccupied with loving the fae to put every word he'd uttered into memory. Though Michael was starting to question if Greyson could really hide this well from him.

Concern replaced any doubts and Michael headed for

Grey's home, skimming through the glen as fast as the heavy foliage would allow. He shuddered to a halt just shy of his mate's door, the intricately carved wood dark against the dimming light. He hadn't realized the sun was nearly below the horizon, staining the clouds a bloody shade of red.

He strode to the porch, drawing a deep breath before banging his fist against the door. "Greyson!"

He waited, straining to hear anything beyond the thick wood, but the home remained silent. He glanced at the windows. Shouldn't Greyson have lights on by now? Surely if the shadows were half as thick within the walls as they were outside, the man would need some form of light to see. Even if the guy used his magic.

He knocked again. "Greyson, please. I... We need to talk." More silence. "Damn it! Just let me know you're okay, and I'll leave. But I'm not going anywhere until you open the door and tell me to fuck off to my face."

A throat cleared behind him and he spun, groaning inwardly at the confused look on Kei and Gabriel's faces. Kei nodded to his mate, obviously indicating he wanted Gabriel to take lead.

His brother sighed. "Michael? Are you well? I'm not sure I've ever seen you dressed like that."

Michael drew himself up, hoping he didn't look nearly as desperate as he felt. He forced a smile, nodding at the men. "I'm..." His voice caught, the words rasping into a grunt.

Kei moved to Gabriel's side, nudging his mate in the shoulder. "If you'd like some privacy—"

"Have you seen Greyson?" Michael took a step toward the couple. "I just wanted to ensure he was all right."

Kei's face scrunched up as he spared Gabriel another quick glance. "Isn't he with you?"

"With me?"

"When you stopped visiting at the same time he left, we just figured…" He waved his hand at the space between them. "That you two were discussing your situation." Kei arched a brow. "So, he's not with you?"

"Initially, yes, but…" Michael tamped down the dread souring his gut. "He left before I woke, and I haven't heard from him since."

Gabriel gave Kei's hand a squeeze before moving closer. "I know you don't want to acknowledge what's happening between the two of you, but whether you admit it or not, you should be able to sense him. Even if you haven't fully bonded."

Michael pursed his lips together. "He's blocking me. Has been since he left."

Fire sparked to life on Kei's skin before he seemed to rein it. "Blocking you? No way. He can't block his true soul."

"Greyson claims differently. And I can attest to the fact that I have no idea where the man is. Which still leaves the question of where he's buggered off to."

Kei's fire sparked again. "You think he's in trouble?"

"Something feels…off. I just want to know he's all right. Then I'll leave. But until then…"

His words died off as a flash of green flared behind Kei and Gabriel. Michael darted forward, palming the hilt of his sword, ready to stand against whatever materialized in the glade only to pull back when two of Oberon's messengers appeared next to the path. Their gazes swung to his hand then back to his face.

One bowed slightly, glancing over Michael's shoulder at the other two men. "Your presence is requested in the hallowed garden by His Royal Highness, King Oberon."

Michael arched his brow, glancing at his brother when the scenery shifted. Pulsing green light radiated around them, blurring their surroundings until they found themselves standing in an older section of the glen, the heady scent of earth and moss filling the lush space.

Michael palmed his sword again, spinning in search of the men, but all that remained was a lingering hint of green in the air not far from them. He moved in beside Gabriel, still scanning the area. While Michael didn't see anyone, he sensed they weren't alone.

"That would be a correct assumption."

He turned, staring at the man standing off to his right, his robe shifting colors with the vegetation as he slowly walked toward them. Long silver hair flowed down past his shoulders, his green eyes clearly assessing every detail.

He stopped several feet away, his gaze focusing on Michael. "I'm impressed. Not many outsiders sense me before I fully lower my glamour." He cocked an eyebrow. "But then you're not really an outsider, are you."

It wasn't a question, and Michael wasn't quite sure how to respond.

The faery grinned. "Forgive the hasty retreat of my kin, but I was hoping we could speak in private. Besides, they'll be recovering for the next few days after having to transport *two* archangels at once. Your grace doesn't like to be forced, does it?"

Michael straightened, removing his hand from his sword. It flickered then vanished. "You could have had them escort us on foot. We would have accepted your invitation either way."

"I had no doubts that Kei and Gabriel would have followed, but seeing as we've never met..." He nodded. "It's an honor to finally meet you, Michael. My son has spoken quite highly of you."

Michael's throat caught at the idle mention of Greyson, but he managed to swallow past the lump forming in his chest. "And you, Oberon. I have to say, Greyson looks a lot like you."

The king's grin widened. "Minus the silver hair. Though I suppose when he's several hundred years old..." His expression sobered. "That's assuming his fate hasn't already been changed."

Michael froze. Oberon knew. Michael wasn't sure if Greyson had told his father or if it was something that ran blood deep, but Michael knew, without a doubt, that the king was aware Michael was Greyson's true soul.

"You seem surprised. Surely my son told you faeries share similar traits to angels. Doesn't your father know far more about you than what you tell him?"

Michael firmed his stance, waving at the garden surrounding them. "Is this your way of saying you don't approve?"

The older fae laughed. "Whether I approve or not has no bearing on the subject. Fate chooses who is blessed with a mate, not I. Though I will admit, the circumstances are most...intriguing. There's never been a fully bonded pairing outside of our realm."

"So Greyson said."

"My son is nothing if not honest. Which brings me to

the reason of why I summoned you. Do you know where Greyson is?"

He sighed. "No. I'm afraid I don't."

"Do you not share a connection?"

"He's chosen to block me."

"Has he?" Oberon wandered across the garden, caressing the flowers that seemed to turn into his touch. "And why would he chose to block you of all people?"

Michael huffed, taking a few, heavy strides toward the king. "Must you take me for a fool? If you know what we are to one another then you know why he's shut me out."

Oberon glanced at Gabriel and Kei then back to him. "You denied the mating, and he's trying to spare you the pain he'll suffer from your rejection."

"It's not that simple."

"Actually, it is." He held up one hand, stopping Michael from interrupting him. "I'm sure you thought you were doing what was best for him, but in this case, it might well cost him and his people, their lives."

"Their lives? What are you talking about? Where is he?"

The man sighed, and for the first time since appearing, fear flashed in his eyes. "Taken."

CHAPTER TEN

"Hey, Princeling! Wake up!"

Greyson gasped as cold water sluiced across his face, stinging a line along his brow. He sputtered through another splash, shaking his head in an effort to clear his vision. The scenery swam, blurring in and out of focus as pain thrummed through his skull.

Rough hands stabbed through his hair, forcefully yanking back his head. "Don't fade on us, chum. It's time for you to meet the boss."

Grey blinked, groaning when a fist connected with his cheek, snapping his jaw to the side. Blood filled his mouth, the metallic taste souring his gut. He leaned forward, spitting most of it onto the stone floor beneath him. It splattered across the uneven surface, the red drops blending in with the varying shades of brown in the rock. Nausea tumbled through his stomach, and he fought the urge to empty it next to the blood.

"Enough, Sezil." A set of boots moved into his field of view. "Our friend isn't much good to us dead." A hand cupped his chin, forcing his head up. Red eyes stared back at him, the pupils narrowed into thin, cat-like strips. "I thought I told you not to mark up his face?"

Sezil grunted. "You're the one who hit him with half a dozen darts. Not my fault he fell."

"So you didn't just punch him?"

"Just trying to get his attention."

"You're an idiot." The man shook his head, letting Greyson's chin bow back to his chest. "Are you sure we weren't followed?"

"Do you have any idea what it took to transport *him* here?"

"I was in the forest with you, for fuck's sake. Yes, I know what it took to bring someone of his strength and light here."

"Well, I'm kinda surprised we all actually made it. So to answer your question, no. No one can follow us. That's why Tharn picked this place for the ceremony."

"Don't say his name. He'll fry our asses if he finds out. Shit, Sezil, have some fucking common sense. Besides, nothing's impenetrable. And our prince has some very powerful friends."

"Trust me. There aren't any rescues for him. Especially from anyone as righteous as those feathered boys."

The guy sighed. "Boss should be here soon. We'd best do one more check, just to be sure."

"Fuck, you're paranoid."

Footsteps tapped around him then faded. Greyson did his best to calm his breathing, wincing as each inhale sent a jolt of pain through his ribs and into his head. Apparently, Sezil had done more than sock him in the jaw. A few broken ribs if Grey's hunch was right.

He released a slow breath, focusing his energy on the ties binding his arms, only to curse as his magic surged then receded, staying trapped beneath his skin. Great. Just fucking great. Either they'd drawn some kind of sigil to prevent him from accessing his magic, or they'd used a spell to bind it. Neither was going to help him escape, especially if he couldn't temper at least a bit of the pain.

Grey clenched his jaw, doing his best to clear his thoughts. He wasn't even sure what had happened. The last thing he remembered he'd been sneaking out of Michael's cabin. He'd needed a few moments to gather his composure before heading back to the faery realm when...

He groaned. He'd been waylaid. And to make matters worse, he hadn't even bothered to glamour himself after jumping off the porch—had just blindly headed into the woods—wings flapping in the breeze as if it were nothing to see a male fae strolling through the human world. The same woods he'd thought he'd heard voices from earlier in the night. He'd been a fool. So wrapped up in the aftermath of not completing the binding ritual, he hadn't taken a single precaution to prevent this very thing from happening. And now, he was tied to a damn chair, with nothing more than his sharp wit as a weapon.

Shame hunched his shoulders. So much for being a warrior of the faery court. Getting snatched as he had—by a couple of red-eyed demons to boot—was nothing less than embarrassing. And definitely not something he wanted to become common knowledge. Which meant he needed to find a way out before he was missed. Damn, he didn't even know how long he'd been gone.

No one can follow us.

Greyson frowned. Where on Earth, or any other realm,

could they take him that others couldn't follow? While Hell wasn't exactly easy to gain entry into, it wasn't impenetrable. Especially considering who was in charge. While Michael didn't have much faith in his brother Lucifer, Greyson doubted the archangel would allow anyone to hurt Michael's mate. Would he? Or had that been the fallen angel's plan all along? Make a connection with his brother only to take away what meant the most to him.

Not mated.

Greyson needed to remember that. Michael had given Grey what he'd asked for, but had never hinted he wanted more. Needed more the way Grey did. Which meant he was on his own.

Another shot of pain pulsed through his temples, stealing his breath. He needed to stop worrying about the past—circumstances he couldn't change— and get his ass out of the chair and on the move. He closed his eyes, concentrating on shifting his arms enough to loosen the straps securing him to the chair. Scratchy fibers bit into his skin, rubbing his wrists raw without giving an inch. He huffed. This wasn't going as well as he'd hoped.

He closed his eyes. While they'd somehow restrained his magic, it didn't mean he couldn't contact someone in the faery realm. Not that he wanted to admit he needed help, but…his options were looking extremely limited.

Greyson pictured Kei, sending out a mental plea for help, only to have the message close back in on him. Grey furrowed his brow. He'd never had that happen before. Sending his thoughts was more a part of him than a direct use of magic. He'd always been able to communicate that way, even before he'd learned how to control his energy.

He tried again, cursing when the message merely bounced back without making it through. The inklings of fear built along his spine, the cold reality of the situation finally sinking in. He hadn't really stopped to consider he was in serious trouble, until now.

He took a calming breath. Panicking wouldn't save him any more than his magic apparently would. He needed to find a way around their barriers. After all, almost every spell had a weakness. All he had to do was discover it and use it to his advantage.

A surge of white light swirled across his skin, tracing the patterns along his flesh before fading into blue as it flickered onto his wings. A familiar voice echoed in his head, only to get cut off as if it had hit a wall.

Michael.

Grey focused, probing the void surrounding him. Images blurred in and out of focus, the constant shifting increasing the nauseous feeling in his stomach. He kept pushing, calling the man's name until the pressure in his head crushed in on him. There was a single moment of clarity—his mate's thoughts joining with his—before the pain splintered through his skull, shattering the connection.

He slumped in the chair, drawing several ragged breaths, despite the searing jolt through his torso with every inhalation. This was more than a just a spell or a sigil. It equated to blood fire for angels, though he wasn't aware of any ancient marking or scroll that held that much power over a fae. Surely if one existed, his father would have shown him long ago.

Greyson raised his head, squinting to bring his surroundings into focus. The chair sat in the center of a small room, the walls and floor comprised of rough stone. But there was something...off. The rocks looked muted, as if most of the color had been drained out of them. He stretched his hands toward the ground. Even if he couldn't use his magic, he should be able to sense the power radiating all around him. Feel the aura. A faint wash of energy pulsed beneath him, then vanished.

It couldn't be. A realm without magic? That inhibited natural abilities?

He needed to leave. Now.

He strained against the bindings, aware he was cutting his skin, but too desperate to free himself to care. Though he didn't know why he'd been taken, the fact he'd been brought to a realm void of magical energy suggested it went far beyond a simple kidnapping. That he was a pawn in a much larger scheme—one most likely involving his people.

Shit, he never should have lowered his glamour. He could have just as easily shared the night with Michael in his alternate form. It'd been selfish. Wanting his mate to see him—hell, accept him—for who he truly was. A romantic notion that the act, itself, might sway Michael's decision. Not that it'd worked. Michael had still rejected their pairing, and Greyson had put his entire kingdom in jeopardy.

A familiar thrill started inside his head, the lilting melody slowly gathering strength. Words joined the notes, mixing together until it felt as if the very air vibrated with the haunting song.

Fuck!

Just his luck. They'd managed to lock up his magic, but the damn song still reached him. He gritted his teeth, mentally shoving away the music. But it only pushed the melody into the background, the mournful rise and fall of the notes continuing. Shit, it hadn't been that long. How the hell was he going to survive the next thousand years with that infernal tune stuck in his head? What if it never went away? Never stopped playing?

Focus, jackass.

He gave himself a mental shake. If he didn't get his ass out of there, he wouldn't have to worry about the ritual or Michael—he'd likely be dead. Or worse.

He worked at the ties again, blood from the gashes in his flesh allowing the restraints to move more freely. Pain seared across his wrists, but he kept tugging, finally managing to wedge one side of the restraint over his thumb then off. The bindings fell to the floor with a soft thud. Greyson leaned forward, untying the ropes around his legs before rising. He grabbed the chair when the room seemed to tilt beneath his feet, holding tight until his equilibrium returned. Pain still thrummed through his head, but at least he could move.

He drew a deep breath, testing his glamour, but it only succeeded in sending more white swirls across his skin. He didn't know why he seemed to be harnessing what looked like a hint of Michael's grace. His mate had been clear that any changes only happened if Michael fully bonded with him. And Grey knew the man hadn't. Greyson wouldn't have been able to resist reciting the words if Michael had given Grey that much of himself.

Grey pushed aside the thoughts. He'd simply have to venture out dressed as he was in only his damn pants and boots—his wings and markings clearly visible. God help him, but he hadn't even grabbed his shirt, not that he could have worn it without being able to manifest his glamour. But knowing he'd left without half his clothes made him feel even more foolish.

He sighed as he took a few stumbling steps toward the opening in the wall. He'd deal with his apparent descent into madness once he'd returned home. Until then, he needed to concentrate on finding a portal back. Cold stone connected with his palms as he tripped against the arch, catching himself as his balance shifted yet again. He didn't know what they'd drugged him with, but it was definitely hampering his ability to walk, let alone fight. And Grey had no doubts he'd have to spill blood before finding his way home.

A pulse of the odd, white light swirled over him, lifting some of the fuzziness from his head. He frowned but straightened. He'd take whatever help he could get, even if he didn't understand what it was. He studied his surroundings. The archway opened into a long hallway, muted light streaming in through another opening at the far end. Several other passageways seemed to branch off of the corridor, most of them cloaked in shadows.

Voices sounded from straight ahead, just beyond the large entranceway at the end of the hallway. Greyson darted out, stumbling his way over to the first passage. He took a quick glance down the length of it then moved into the dark recess near the edge, pressing his back against the wall. Footsteps tapped closer, slowing as they neared his hiding spot. A startled gasp lit the air.

"What the fuck? Where…"

Sezil's voice sounded a moment before he and his partner raced past, their boots pounding against the stone. Greyson didn't waste the opportunity as he dashed out behind them, running for what he hoped was the exit. While a part of him screamed at him to turn and fight, another recognized the futility of it. They were bound to have weapons, and he was lucky he hadn't tripped. Shouts echoed behind him, but he chose to lower his head and push harder.

He'd nearly reached the archway when another demon walked through it. Grey reacted, twisting sideways as he slid onto his side, skidding past the creep and into the opening. The man snarled and turned, reaching for Greyson when he managed to push to his feet. The demon grabbed one arm only to recoil as his body jerked forward, then fell, another one of those strange darts sticking out of his back.

Grey snagged the man's blade, chancing a look down the hallway. His captors charged toward him, matching blades in their hands. White light gathered on Grey's palm, and he aimed it toward the two demons, inhaling when it shot forward, knocking them both down. A wave of dizziness spun the scenery, but it receded, leaving only a lingering hum of power strumming across Grey's flesh.

He gathered his bearings then ran, boots crunching across hard-packed dirt. A shadowed copse of leafless trees stood off to his right, the bare branches creaking in the strong breeze. A mixture of sulfur and smoke filled the air, the pungent aroma souring his gut.

He increased his pace, nearing the trees when a mass of demons emerged from the thick bramble, effectively blocking his way. He skidded to a halt, spinning in a circle as the creatures closed in on him, swords gleaming in the dull light. He glanced up. Nothing but gray clouds filled the sky, all hint of color bleached out.

He stretched his wings. While they were a physical part of him, his ability to fly was largely due to his connection with nature. A byproduct of his magic. Without access to it—he wasn't convinced he'd do more than hover for a few seconds then fall. And he couldn't afford to leave himself vulnerable like that.

Grey raised his weapon. While he preferred to use his magic as a means of defense, he knew how to handle a blade. The demons continued circling, none seemingly willing to make the first move. They were obviously buying time. Stalling long enough for others to arrive.

He took the initiative, striking out at the closest man. The demon parried his attack, landing a few hits on Grey's sword before falling as one of Grey's thrusts hit home. Another demon took up the fight, crumpling to the ground after only a few swings. But as quickly as he cut the creatures down, more took their places.

He cursed. He'd tire long before he'd done more than kill a few dozen demons. His magic thrummed beneath his skin, manifesting as a flash of white light. The glow traveled along his torso, ending as tiny arcs across his wings. He sighed. He'd have to chance flying, or he'd never get free.

Another red-eyed bastard fell, opening up a small strip off to Grey's right. He turned, sprinting a few steps before leaping. He tipped his wings up then down, trying to garner a fraction of lift as a small flicker of pale-blue light cascaded along the surface, highlighting the swirling veins. He'd gained about ten feet when a soft twang sounded behind him.

Understanding dawned, and he swooped right, narrowing avoiding the arrow only to get struck by another. Burning pain exploded across his shoulder, dropping him harshly onto the ground. Dirt and stones bit into his skin as blood washed down his flesh. Rough hands flipped him over, silver eyes staring down at him.

"Now, now, young prince. I can't let you leave before the main event, can I?"

Greyson gasped. "You? But your kind is bound to the shadow lands, you can't be..."

His words morphed into a scream as the creature grabbed the end of the arrow and yanked it free. Blood sizzled along the triangular head, sending up tiny tendrils of smoke. Iron.

The entity smiled, a sickly mixture of perfect lips and bone-white teeth. "Your father was wise to hide you for as long as he did. Too bad you weren't as smart." A cruel laugh echoed around them. "An heir with wings. We've been waiting for you."

CHAPTER ELEVEN

Michael's stomach dropped to his feet as a dull ringing sounded in his head. He tried to speak, but only managed to take a staggering step toward the king. Gabriel grabbed his arm, stopping Michael from tripping onto one knee as his brother braced some of his weight, waiting until Michael had regained his balance before slowly releasing him.

Michael whispered his thanks, focusing once again on Oberon. "You're not making any sense. I was just with..." He forced himself to take a calming breath before continuing. "What makes you think Greyson's been taken?"

Oberon's expression never wavered. "I know." He held up his hand when Michael went to speak. "I'm sure your father knows when one of His angels is in peril. I know when my people are suffering." He sighed. "I'm afraid it's begun."

"Greyson's suffering? How? And what's begun?"

Oberon merely stared at him, tilting his head as if

measuring Michael's worth. And Michael didn't need any special powers to surmise that the King of the Fae most likely found him lacking.

Michael drew himself up, allowing his grace to lightly color his skin. "I'm done talking in riddles, Oberon. If you have reason to think Greyson's in danger, just tell us. We can't help him if we don't know what's wrong."

The man's lips pulled tight, deepening the fine lines around his mouth. He looked tired. Or was he scared? "If you truly wanted to help my son, you wouldn't have rejected him as your mate."

Guilt washed over him, constricting his throat and tensing his shoulders. His wings snapped with annoyance as a deep ache settled in his chest. He clenched his jaw, knowing there was nothing he could say to justify his actions. Not when the man was right. He glanced at Gabriel and Kei. They wore similar expressions, though Michael knew they'd never voice their judgment. At least, not in front of Oberon.

Mixed emotions warred inside Michael, another hollow echo of Grey's voice in his head finally drawing him out of his thoughts. "What's between Greyson and me—"

"Are you denying he's your true soul?" Oberon crossed his arms, arching a brow in challenge. The foliage scattered throughout the garden shook as a tremor rumbled the earth. "Are you prepared to forsake him as I bear witness?"

"Why are we wasting time discussing this when you claim he's in danger? Do you know where he is or not?"

Oberon continued to stare at him, eyes narrowed, an earthly glow softly gathering around him. A clap of thunder rolled overhead, followed by a flicker of light. Michael's grace answered in kind, whirling eddies of dust and leaves around the glade as clouds gathered overhead. Bright, white light gleamed from his skin, chasing away any vestige of darkness.

He took a step forward when a hand landed on his shoulder. He glanced back, his gaze clashing with Gabriel's. His brother's grace glimmered around him, more orange than the golden color it used to be, as it mixed with Kei's magic in a testament of their union. Gabriel gave him a curt nod, mentally telling him to pull back as he motioned toward Oberon.

Michael bowed his head, exhaling as his power spiked then dimmed, slowly sinking beneath his skin. The wind eased, leaving a trail of leaves strewn across the glen. Exhaustion drooped his shoulders, the strain of denying the truth weighing heavy on his soul.

He gathered his composure, lifting his chin until he could look Oberon in the eyes. "All I want is to know that Greyson is well."

Oberon held his gaze as he moved toward him, his graceful form flowing over the glass and flowers until he stopped an arm's length away. The man's violet eyes saddened. "If you truly want to help Greyson—stop the prophecy before it reaches fruition—you're going to have a make a choice, Michael."

Fear sluiced through his veins. "Prophecy? What prophecy?"

"Your decision, first. Are you Greyson's mate, or not?"

"And that matters how?"

Oberon remained silent.

Impatience bled through Michael's reservations, the

sheer agony of his denial finally cracking his defenses. "Fine!"

He threw up his arms as he tipped his head toward the heavens, knowing this was a moment he couldn't take back. That saying it out loud would bind him to the fae as surly as if he'd given Greyson his grace. That it would only be a matter of when, not if.

He returned his focus to Oberon. "Yes. Greyson is my soulmate, my true one, and shall be as long as I draw breath. Whether you approve of the union or not, I will watch over him. Give my life for his if needed. He is my beginning, and my end." He narrowed his eyes. "Now tell me... Where. Is. My. Mate?"

The king's lips quirked at one side. "So be it." He waved his hand. "Please, follow me."

A warm glow surrounded them, fading into a room Michael had never seen before. Rows of leather-bound tomes lined each wall with light streaming in from translucent panels above them. Rough stone lined the floor, and Michael could have sworn the entire room breathed once before settling.

Oberon stood behind an old desk, fronted by three vine-covered chairs. He motioned to them without looking up, his gaze focused on a piece of parchment spread out across the surface. Michael covered the short expanse, taking the chair on the far right as Gabriel and Kei claimed the other two. An uncomfortable silence enveloped them, nothing but the whisper of breath sounding through the room. Michael glanced at his brother, but the man seemed content to wait for Oberon to speak.

Oberon finally raised his head, defeat shadowed in his

eyes. "If I knew where my son was, I'd tell you. I'm afraid things aren't as simple as you'd like." He tapped his finger along the paper. "Greyson went to the human realm three nights ago. I assume he went to spend the time with you?"

Michael furrowed his brow. "He did. But how…"

Oberon chuckled. "I sensed him traveling through the wards."

"Strange, he said the same about me."

"Fae are sensitive to those we love, whether it be kin or mates. I can tell you that he never returned."

"What?" Michael pushed to his feet. "He's been gone for three days and you're just now summoning me?"

"I had hoped for the best. That the barriers I sensed were to give the two of you privacy. Mating can be a very…intense time for the couple. But when the sun set like a bloody stain in the sky this eve, I knew."

"Knew what? By all that's holy, can you just tell me what the hell is going on?"

Gabriel sighed. "Easy, brother. We'll do all we can."

Michael turned. "If it were Kei? Would you be this patient, then?"

"Probably not. But I have no doubts that you'd ensure I maintained an even composure."

Michael muttered a curse under his breath. Damn, he was obviously spending too much time listening to Lucifer ramble inside his head. Now, he was starting to sound like the man.

Oberon palmed the table. "Tell me this. During your encounter, did Greyson lower his glamour?"

Michael looked up, uncertainty crawling along his spine. He didn't like where this conversation was heading.

"Yes, as did I. Not that I understand why he chooses to hide. He's quite magnificent."

Kei cleared his throat. "Hide what?"

Oberon released a weary breath, spinning the parchment toward them. "It's no secret that the Fae are an ancient race. That we once shared the human world until their blatant disregard for nature compelled us to seek refuge within our own realm—a mere veil separating our two worlds. The majority of my kind bear humans no ill will. After all, they are a young race still learning their way. And without access to the magic that strums around them…" He shrugged. "They're hardly a threat. But there were those among my people who wanted nothing more than to enslave what they considered inferior beings."

Oberon nodded toward Michael and Gabriel. "As you can imagine, your father didn't take lightly to the notion of a war between our realms. He made it quite clear that He'd use whatever means was necessary to stop His children from being harmed."

Michael frowned. "He would have sent us."

"Precisely. Thus, in an effort to avoid bloodshed between the Fae and the angels, we signed a treaty of sorts. All seemed well until a sect within the Fae rose in opposition to this agreement. They used dark sorcery to conjure up armies of creatures so vile, the very earth bled in despair. In the end, the only way to stop the dark forces was to banish them to the shadow lands, where they have spent the past few millennia festering like an open wound. Waiting for their chance to return and claim both our realms."

Kei frowned. "While that's a fascinating history lesson, I don't see what it has to do with Greyson."

"During the final battle, Belfrey, the leader of the dark fae, realized he wouldn't be able to win against the forces of light. In desperation, he used what was left of his life force to cast a curse upon the royal family. That one day, a male heir would be born with wings of pearl-like essence and swirling runes upon his skin reminiscent of the vines that still bar the entrance into the shadow lands. It is foretold that he will be the one to free the dark fae, and bring devastation to all. And the bloody sunset tonight was the sign that the prophecy has begun."

"But…" Kei looked at Michael. "Don't get all defensive on me, Michael, but I've see Grey naked. Jackass used to skinny dip all the time. He doesn't have wings or any kind of marks on his skin."

Oberon focused on Michael.

Michael's stomach dropped as Oberon's words repeated in his head. He stared at the king, noting the regret in the lines around the man's eyes, before turning to Kei. "Actually, Kei…he does." Michael gave the mage an apologetic smile. "He glamours himself. To hide his true form." Anger burned beneath Michael's skin as he faced Oberon. "You never told him. All this time, you made him think he should hide because he was different. Why?"

Oberon sighed. "Believe me. His mother and I wanted to tell him, but…in this case, we feared too much knowledge would only send him down the very path we'd hoped to avoid. Like it or not, even fae have a way of self-prophesizing."

"So you chose to leave him in the dark? Oblivious to the danger?"

"There was one ray of hope. Using the dark arts comes at a high price, for one cannot invoke that much negative energy without giving up something in return. In this case, the prophecy states that if the heir mates before he's discovered, the curse would be lifted. When we realized you were his intended mate..."

The fae's words washed over Michael like an unforgiving rain, chilling him to the bone. He stumbled backward, catching himself on a pillar as his legs buckled beneath him. The rough wood bit into his palm as he bridged his weight, the scenery fading in and out of focus. An arm wrapped around his chest, easing him upright as a chair scraped nearby. His ass hit the surface, his vision finally clearing.

Michael blinked, tears burning his eyes as he fought just to draw a single breath. "I did this?"

Kei gave him a shake. "This isn't your fault. You had no way of knowing he was a target—"

"I removed the warding, Kei. Made him visible, and all because I didn't want to admit the truth. Believe he'd be able to find my sanctuary if I merely sent him a mental image of where I was."

"He chose to lower his glamour. Had you known he was—"

"I knew enough. I *knew* who he was. *What* he meant to me, and yet, I rejected him. Held him at arm's length because I feared I'd be responsible for his death, all the while the reasons I had for denying him were the ultimate cause of his capture." He rested his face in his hands. "I saw how hard it was for him to fight the mating. To keep the words at bay and still, I denied him. I went so far as to heal him just to soothe my conscience." He shook his head. "Dear God, what have I done?"

Oberon grasped his shoulder, waiting until Michael

made eye contact. "All is not lost. There's still a way for you to save him."

"How?"

"Before I lost all contact with my son, I sensed a change in him. A hint of power that wasn't his. You said that you healed him. I assume it was when the flute was playing inside his head? When he started repeating the binding ritual?"

"Yes, but…"

"So, you gave him some of your grace?"

"It wasn't enough to fully bond us. And he never finished reciting the words."

"That doesn't matter. The process was started. Your light still lives within him. Like a barrier. If you can reach him and finish the bonding before the sun sets on the day he's infected with the darkness, you can still save him. Stop this. That's why I brought you here. You're the only one who can break the curse."

"What if he's changed his mind? If he's unable to recite the words?"

"It's not his devotion that's required. Your grace is what will break the curse. And for the record, faeries never change their mind where their mate is concerned." Oberon's expression sobered. "But know this—there'll be no turning back. If you're successful, you'll be his mate for life. You must be very certain, Michael. If you deny him again…" Oberon eased back. "Fae have been known to die of a broken heart."

"I think I've failed my mate enough for one lifetime. Just tell me where he is, and I'll get him back."

"That is a question only you can answer."

"Me?" Michael shook his head. "I'm cut off. I don't know where he is."

"Are you? Have you sensed nothing from him? Not even an echo of his voice?"

Michael froze. "Passing through the wards, I heard him call my name. Then again in the glade. But it only lasted a second. Not long enough for me to pinpoint his location. Even now, I feel nothing."

"In order to turn someone as powerful as Greyson against the light, they'll have to take him somewhere that hinders his natural abilities. Isolates him from his magic. It's the only way for the sickness to manifest against his purity. For the darkness to destroy the light."

"A place void of magic? Of energy? No such place exists in Heaven or on Earth. Can they take him to these…shadow lands?"

"The way is sealed until Greyson breaks the warding. They will use someone skilled in the dark arts to transport him to a realm of desolation. A fae sympathetic to their cause or an ancestor of a warrior who escaped the banishing. There have always been rumors of those that were missed. Who hid in the shadows, preparing for the return of their kin."

"Is there any way they could be here? Ward off a section of your realm?"

Oberon shook his head.

Michael huffed. "Then where in the hell…" He paused as a possibility blossomed. Dread sickened his stomach. If they'd truly taken Greyson *there*… Greyson's voice echoed in his head, the silent plea confirming Michael's greatest fears.

Gabriel shook his head. "I know what you're thinking,

brother, but…he can't be in Hell. While it might not be pleasant, it isn't devoid of magic. You'd still be able to sense him, and knowing Greyson, once he realizes he's in trouble, he'll do all he can to make contact."

Michael nodded. "I realize that. There's no way Lucifer wouldn't have sensed that amount of dark energy breaking through his wards. He would have told me if he had."

Gabriel frowned. "Told you?"

Michael waved the question off. "That's not important. He is. He's the key."

"Who's the key? You're not making any sense."

Michael straightened, all his doubts fading away. "I know where Greyson is, but I can't get there alone."

Gabriel clasped his hand around Michael's forearm. "Whatever you need, we'll help you."

"You might not feel that way once you know what's involved. *Who's* involved."

Gabriel quirked his brow.

Michael turned, heading for the doorway. He stopped at the threshold, glancing back at the men watching him as if he'd lost his mind. He focused on Oberon. "Do you know how long I have?"

The king's expression fell. "Until sunset tomorrow. But you must return him to where he was taken to complete the circle."

Michael nodded. "Then there's no time to waste."

Gabriel took a step toward him, confusion still creasing his face. "Where are you going?"

Michael gave his brother a grim smile. "To summon the only person who can help me. It's time to talk to Lucifer. Face to face."

CHAPTER TWELVE

"So, you're Greyson. I've heard a lot about the young Prince of the Fae. I will say...you're the spitting image of your father. Except for the wings and markings, of course. That part belongs to us."

Greyson clenched his jaw, grinding his teeth against the pain as every tiny twitch of his muscles brushed the iron chains against his flesh, leaving another burning welt across his skin. A deterrent to attempt another escape, he supposed. As long as he remained still, submissive, the iron stayed pressed against a layer of cloth. But as soon as he moved...

His magic thrummed in protest, wanting to break free but still somehow trapped inside him. He looked up at his captor, secretly wondering if he were hallucinating the entire ordeal. If the strain from not mating with Michael had driven Grey mad, and this was all a figment of his imagination.

The iron brushed his wrist above where they'd wrapped his skin, the resulting flash of pain proof enough that this was all very real. Though, he still didn't know why he'd been taken. How an obvious descendant of the dark fae had escaped the barrier. A hand gripped his chin, jerking up his head until he made eye contact.

He twisted his jaw free. "Nothing I have belongs to you."

The faery shrugged, running his finger along the upper line of Greyson's wing. "Not yet. But soon."

Greyson grunted, the man's touch souring his gut. While the gesture was wildly hot where Michael was concerned, having another caress him in that fashion made him sick.

The fae chuckled. "Something tells me you don't enjoy having your wings played with. That will change. Once you join us, you'll learn to embrace every part of yourself. Get off on the sheer pleasure of having slaves service your every whim. You won't hide from who you are any longer."

"I won't join you. I'll die first."

"Oh, you light types are always *so* damn dramatic." He shook his head, glancing toward the ceiling then back. "No wonder you haven't found a mate. You've already got a giant stick up your ass. No room for anything else. Though, I'm thankful you haven't. It was the one act that could have broken the curse. Saved you from your fate, but I guess you never found anyone to man up and claim you." He grinned. "Didn't realize you swung that way until my scouts found you." He tsked. "An angel? Really? That's your idea of a good time?"

Greyson merely stared at the man, doing his best to hide the fear beading his skin with goosebumps. They knew about Michael, though perhaps not his true identity.

But that didn't stop Grey from wondering if they'd hurt his mate, especially if Michael could somehow undo this curse the dark fae kept talking about. If that was the reason Grey couldn't make contact.

The bastard sighed. "Don't worry. If angels are your thing, we'll see you have a harem of them to please you. Once we seize control of both the faery and the human realm, you can have anything you desire."

"If you think my father will hand over his crown, his people, in exchange for me, you've wasted your time... Tharn, isn't it?"

"I obviously need to hire better help. There's power in names." He glared at someone over Greyson's shoulder. "Something demons seem to forget. They have this notion they're far more powerful than they really are. But since you already know..." He straightened then performed a sweeping bow. "Tharn, son of Darol." His lips kicked up into an evil grin. "Great, *great*-grandson of Belfrey."

"The dark king. And here I thought they'd caged all of you."

Tharn lunged at Greyson, rattling the iron against his flesh. He smiled at Grey's obvious pain. "Close, but not quite." He eased back, scratching a line across Greyson's shoulder next to the gaping arrow wound that continued to drip blood down his chest. "A small contingency of his followers escaped, including his pregnant mate. They sought refuge in the very world they detested. Living amongst the humans as if they were remotely worthy of being in my ancestors' presence. All the while, practicing their dark arts. Strengthening their power so they'd be ready when the chosen one arrived."

"Chosen one? You do know that wielding that much

darkness stains your soul, don't you? That it eventually leads to madness, then death. That's assuming you were ever sane to begin with."

Tharn arched a brow, sliding one finger across the open laceration. He pushed against the wound, laughing at the strangled groan that made it past Grey's clenched lips. "The prophecy only states that you need to be alive to be turned. It doesn't say anything about how close to death I can take you. You might want to keep that in mind before you speak ill of my family."

Greyson gasped, allowing his chin to drop to his chest as he fought the need to scream. Tremors racked his limbs, a hint of gray closing in around him. He blinked, vowing he wouldn't give the bastard the satisfaction of seeing him crumble. He moistened his lips, hoping his voice didn't crack. "Prophecy? You're crazy. There's no prophecy."

"Oh, but there is. One with you in the starring role. Let me guess...Oberon never told you that his firstborn son was destined to destroy his kingdom? Sentence his people, and the humans they shunned us for, to death?" Tharn tapped a finger against his chin. "Makes me wonder why. Was he sparing you the knowledge that you'd betray him, or was he planning on killing you before the prophecy could come to fruition? It's a shame, really. If you'd known the dark fae would be searching for you, perhaps you would have taken better care not to expose yourself. Removing your glamour for an angel? I hope he was worth it, Prince."

"It doesn't matter what you do to me. I won't join you."

"Afraid I'm not asking."

He reached into the pocket of his tunic and removed a red velvet bag. A punch of dark energy burst from the pouch the moment Tharn opened it, billowing around the room like a menacing cloud. Grey turned his head when the red essence whirled around him, drawing a hint of his magic to the surface. Soft blue colored his skin, the shade noticeably lighter than Grey remembered.

Tharn waited until the glow dimmed before removing a silver-colored pendant from the bag. A sphere-shaped globe hung on a leather cord, a series of delicate swirls adorning the surface. A blood-red stone sat inside the center, the color nearly black against the shiny gray. Tharn grinned and held the amulet toward Greyson. The dark energy coiled around the sphere, finally sinking into the stone with an eerie flash of crimson.

Tharn cocked his head to the side. "Don't suppose the pattern looks familiar."

"Fuck you."

"Perhaps later. You're far too pure for my tastes the way you are."

He bent toward Grey, draping the amulet around his neck. White-hot pain seared across his flesh, drawing a reluctant scream from deep within his chest.

Tharn tousled his hair. "Easy. The iron will only burn for a few minutes. Just long enough to draw some of your blood into the stone. Once it has absorbed enough, the sensation should subside."

Grey squeezed shut his eyes, grunting through the pain. He wouldn't give in. Wouldn't turn against his kin, no matter how much it hurt.

Tharn tsked. "Fight all you want, Greyson. All it does

is delay the inevitable. And I've got nothing but time." He leaned forward. "Now, for the second part."

He removed a knife from his belt, then used the edge to cut a slice across his finger. Blood welled up from the wound, the color matching that of the stone. He placed his finger against Greyson's pec, then traced the outline of a sigil across his skin, more of the same swirling patterns incorporated into the design.

Tharn took a step back once he'd finished. "Perfect. Just one more ingredient, and we're done."

He clapped his hands. Sezil appeared a few moments later, a heavily adorned box clasped in his fingers. He held out the offering to Tharn, immediately retreating once the dark fae had taken the chest. Tharn set the box down at Greyson's feet, then opened the lid, revealing a glass-like vial. A black essence pulsed within the container, the constant shifting reminiscent of ripples on the water.

"Tell me, Prince of the Fae, do you know what this is?"

Greyson barely managed to make eye contact before another jolt of pain stole his breath. He clenched his jaw, groaning when it only seemed to increase the burning sensation. "I'd say your soul, but you obviously don't have one."

"Very funny, yet fairly close. This is the very life force of Belfrey. The same dark power he used to curse the royal family all those millennia ago. The one that foretold of your coming. Once I release it, it will infuse the amulet around your neck, and slowly take control of your body—melding with your blood until nothing of your magic remains. Until there's only blackness within your heart."

"Never."

The bastard chuckled. "I'll admit. I like your tenacity.

It'll make watching your turn all the sweeter."

He crouched beside the box, glancing at Greyson again before opening the vial. The black essence swirled inside the glass then exploded into the air, flashes of red light arcing within the mass. It snaked around the room then shot toward the amulet, snapping Greyson's head back from the force. A searing cold stabbed through his chest, constricting his throat until his breath simply stalled. Black dots edged his vision as a dull ringing sounded in his head.

His magic flared in protest, freeing him enough he gasped in a ragged breath. The musky scent of blackthorn engulfed the room, staining the very air with its aroma. A dull red encased the pendant, slowly spreading across his chest. He focused every ounce of strength on countering the icy progression across his torso, doing his best to build a mental barrier. An unholy growl lit the air, followed by a blast of cold air.

Greyson's magic flickered, small streaks of crimson weaving through the strands. He fought against them, vowing he'd die before giving in, when a pulse of pure white light flared across his flesh. It pushed against the darkness, holding it at bay as it swirled along the patterns adorning his skin. The ghostly echo of a flute played inside his head, blocking out the evil murmurs as the pain gradually eased.

"What the hell?" Tharn muttered something under his breath, leaning in close but not touching Greyson's body. "Looks like you have something other than just faery magic inside you. Sezil. Get your ass over here."

The demon appeared in front, hands fisted at his side. "What?"

Tharn swatted the man in the face. "Don't take that tone with me unless you want to spend the next thousand years as a toad. Do you know who our guest was visiting when you snatched him?"

Sezil frowned, rubbing his cheek. "I told you. Some angel. Blond hair. Wings."

"His name. Do you know his name?"

"You said you wanted the fae, not the feathered freak. They all look alike to me. He was wearing jeans, I think."

"You should have found out." He pursed his lips as he watched the white glow arc across Grey's skin. "There's something odd here. If I didn't know better, I'd say the angel left a piece of his grace behind. But that would imply the man was more than just a quick fuck. And I know, firsthand, there's never been a pairing outside the faery realm. I don't see Oberon making an exception where his son is concerned." He frowned. "Still…"

He sighed, crossing his arms over his chest. "It matters not. The darkness will still creep into your soul. It just might take longer than expected. Nothing and no one, can save you, now."

Grey shook his head, drawing strength from the warm glow of Michael's power as it tried to shield him. "I won't give in."

"You don't have a choice."

"I'll die first."

"Don't make promises you can't keep." Tharn backed up. "But just to be safe, I think I'll take a short trip back to the human world. See if I can unearth who this mysterious angel is. But I'm afraid Lucifer himself couldn't help you." He grinned. "Welcome to the age of the shadows."

CHAPTER THIRTEEN

"Are you sure about this, Michael?"

Michael glanced at his brother, noting the tight press of Gabriel's lips as he stood several feet away, feet braced apart, his arms crossed over his massive chest.

Gabriel glanced around. "Not only are you summoning Lucifer, but you'll be exposing the location of your sanctuary to him. Neither should be done lightly."

Michael focused on Kei, judging the other man's reaction. The mage matched Gabriel's stance, his shoulder brushing that of his mate's in a visible show of support. Another wash of guilt filled Michael's chest. If he hadn't been so foolish, so afraid, Greyson wouldn't have been taken.

Gabriel sighed. "You don't know that. More likely, he would have been killed outright when they discovered he'd already mated."

Michael glared at his brother. "It's bad enough Greyson can read my thoughts, whether I try to block him, or not. And it seems Oberon can sense them, when we're close. Must you listen in, as well?"

"You're privy to mine, if you choose to be. And right now you're too focused on everything else to erect a barrier. At least toward me."

Michael narrowed his eyes. Did Gabriel, also, sense the barrier he'd erected to keep Lucifer out? Or was it more of a generic statement? He pushed aside the thought. None of that mattered, anymore. Not when he was about to call on the man for help. And knowing Lucifer, he'd get great joy in telling Gabriel about their conversations over the past few months.

Michael merely nodded. "I don't have a choice. Greyson doesn't have much time left if Oberon's correct. And I have a feeling he's rarely wrong."

Kei shuffled his feet, looking slightly out of his element. "You could just tell us where you think they've taken Grey. We might be able to get you there without summoning...well, without *him*."

Michael gave them both a tight smile. He couldn't divulge where he was going until it was too late for either of them to stop him. Not when he suspected Gabriel might try to reason with him.

"Please, just trust me. I'll explain everything once Lucifer's here." He motioned them to back up. "You might want to give me a bit more room. I don't imagine this will be pretty."

"I could summon him." Kei's voice sounded strained, as if he'd had to force the words out. "I did it once before and lived to tell the tale. And spells are kinda my thing."

"From what I understand, you were lucky my brother didn't shred your soul in the process." Michael shook his head. "Greyson's my responsibility. If I want Lucifer's help, I need to have the courage to summon him myself."

Gabriel huffed. "Greyson's our friend, as well. I realize he's your mate, but that doesn't mean you have to be alone in this. We can all fight."

Michael nodded, aware there wasn't anything he could say to lessen Gabriel's determination. "Ready?"

He lowered the barrier separating him from Lucifer, using their connection to pinpoint the archangel's location. His grace strummed around him, the white light increasing as he directed his energy into the sigil he'd drawn in the dirt. He chanted the summoning ritual, fueling the spell with his power until the ground shook beneath them. The earth split, vents of steam hissing into the air as heat billowed around them, a hint of brimstone wafting along the breeze. There was a moment of oppressive silence before a growling hiss sounded around them, a loud thunk resonating across the space.

Michael reined in his power, panting against the strain as he stared at the man kneeling within the markings. Smoke rose off his pale flesh, his torso bare. Part of his pants had gotten torn, revealing the tops of his shoes. He rolled his shoulders, then slowly uncurled his body, arching his back as he reached his full height.

He shook his head, his gaze fixed on Kei and Gabriel. "Oh for fuck's sake. Did you seriously just summon me? Again? I was in the middle of charming a rather beautiful young lady and her male partner into my bed, and now..." He waved at the surrounding landscape. "Now, I'm back on Earth. And by the looks of it, we're pretty damn close to the last godforsaken place you made me appear. Fuck, the least you could do was pop me up somewhere nice."

He crossed his arms over his chest. "Call me crazy, but either you've learned how to fully tap into Gabriel's grace, or you weren't the one driving the spell, because that..." He whistled. "That was a thing of beauty, even if I'm pissed about being here."

Michael took a fortifying breath. "Kei didn't summon you. I did."

Lucifer glanced over his shoulder before grinning. He turned, giving Michael the once over. "Mikey. I should have recognized that hint of overly pure essence in the energy. Glad to know you've made a full recovery since our last meeting."

Michael stilled. Had Lucifer just passed on an opportunity to flaunt their connection?

Lucifer winked at him, looking at Kei and Gabriel as they moved closer to Michael. "What's the occasion? Is it Thanksgiving already? Don't tell me I missed a birthday."

"Must you be an ass?"

"It's one of my true gifts." He smiled. "Now, not that I don't love these little family reunions, but... I've got deals to make. Souls to torture. Sex to have. So, perhaps we can skip all the small talk and awkward silences and get to why the hell I'm here."

Michael took a deep breath. This was it. A moment he'd never be able to take back. If he thought admitting to Oberon that Greyson was his mate had held serious ramifications, it paled in comparison to what he was about to do. What would be needed to garner Lucifer's help.

He steeled his resolve. He'd do anything and everything to get Greyson back. Period. "I need your help."

Lucifer arched his brow, the hint of a smug smile curving his lips. "I'm listening."

"There's a...situation."

"Situation?" He groaned. "Shit, you didn't lose the book, did you?"

"Book?"

"The *book*! The one keeping Abaddon from destroying my little section of reality. Is that why we're so damn close to where it all went down?"

"What? No. It's safe. This is..."

"This is what?" Lucifer laughed. "Oh fuck. This is your sanctuary, isn't it? Damn, Mikey, it's like that whole thing was an act of providence. Fine, then why am I here?"

"It's Greyson. He's been taken."

Lucifer snorted. "Greyson. Your mate...oops, sorry, fae with benefits. Someone took him?"

"Wait." Gabriel edged closer. "How do you know about that?"

Michael huffed. "None of that matters. What matters is that he's been abducted, and I need your help to get him back."

Lucifer scoffed. "My help? Why on earth would you need my help? You have Gabriel and Raphael at your disposal."

"They can't help me get where they took Grey. I need...you."

"Really? Makes me wonder where you think they took your friend. Or have you admitted he means more to you, yet?"

"Damn it, Lucifer, we don't have time for this petty arguing. Yes, he's my mate. And yes, I'll do whatever it takes to get him back." He straightened, holding his head as high as he could. "Now, I don't expect you to simply help me out of the goodness in your heart, so I'm prepared to make you a deal."

"You? Make a deal with me? Oh, Mikey, it's like Christmas all over again. Gives me fucking goosebumps." Lucifer moved closer, stopping just a foot away. "Why don't you tell me where you think they took your boy, and then we'll talk deals. Because, honestly, I can't think of anywhere you can't gain access to all on your own." He frowned. "You don't think *I* took him, do you? Because I didn't. The last thing Hell needs is an overly righteous faery who has the hots for my big brother."

"Damn it." Gabriel moved in beside Lucifer. "We already know he's not in Hell. Michael seems to believe you would have told him if Greyson had been taken there. Though, I'm still confused on that part, as well as how you even know Michael has a mate. But that's obviously not the point of this conversation. Oberon said that Greyson's been taken to a realm void of magic, which rules out Hell."

Lucifer glanced at Gabriel then turned back to Michael. "Void of magic? But there's nowhere... Shit!" He spun, taking several heavy steps away before turning back. "You seriously think someone took him *there*? Of all places?"

"Where's there?" Gabriel threw up his hands. "Would one of you please just spit it out? Where do you think he is?"

Michael sighed when Lucifer waved at him. He twisted to face Gabriel. "Purgatory. They took Greyson to Purgatory." He released a weary sigh. "It's the only realm void of magic, and the one place I can't follow, which is why I need Lucifer."

Gabriel's mouth gaped open as his gaze shifted between his brothers. He shook his head. "No."

Michael gave Gabriel an apologetic smile. "Gabriel—"

"No, Michael. I know that you want to save Greyson, but this..." He waved his hand violently between them. "Do you know what it will take to send you to Purgatory?"

"Yes, which is why I didn't tell you before. Why I'm standing here prepared to make a deal with Lucifer. He's the only one who might have the power to get me there."

"At what cost? Nothing pure can go there. You'd pretty much have to fall in order to gain access." Gabriel raked his hand through his hair. "Shit, the amount of dark magic they must have used to get Greyson through the wards... to mask his power." He closed his eyes as sadness creased the lines around his eyes. "I'm not sure he could have survived it."

"He's not dead." Michael held up his hand. "I know. I *feel* it, even if I can't communicate with him. He's alive, but he won't be for much longer." Michael focused on Lucifer. "Are you willing to help me, or not?

Lucifer clenched his jaw, looking uncharacteristically unsure of himself. "It's not so much a matter of willing. We're talking about Purgatory."

"I'm well aware of what I'm asking you to do."

"Are you?" Lucifer stormed over, invading Michael's personal space as he tapped a finger on Michael's chest. "There are only three ways to get into Purgatory. One. You're a monster or a demon or something equally unholy, and you die, which is the only easy way, in case you're wondering. Two. You use an obscene amount of dark magic and pray you don't shred the fabric of reality on the way through or…" He gave Michael's chest another hard jab. "Or you use an extremely powerful banishing spell, which is no easy feat to achieve. Trust me. I've tried. It didn't turn out that great for the poor son of a bitch who wanted to go there. In fact, I think his intestines are still baked into the rock where we gave it the old college try, and I was minus one soul."

Michael held firm. "I'm not some ordinary human."

"No! You're God's fucking Warrior. You're as pure as they get." He laughed. "Christ, this is so absurd it's actually funny." He shook his head. "What you're asking…"

"Are you saying you can't do it? Or are you worried it might kill me, because I thought that would just be an unexpected perk."

Lucifer's expression sobered, any hint of amusement quickly fading. "I'll admit, there are times I'd give anything to see your blood stain my sword, but this…" He backed away slightly, breaking eye contact. "Not like this, Michael."

The inklings of panic prickled Michael's skin. If Lucifer refused to help him, he'd lose Greyson forever.

Michael reclaimed the lost inches between them, forcing his brother to meet his gaze. "I'm begging you to help me. Please, brother." He cursed inwardly when Lucifer merely stared at him. "Fine. If you won't do it for me, then do it for yourself. If I don't reach Greyson before the sun sets tomorrow, then everything you hold dear will come to an end."

"What the hell are you going on about now? What has Greyson got to do with me, other than becoming another annoying in-law?" Lucifer rolled his eyes. "Like a damn fire mage isn't bad enough. Now, we have to add a faery prince to the mix?"

Michael ignored Gabriel's irritated huff. "This isn't just because he's my mate. If I don't rescue him, the prophecy will come true, and the age of shadows will rise."

"Prophecy? Age of shadows?" Lucifer scrubbed a hand down his face then inhaled roughly. "Wait." He held up his hand, shaking a finger at Michael. "Your little fae doesn't have wings, does he? And runes..." he waved at his sides, "...up and down his torso? Swirly things that look like tattoos only they're not?"

"How did you know—"

"Oh for God's sake! Doesn't *anyone* read anymore?" Lucifer stormed away again, spinning when he reached the edge of the sigil before marching back over. He gave Michael a shove. "Are you fucking shitting me? Not only do you somehow break faery tradition and become the mate of their prince—something that has never happened in all of their existence—but your true soul turns out to be the fated destroyer of prophecy? The one that will likely obliterate Earth in the process, which means Hell right along with it?" Lucifer chuckled, as he shook his head, again. "This has got to be some kind of joke." He tipped his head back. "Really, Dad?"

"This has nothing to do with Father. He doesn't choose our mates."

"No? Well, maybe He should start." Lucifer kicked at the dirt, a few flames flickering along his arms before winking out. "This changes everything. Fuck, I hate this shit. Fine. You think you can survive the trip to Purgatory, I'll do my best to send you there. But don't think that you're going to like what it takes, or that this is going to be easy. Thank Christ, I'm at least at full power when I get summoned to this shithole. You can't access Purgatory from Hell."

"Name your price."

"Let's just see if you survive long enough to make me a deal, okay? Because I'm not convinced you will."

He lowered his head, muttering a series of words under his breath. The air warmed around them a moment before a book materialized on the ground. Lucifer bent low, grabbing the tome then flipping through the pages. He stopped halfway through.

He drew his finger across the page, tapping on the old paper. "This is it. A one-way ticket to Purgatory. I'm going to need blood. Or course, it has to be mine, fucking bastards. An ancient banishing coin." He snapped his fingers, holding up a tarnished medallion. "Like this, and..." He looked at Michael. "Your grace."

Gabriel gawked at Lucifer. "His grace?"

"Did I stutter?" Lucifer exhaled with what sounded like forced patience. "You said it yourself. Nothing pure can enter Purgatory. And Michael's got enough grace to light up the entire place. He can't go there glowing like a damn beacon from Heaven."

"But if he gives you his grace, it'll be the same as if he'd—"

"Fallen. Yeah, I know what it means to give up your grace, Gabriel. But it's the only way to get through the wards without dying. Even then, I can't make any promises."

"This is insane."

"Look on the bright side. It's only a temporary fall. I'll

keep his grace safe until he gets back." Lucifer glanced at Michael. "*If* you get back."

Gabriel shook his head. "Why you?"

"Because it's part of the spell, jackass. You think I like this? Having all that sickeningly sweet light living inside me? I'll probably end up crapping out rainbows for a week."

"No." Gabriel held up his hand, stopping Michael from replying. "The whole point of this is for you to break the curse. You can't bond with Greyson without your grace."

"If you'd let me finish, I'd explain the rest of the plan." Lucifer glared at Gabriel before focusing on Michael. "I can let you keep just enough to complete the bond and get you back here by giving you a bit of mine to mask the purity. At least, that's what I've read. No idea if it'll work or just guarantee you die on impact."

Kei grabbed Gabriel's arm, motioning for him to stand down when he looked as if he were going to argue again. The mage nodded at Lucifer. "Not to play the devil's advocate here, but...you promise to give it back, right? This isn't a ploy to make yourself stronger?"

Lucifer laughed. "What are we, five? It doesn't matter what I promise. I can always break it. Fallen, remember? In the end, it comes down to what Michael wants to risk more. His grace, or his mate. But if it makes everyone feel better..." He smiled, holding up his hand. "I can pinky swear."

Gabriel snorted. "You can't risk your grace, Michael. Let me perform the spell. At least, you know your grace will be safe."

"For crying out loud." Lucifer shook the book. "It's a

banishing spell. It's not quite full-blown dark magic, but it does require less than pure energy to cast it."

Kei stepped forward. "Then I'll do it."

"Right. Let's have the fire mage cast the spell instead of the fallen fucking angel. Are you high? Your power doesn't come close to mine. I'm the exception to the rule. The only one who's been cast out but kept their grace, albeit stained."

"Enough!" Michael moved in beside Lucifer. "There isn't anything to debate." He nodded at Lucifer. "If I have to fall in order for you to send me there, so be it. Just do it now."

"If you insist, big brother." He snapped his fingers again, holding up the sigil-covered knife that materialized in his hand. "I'll make a small cut on both our forearms. As I recite the transfer spell, you'll feel an odd, tingling sensation. It's only temporary. Ready?"

Michael nodded, thankful he didn't have to actually cast himself out of Heaven—experience all the other side effects of falling—in order to give Lucifer his grace. Not that the result would be any different. He'd still be a fallen angel.

Lucifer gave him one last hard look, then lowered the knife, burning a line across Michael's skin. Blood welled along the edges, accompanied by a flash of white light. Lucifer followed suit, pressing their cuts together as he chanted in a language Michael didn't recognize. The burning sensation intensified, nearly dropping him to his knees as his grace surged forward, casting a blinding glare across the space before rushing at Lucifer. It coiled above his arm, pulsing wildly then quickly sinking beneath the man's flesh.

Michael sagged from the strain, thankful when two sets of hands grabbed his arms, keeping him for collapsing onto the dirt. He took a few deep breaths, blinking until his vision returned to normal. The cut on Lucifer's arm glowed, the white color bleeding into red along the edges.

Lucifer whistled. "Wow. How the hell do you stand this much goodness inside you? God, it's like bathing in holy water." He tossed Michael the coin. "Now listen carefully. The coin is your link back to this plane. If you lose it, you'll be stuck there unless someone else ventures over to save your sorry ass. So don't.

"Once you find Greyson and break this curse, you need to return to wherever it is you pop up. Place the coin on the ground then use what's left of your power to activate it. It won't be easy with the whole place trying to block your energy, but with so little left, you should be able to wield it. The retrieval spell is fueled by grace, so make sure you keep some for yourself, otherwise you might not return. But if it all goes according to plan, once you activate the coin, a portal should appear and toss you both back here."

He bent over, carving out an odd-looking sigil on the ground. Then he made another cut on his other arm, allowing his blood to drain into the grooves until the lines gleamed red.

He straightened motioning to the markings. "If you'd be so kind as to step inside..."

Michael stumbled across the lines, careful not to touch them before going to his knees. Weakness gnawed at his determination, but he focused on Greyson. On how he'd never survive failing his mate.

Lucifer cleared his throat. "If you're done with the

self-pity... There're a few other things you should know. While you're there, you won't have access to your usual abilities, seeing as you're lacking your mojo—maybe some increased strength, a bit faster than normal healing, but nothing like what you're used to. Remember...fallen angel. Unfortunately, as you already know, Greyson can't access his magic, either. Which means you'll both be essentially mortal. So don't go and get yourselves killed. The bit of my power that I exchanged with you might fuel the odd spell, but don't count on it for protection. Thankfully, your sword will make the transition with you, though, it won't remain hidden. And lastly, your wings."

Michael raised his head to stare at his brother. "What about my wings?"

"Without your grace to protect them, I doubt they'll make it to the other side completely intact." He held up his hand at Michael's gasp. "Again, all temporary. Once you zap your ass back here, your grace will heal the worst of the effects. And we can fix the rest. At least, I hope that's how it works. Either way...I thought you should know. Full disclosure and all that bullshit." He arched a brow. "Still determined to save your mate?"

"If my wings are the price of saving Greyson from a life of darkness, then so be it."

"Wings. Grace. In for a penny, I suppose."

Lucifer rubbed his hands together, then held them toward the ground. He bowed his head then jerked it up, reaching into his pocket. He took a couple of steps toward Michael, handing him a folded piece of paper.

Michael turned it over in his hand without opening it. "What is this?"

"The ritual your faery friend has to recite in order to bind you together. Thought it might come in handy."

"How do you know about all of this?"

Lucifer shrugged. "I can't take over every realm and become supreme ruler of all if I don't study."

"That's not funny, Lucifer."

"Actually, it is. Okay, here we go." He extended his hands toward the ground again. "Please keep your arms, legs and wings inside the sigil at all times and whatever you do...don't try to disembark until this ride has come to a full stop." The red glow returned as fire danced from his hands. "See you on the other side, bro."

There was a flash of red, then a blinding white light. The air crushed in around him, sparking pain through his chest as he fought just to breathe. Heat seared through his flesh, burning all the way to his bones as the earth dropped out beneath him. He fell, nothing but blackness closing in on him, the air howling around him. Streaks of red appeared amidst the darkness, rushing toward him. He braced against the inevitable impact, grunting loudly when he hit solid ground just as the streaks skimmed across his flesh, leaving large welts wherever they touched. Pain flared through his back and shoulders before slamming into his head. There was a moment of intense pressure, then silence.

His pulse pounded inside his skull, the steady throb one of many that coursed through his body. A burning sensation built in his chest, until he realized he was holding his breath. He inhaled, groaning as the simple action sent a stabbing jolt through his ribs. Dots flickered across his vision, his consciousness fading.

Sharp stones bit into his cheek, the dusty taste of dirt

finally snapping him back. He blinked, waiting for the scenery to stabilize before squinting his surroundings into focus. Dull, gray earth spread out in front of him, pockets of spiny trees dotting the landscape. Dark clouds filled the pale sky, the pungent stench of rotting meat filling the air.

Michael pushed onto his hands and knees, doing his best to ignore the accompanying roil of his stomach as the colors seemed to wash together before settling. He glanced at his arms, cursing the series of welts laced across his skin, dots of dried blood caking his flesh. He reached inwardly for his grace, but only succeeded in making the wounds burn more.

He sighed. He needed to remember he wasn't an archangel, anymore. That he couldn't rely on his grace to save him. That he was just a man. A thrum of pain echoed the thought as he gained his feet, swaying a few times before finding his balance. He pushed his shoulders back as his hands fell to his sides. At least, he'd made it alive.

He braced himself then did a long sweep of his body. Patches of his jeans had been torn away, the skin beneath scraped raw. Purple bruises lined the left side of his ribs, ending in a laceration across his hip where the band on his pants had gotten ripped. But those injuries were nothing compared to his wings. Half the feathers had been charred during the spell, with sections hanging limp at his side. He tried to spread them only to trip forward onto one knee as pain stabbed through his back and into his chest.

Michael fisted his hand, slowly lifting his gaze. While he knew he couldn't fly, it didn't mean he couldn't fight. His sword jabbed against his waist as he stumbled to his feet, the silver color more gray in the dull light. He palmed the hilt, focusing on the smooth glide of metal beneath his hand. The familiar weight of it as he drew it close to his chest. He didn't need wings, or grace. All he needed was that one blade, and the courage to take his first step.

He closed his eyes and listened. Even without his power, he couldn't shake the feeling that he could still sense Greyson. That their bond went beyond magic and grace. That simply being in the same place would reopen their connection. Twigs snapped in the encroaching forest as hushed footsteps circled his location. A low growl drifted along the breeze with hints of sulfur and smoke. He pressed harder, feeling creatures move toward him when a single image exploded inside his head—iron chains looped around a solitary chair. A pulsing red amulet filled with an evil black essence. Numbing cold slowly sinking beneath Greyson's flesh as the stone room dissolved into emptiness. His light consumed by the dark.

Michael jerked back to his senses as he spun to his right. A hint of blue hung in the air, the otherworldly glow trailing off toward a thick section of forest. He glanced behind him, aware of the monsters slowly closing in on him. Jaws snapped in a show of defiance, their numbers quickly increasing.

A sense of calm washed over him as he turned to face the horde. They were just a temporary distraction. The price he'd have to pay to prove his worth before he reached his mate. The ultimate test.

I'm coming, Greyson. Hold on.

A growl echoed through the open space as Michael readied his blade then attacked.

CHAPTER FOURTEEN

Cold. God, he was so damn cold.

Icy fingers scratched along Greyson's chest, slowly picking away at the barriers he'd erected. The ones barely holding on to the light still living inside him. A low growl echoed through the room, followed by a stab of pain through his heart.

Sweat beaded his brow, his breath ragged pants in the oppressive stillness. His limbs shook from the strain, but the resulting burn of iron didn't compare to the searing pressure pushing against his resolve. And he knew it was only a matter of time before the darkness won.

A ghostly echo of Michael's voice whispered through his head—a promise Greyson knew the angel couldn't keep. No one was coming to save him. Not here. Though it'd taken him a while to figure out where Tharn had hidden him, the answer had suddenly become crystal clear. There was only one place strong enough to hinder his magic. To sever the link to his mate.

Purgatory.

If he were honest, he hadn't really believed such a place existed. That there was evil powerful enough to cripple him. But then he hadn't thought the dark fae would ever rise again, either. Especially with him as their savior.

He squeezed shut his eyes against the overwhelming guilt. Why hadn't his father warned him? Told him his wings, his markings, were far more than traits from a lost age? That they were signs of a coming apocalypse. That he was no better than Abaddon. A curse upon his people that would end in death and darkness.

The haunting melody of the binding flute wavered at the edge of his consciousness, the song still trying to play. Greyson listened to the simple rise and fall of notes, smiling at the momentary peace it brought him. He'd gotten so close. If he'd only be able to finish the ritual...

He sighed. It was better this way. If he'd managed to bind Michael to him, the angel would have suffered unspeakable pain from the loss. Now, Michael would be able to move on. Greyson's death would sever their connection—allow Michael to find another mate worthier of his soul. Find a way to stop the dark fae from claiming the Earth for their own, evil purpose.

The amulet pulsed, as if sensing his thoughts, sending out a sharp blast of energy. It swirled around the room, slamming into Greyson's chest like a damn battering ram. He jerked back from the impact, losing some of his hold on the barriers. The numbing chill intensified, crushing in on him, extinguishing more of his light. Exhaustion wove through his muscles, and he wanted to simply let go. Fade into the blackness that wrapped around him like an evil fog.

Footsteps clicked across the floor, a set of boots stopping in front of him. Sezil's face appeared amidst the shadows as the demon bent low, getting close without actually touching Grey. The other man frowned, looking at the pendant then back to him. "How the hell is he still hanging on?"

A disgruntled huff sounded off to Grey's right. "He *is* the Prince of the Fae. Did you really think he'd break easily?"

"Tharn seemed to think so. That was enough for me."

"Well maybe Tharn doesn't know as much as he claims. He's been gone for almost twenty-four hours. You'd think someone as powerful as he is would be able to track down one fucking angel by now. I mean, we gave him the exact location of where we picked the good prince up. That angel's cabin was out in the open."

"Maybe the guy wasn't home. Angels aren't normal." Sezil straightened, nothing but the man's lower torso visible. "How should I know? Not that it matters. Our friend here's getting ready to crack. Just look at him. Prince or not, he can't hold out much longer. That black patch on his chest has nearly consumed his entire torso. Another hour, tops, and anything remotely good will be long gone." He laughed. "All that suffering only to lose in the end. That's gotta sting."

Greyson raised his head enough to glare at the demon. "Fuck you."

Sezil leaned in closer. "Sorry, but Tharn made it clear you're his, lucky bastard. You are pretty to look at, even busted up the way you are. Maybe after he's done with you, I'll..." He paused as shouts rose in the distance. "What the fuck is it now? Hey, Ezra. Stay here and keep an eye on the princeling. I'll go see why everyone's yelling. I swear, if it's another goddamn werewolf pack…"

Erza merely grunted, staying out of Greyson's field of view. Grey glanced toward the end of the hallway, an odd sensation gathering in his chest. Something was off. He felt…warmth. But not the kind that burned. This was… comforting. Healing.

The telltale clatter of swordplay rose above the chorus of voices, the dull clanging sound echoing through the room. Frantic footsteps thundered beyond the doorway a moment before Sezil appeared in the graying light. A bloody gash marred one shoulder as he raced toward them, a curved dagger in his hand. He skidded to a halt, glancing over his shoulder as if expecting to see something.

Ezra grabbed Sezil's arm, roughly twisting him. "What the hell? Why—"

"We don't have time. He's here, he's…" Horror flashed in his eyes. "He killed everyone. Every demon, every damn monster. We…" He shook his head. "Tharn said if anything went wrong, we had to try to force the process along, even if it meant the faery might not make it." He turned the dagger over in his hands. "I hope this works."

He struck, plunging the knife deep into Greyson's shoulder. The iron blade burned through Greyson's flesh, the strange markings on the shaft amplifying every sensation until even screaming didn't lessen the crushing pain that coiled deep inside his soul, breaking through the last of his barriers. The amulet flashed red, its icy chill quickly seeping into Greyson's chest as the darkness consumed him, fading the room into black.

He slumped forward, not even the burn of the iron

against his wrists overshadowing the empty feeling inside him. As if a part of his soul had simply vanished. Fear prickled along his spine, quickly turning to rage as the energy from the amulet gathered strength, manifesting as a grating voice inside his head. It hounded Grey, demanding he seek justice—make his people pay for leaving him there to die. For abandoning him when he needed them the most.

They'd never accepted him. Embraced that he was different. He deserved to be king, not Oberon. But Grey couldn't rule alone. He needed people he could trust. Fae like him. Outcasts. An image formed in his mind. A collection of vines in the farthest corner of the sacred garden. The barrier between light and dark. All he had to do was open the lock—release his kin. It all made sense, now. Why had he resisted in the first place?

Footsteps sounded in the distance, followed by a series of anguished cries. Someone called his name, but it got lost in the looping words inside his head. They were all that mattered. What he needed to focus on.

"Greyson! Dear God, what have they done to you?"

He frowned. Why did that voice sound so familiar? Why did it ease the pain still coursing through his body? Fill the hollow in the pit of his chest? A surge of dark energy scattered the thoughts. He had to free his kin. That was his only mission. Hands brushed along his limbs, tugging at the chains. Pain teased his senses as the iron fell away, allowing his arms to fall to his sides. His shoulders burned as his muscles protested the movement, and he swayed when the room seemed to flip-flop.

Fingers stopped him from falling, the soft brush of skin across his sending a shiver along his spine. A flute began softly playing in the darkness, the melody quickly crushed by the power pulsing within the amulet. Hands cupped his face, lifting his chin as thumbs stroked his cheek. He felt a gentle press of lips on his forehead followed by a delicate kiss on his mouth.

"Greyson. Open your eyes."

Grey blinked, somehow managing to pry open his eyelids. An angelic face peered back at him, with eyes so blue it made the room fade into gray. His blond hair hung in tousled strands around his head, the ends grazing his bare shoulders. Warmth bathed Greyson's face, a hint of light appearing in the darkness.

The voice inside him howled, dropping Greyson's head onto the other man's shoulder. Pain ricocheted through his skull, taking him to his knees when the guy tried to lift him. Images spun through his mind—an isolated cabin, bare skin gleaming in the moonlight—but it all bled into black.

A white glow brightened the shadows, forcing Greyson to meet the man's gaze. The light covered his skin, and all Greyson could think about was how it paled to what it should be. How it was only a fraction of what the man held within him. The thought angered Grey. Why was the guy holding the rest back? Was Greyson not worthy of all of it?

The man frowned. "Greyson? Don't you remember me?"

The man's name hit Greyson like a physical blow. His head snapped back as the energy inside him raged in protest. A surge of power pushed him to his feet. He shook off the guy's hold as he took a few steps back, knocking the chair to the floor. It clattered across the rock, jiggling the chains in the process. Blood still oozed from the wounds on his shoulder, but none of it seemed important. He'd live long enough to break the lock. That was enough.

He sneered, letting the darkness inside him flow around him. "I know who you are, *Michael*. You're the man who didn't think I was worthy of being your mate."

Michael flinched from the words, the malice in Grey's tone impossible to miss. Confusion clouded the guy's face as his gaze dropped to the amulet then back up. "That isn't you talking. It's the evil inside you." He gained his feet, maintaining their distance. "You have to fight it, Grey. You're stronger than it is. I know it. Come back to me."

"You think I'm weak, now?" Greyson laughed. "What I was before was weak. Serving my father. Hiding." He shook his head. "I should be king. Watch my people bow at my feet. Watch you bow."

"Is that what you think will happen? That you'll be ruler?" Michael crossed his arms over his chest. "It's nothing but a lie. You won't live long enough to rule. Look at your wounds. If the darkness inside you really wanted you to be king, wouldn't it heal you? Guarantee you survived to sit on the throne?" He took a step forward. "It's using you. You're nothing more than a pawn. A vessel to break the wards, free the dark fae. Then their leader will claim the throne, not you. They'll watch you bleed. Die. And you'll never be spoken of again."

Grey shook his head, feeding off of the evil pumping through his veins. "No. I'm their savior. They need me. Unlike you." He spat the words out, allowing all the pain to flow from him. "You never needed me. Never saw me as anything more than a one-night stand. You're supposed to be my mate!"

He tipped back his head, grinning when streaks of red burst across his skin. They raced along the ruins marking his flesh, burning the blues and greens into black before spreading across his wings, turning the once translucent surface into bloody crimson. He watched them flutter behind him, like shadows rising from his back, then turned to Michael.

He arched a brow. "You denied me. Do you know how much that hurt!" He took a menacing step forward, arcs of fire sparking along his skin. "How I've had to listen to that fucking flute play over and over and over, knowing there'd never be an end. That I'd never be free of that infuriating song. And I would have done it. I would have suffered for a thousand years just to spare you the pain, but not now." He stretched his arms out to the side. "Now, I see the world for what it is. Cruel. Just like you."

Sadness flashed in the angel's eyes, but he stood his ground. "You're right. I was cruel. And selfish. I only focused on how scared I was. How broken and unworthy I felt, instead of how pushing you away affected you. I didn't want to need you. Didn't want to love you—but I do." He drew himself up. "I failed you once. I won't fail you again. You *will* leave here, but not like this. You'll leave with me. Pure. Whole. No matter what it takes, I'll drive that vile essence from your soul and send it back to the far reaches of Hell where it belongs."

"You're not powerful enough. You barely have enough grace to save your own soul, let alone mine. And your wings..." He laughed again. "You can't even fly."

"I don't need either to heal you. I have something far more powerful."

"Let me guess...love." He rolled his eyes. "You're going to heal me with your angelic love, aren't you?" He spat on the floor. "That's what I think of your love. Besides, I doubt you're even capable of loving anyone other than yourself. Or your father. Or your fucking duty. I never had a chance."

"Then come to me if you're so certain I can't change you." Michael arched a brow. "Or are you afraid?"

"Not anymore." Greyson bent over, grabbing Sezil's sword. He turned it over in his hands, judging the weight of it, then pointed it at Michael. "If you truly want to save me, you'll have to win."

The muscle in Michael's jaw jumped. "I won't fight you, Greyson."

"Then you'll die."

CHAPTER FIFTEEN

Michael stood there, staring at his mate—watching as the man readied his blade—and knew there wasn't any way in which he could engage and win. If he didn't fight, he had no doubt Greyson would kill him without so much as a second thought. But if he did...

He glanced at Grey's battered body. The gaping wounds on his shoulder that still bled. The numerous welts along his arms and legs. Greyson's only saving grace, if it could be called that, was that most of the injuries had been the result of iron, which had cauterized the majority of the flesh, limiting the actual amount of blood loss. Not that it would matter in the end. That amulet around his neck... Even with his limited power, Michael sensed it feeding off of Greyson's life force. Stealing more of his energy until there'd be nothing left but a withered shell.

Michael cursed under his breath. He wasn't sure if he had enough grace left to heal the man, though he could ease some of the pain. Give Greyson the strength he needed to return to the summoning spot. Though, his mate would have to initiate the reversal spell. Channel Michael's grace with enough precision to activate the coin.

He pushed aside the thoughts. Greyson was strong. Skilled. All Michael had to do was break the amulet's hold, and he was confident his mate would be able to make the journey back. It didn't matter if Michael joined him or not. As long as Greyson lived.

Greyson nodded at Michael's sword. "I'll give you one last chance to ready yourself before I strike."

"I'm not fighting you. I'd rather die than hurt you."

"It's a bit too late to make that promise."

Greyson lunged at him, the man's blade slicing through the air in clean, efficient strokes. Michael blocked the first sequence, dodging to his right in an effort to increase their separation. But the room was barely large enough to contain them standing still, let alone parrying each other. Greyson smiled at Michael's reluctance, the fae's next attack catching him across the shoulder. Blood welled along the laceration, dripping steadily down his back.

Grey chuckled. "You're going to have to up your game, or you won't last long."

Pain flared across the wound, a reminder that they were both essentially mortal, though Michael wondered how much of the amulet's power Grey could manifest in this place. If it was only pure energy that was hindered. More of those strange red arcs crackled across Greyson's arms, as if in defiance.

Michael circled to his left, glancing at the chains scattered along the floor. While he didn't want to so much as scratch Greyson's flesh, Grey was right. His mate was more than skilled with a blade and would certainly do far worse than cut Michael's shoulder if he didn't start fighting back. He needed an alternate solution.

He motioned to the pendant. "Why don't you take that amulet off, and we'll see if you still want to kill me."

"This?" He flicked it with his hand, seemingly indifferent to the slight burn it left behind on his fingers. "On. Off. It doesn't matter. I've seen the truth..." he hit his fist on his chest a few times, "...in here. This is nothing more than an empty trinket, now."

As if to prove his point, Grey yanked the pendant off and tossed it across the room. It clattered against the far wall, the stone in the center turning black. Michael's shoulders drooped slightly. He'd really hoped removing the necklace would break the connection. If he'd only arrived sooner.

He played a few scenarios over in his head, his only solution settling hard in his stomach. He'd already hurt Greyson enough. Even minor injuries in an effort to save him didn't feel right.

Grey struck again, this time catching Michael's left wing when Michael checked his swing, avoiding a stroke that would have left a gaping wound along his mate's side. Michael tripped against the wall, breathing through the resulting surge of pain. If he kept this up, Greyson would kill him.

Greyson tsked. "I warned you. But you're too pure, aren't you? Always the good son. Is that why you haven't blocked Lucifer? Do you like the constant reminder of how much better you are than him? Does it give you the redemption you're looking for to allow him to feel your light?" He shuffled sideways, lining up another strike. "Or are you just too fucking weak to push him out?" Grey flashed him an evil grin. "I think it's the latter."

He dove at Michael, missing by a few inches when Michael rolled across the floor, grabbing the iron chains as he went. The cold metal felt heavy in his hands, a stark reminder of all he had to lose. How much Greyson had suffered because of Michael's failures.

Grey recovered quickly, spinning toward him. Grey's blade sliced through the air, this sequence far more intricate than any Michael had seen his mate utilize yet. Michael dodged as best he could, using the chains to deflect the last couple of swings. Greyson snarled, lunging for his chest. Michael waited, allowing the tip to catch him in the side before twisting away as he looped the chains around Greyson's arm, pinning it and his sword to Grey's torso as he spun in behind his mate. He pressed his chest to Grey's spine, his hands white-knuckled around the iron in an effort to maintain control of the other man.

The iron sizzled against Greyson's skin, the sound making Michael's stomach heave in protest. His mate thrashed against his hold, taking them both to the floor. They hit hard, the force of Greyson's body landing on his, stealing Michael's breath. Black dots danced across his vision, the edges slightly grayed. Greyson stilled for a moment, groaning as his head hit the rock beside Michael's shoulder.

Michael moved, tossing the chains aside then shifting his grip to Greyson's wrist as he flipped them both over, trapping Greyson beneath him. The other man's wings beat against his sides, leaving bloody gashes along

Michael's ribs. But he held on, knowing he only had one chance to save his mate. To drive away the darkness.

"I'm not going to lose you again, Grey. Not this time."

More red sparks danced along Greyson's arms. "I'm not yours!"

"You will be."

Michael brushed his mouth against Greyson's ear, allowing what remained of his grace to shimmer to the surface. A muted glow shaded his skin, the white color fading into a light blue. Peace filled his soul as he closed his eyes and said what he never should have held back.

"Unlike faeries, archangels don't have to say any words to bind their mate to them. It's a giving and sharing of grace that completes the bond. I'm not sure I have enough left to offer you, but whatever I have is yours."

His energy surged forward, skimming along Greyson's flesh. It hovered above the dark patches, slowly sinking beneath the surface. Greyson stiffened within his grasp, a ragged scream tearing from his chest. A hint of blue colored his skin, only to fade into red.

Michael waited, but nothing changed. He sighed. To fully bind them, his mate needed more. Michael adjusted his grip, counteracting the growing weakness as best he could as he channeled the last of his grace into Greyson. Tremors racked his arms, and Michael knew that it was only a matter of time before Grey broke free. If Michael couldn't vanquish the dark energy before then…

Greyson's head bowed forward, his forehead connecting with the floor. The man's frantic breathing sounded around them, a rash of goosebumps covering his flesh. He shook his head, groaning in apparent pain. "The voice. It's telling me I have to free—"

"Yourself. You have to free yourself from the darkness inside you. Return to the light. The only voice you need to hear inside your head is mine. I'm yours."

Grey whimpered, then screamed as a blast of energy lifted Michael up and flung him across the room. He slammed against the wall then fell to the ground, the room blurring out of focus. Rough hands flipped him onto his back, sparking more pain through his head and shoulders. He blinked just as Greyson straddled him, a curved dagger in his grasp. He glared down at Michael, holding the blade in both hands as he pressed the tip against Michael's chest.

His mate's arms shook as he sat there, seemingly unable or unwilling to make the final strike. "I can't abandon my mis..." He grimaced, his head drooping slightly. "The flute. Do you hear it?"

Michael placed his fingers over top of Grey's. A flash of light brightened the shadows, the haunting lilt of a flute sounding around them. "I hear it. It plays for us, Greyson."

He shook his head. "It's a trick."

"No, it's fate. All you have to do is say the words."

Anger creased his brow. "You denied me."

"I was foolish. Afraid. I'm not afraid anymore."

"It wants me to kill you. I *should* kill you."

He gave Grey a genuine smile. "If my life is what you need to return to the light, then take it. I love you, Greyson. Alive or dead, that will never change. You are my sun, my moon, my darkest night. You are the light that brightens the shadows." He arched his brow. "Would you like to continue, or shall I?"

Greyson's eyes widened, the knife shaking in his grasp.

He dropped his gaze to where the tip of the blade scratched Michael's chest, blood already dotting along the lines. His mouth gaped open then his head tipped back, an anguished cry rumbling free. He arched backwards, the black staining on his skin exploding upwards. It gathered above them, long finger-like threads still clinging to Greyson's flesh.

Michael freed the knife from Grey's fingers, quickly flipping the dagger and swiping at the tethered ends. The edges sizzled then snapped, coiling up into the whirling dark mass. An unholy growl sounded around them before the essence retreated, circling the room a few times then slamming back into the amulet. The stone lit up a bloody shade of red, casting the strange markings as shadows across the ceiling before winking out.

Greyson shouted Michael's name, then collapsed. Michael managed to catch most of the fae's weight before he hit the floor. He cradled Grey's head gently in his hands then rolled, placing his mate on the stone. The black lines faded from his skin, all traces of the dark energy dissipating.

Michael gave Grey a light shake. "Greyson?"

His mate groaned but didn't rouse.

Michael sighed, bending down before giving Grey a fleeting kiss. "Rest. I'll take us somewhere safe, for now."

He'd passed a river on the journey there. There'd been another deserted dwelling hidden amongst the trees next to it. With any luck, he'd be able to ward the small structure with enough ancient markings, he could buy Greyson a bit of time to recover.

His muscles throbbed in protest, reminding him Greyson wasn't the only one who needed to recover. And now, with only Lucifer's essence still fueling Michael's body, it would take twice as long to heal. The new wounds burned as he bent over to retrieve the amulet. He didn't want to chance it could infect anyone else. He'd find a safe place for it once he'd returned. That or destroy it.

If he returned.

He sighed. Now wasn't the time to fill his head with negative thoughts. He could worry about activating the coin once Grey was better. He moved back to his mate, shuffling Greyson into his arms. Then he lifted the man across his good shoulder, doing his best to evenly bridge his weight. Michael focused on trying to retract what was left of his wings. But it only added a sharp sting to the pain already strumming through him.

He'd just have to leave them out, hanging limp at his side. God, he prayed Lucifer was right. That if they made it back, his grace would restore him. That's if his brother decided to give it back. And with all his grace gone...

He tipped back his head. For someone who wasn't supposed to be filling his mind with negative thoughts, he wasn't doing a very good job of staying positive. He drew a deep breath, then picked his way down the corridor and back outside. Bodies were strewn across the ground, the stench of blood and death heavy in the air. He couldn't remember the last time he'd done this much damage— killed this many creatures. He just hoped it was enough. That they wouldn't face an equal number of monsters on the way back. Under the circumstances, Michael knew they wouldn't fair well.

An eerie howl sounded in the distance. He headed for the tree line. If he kept to the edge of the forest, he might be able to reach the other structure before anything caught their scent. He wove through the branches, careful not to knock Greyson as he headed back toward where he'd landed. The dull sky looked darker, though it was impossible to tell what time of day it was, and he wondered if the muted sun ever set? Or if the damn place was just a never-ending twilight.

Footsteps sounded in the distance, followed by the rustle of leaves. Michael ducked behind a gathering of bushes, cradling Grey in his lap as he scanned the surrounding area. The air thickened around them, a blast of otherworldly power prickling the hairs on his neck. He palmed the hilt of his sword, readying himself to launch an attack, when a black, bubble-like cloud materialized in the clearing off to his left. It swirled counterclockwise, slowly dissolving into the ground. Two men stood in its place, their stark beauty matched only by the dark energy thrumming off them.

They were both pale, with long ebony hair extending down to their waists. Black markings swirled across their skin, curling up their ribs, along their chests then over their shoulders, continuing the length of their wings. Where Greyson's were light, nearly transparent in nature, theirs were more like moving shadows, the surface constantly rippling like waves on the water.

Michael frowned. He hadn't expected the dark fae to be beautiful. To mimic the qualities he admired in Greyson's kin. He glanced at his mate. There was no mistaking the similar physical attributes—the wings. The runes. But that's where it ended. Greyson's heart was pure. His soul unstained by fear and hatred. Even in this place, the light within him fought to burst free. To banish the surrounding darkness.

Michael groaned inwardly. It was that very source of light that could give them away. Reveal their position. And he wasn't sure if he had the strength to fight them off. Not if they could harness their power. The fae turned when two more men burst through the foliage, stopping before them.

They bowed, the taller one pointing toward the cabin where they'd held Greyson. "The Prince is gone. Nothing but dead left behind."

One of the newcomers arched a brow. "He can't be gone. He has no way of leaving this place." The fae tapped his finger on his chin. "The process must be complete. Tharn most likely returned and took him somewhere safe to await the second coming after allowing the Prince to enjoy a bit of sport. Hone his fighting skills."

"What if he escaped?"

The other man laughed. "Escaped? How? He was bound in iron."

The guy looked at his partner then shrugged. "What if he had help?"

"From who? None of his kin can come here without the use of dark sorcery. And Oberon would never make himself vulnerable like that."

"There was talk of an angel—"

"An angel? Don't waste my time. They're far too pure. Their grace would tear them to shreds when it hit the barriers." He silenced any further retort with a wave of his hand. "Enough. Ready your followers. Once we control the faery realm we'll need your help to conquer the humans."

The guy nodded then headed off, branches cracking as he cut through a thicker section of the forest. The fae glanced toward where Michael crouched behind the foliage, the silver in his eyes impossible to miss. He seemed to stare directly at them then continued on, twisting to whisper to his companion. The other man nodded, swirling his hands in the air. A purplish light appeared above his palms, slowly increasing until it engulfed them. Another blast of power rippled through the forest, swirling in on itself until the dark faeries vanished.

Michael waited a few moments to ensure they were truly gone before heaving Greyson back on his shoulder. Fatigue gnawed at his muscles, but he started moving. At least Greyson's disappearance wouldn't be missed. Not until they discovered that this Tharn didn't have him. Once that happened...

Michael just needed a few hours. Time to rest. Heal. And if he was fortunate enough to return, he'd deal with Tharn and the dark fae one last time.

CHAPTER SIXTEEN

"The voice. It's telling me to kill you. I should kill you."

"If my life is what you need to return to the light, it's yours."

"You denied me."

"I love you. You are my sun, my moon, my darkest night."

"Michael!"

Greyson gasped as he opened his eyes, the echoed voices still ringing in his head. His. Michael's. Snippets of conversations, though Grey wasn't even sure if it was real, or something he'd imagined. He frowned. Had Michael said he loved him?

Grey tried to turn, inhaling against the pain that throbbed through his body. Pieces of the past few days came rushing back, one cold truth hitting him hard. He was in Purgatory, which meant the ghostly words had been nothing more than wishful thinking, even if some of the words felt wrong. As if someone else had spoken them. Footsteps scuffed nearby, followed by the soft brush of a hand along his cheek. It was loving. Warm.

He blinked, furrowing his brow when Michael's face

wavered into view. Tears stung his eyes, and he looked away in an effort to keep them at bay. "Must you haunt my waking dreams, as well?"

Michael chuckled. "Is that what you think I am? A figment of your imagination?"

Grey made eye contact again. God, the man looked so real. He reached for his jaw, stilling when he connected with smooth flesh. "You feel...real."

Michael's hand covered his, holding Grey's palm tight to his cheek. "That's because I am. Real."

"But..." Grey shook his head. "You can't be. Not here. Either I'm dreaming, or I'm dead and this is Heaven, though I'm not sure faeries go there."

Michael's eyes welled up, but he blinked away the wetness. "You're not dreaming, and you certainly aren't dead, though you came pretty damn close." He glanced around at the stone walls. "And we're as far from Heaven as we can get."

Greyson swallowed as he did his best to scan the surroundings. They were in a small, stone structure, much like the one Tharn had taken him to, only it appeared to be a solitary room. A fire blazed in a hearth not too far away, the crackle of wood suddenly filling the emptiness.

He gazed up at Michael, groaning as the scenery flip-flopped. "We're in Purgatory? But how..."

Michael tilted his head, looking at Grey as if he thought Grey was crazy. "Did you really think I wouldn't come for you?"

Fear prickled Greyson's skin. "I..." He glanced around, again, wondering if this was really some kind of ploy. A way to trick him into accepting his role in the prophecy.

Michael sighed. "This isn't a trick. Promise. Yes, we're still in Purgatory. But you beat the darkness."

"You can't be in Purgatory." He frowned when Michael chuckled. "It's not funny. Nothing pure can get through. They used dark magic on me to get me through the barriers, but you... Even you couldn't break those wards."

"I didn't."

"Then how..."

Michael's head bowed toward his chest, a hint of defeat in his shoulders. "There's more than one way to get to Purgatory. And thankfully, I happen to know someone very skilled in banishing spells." Michael met Grey's gaze. "He's also extremely powerful and less than pure."

Greyson's breath caught in his chest. Surely Michael hadn't made a deal with...*him*.

Michael shrugged. "Not an official deal, yet. My brother wasn't convinced I'd survive."

"You went to Lucifer?"

"He was the only one who could send me here. I didn't have a choice."

"How about simply not coming?"

"That was never an option."

Greyson stared at the man, finally seeing beyond his shock. Fatigue creased the angel's brow, the fine lines around his eyes deeper than usual. Blood caked his skin, some wounds still oozing, but those weren't what held his attention. Michael's once pearl-white wings had been shredded. Blackened and torn, they hung at an odd angle to each side, the left one ripped nearly in half.

Michael glanced at him. "They're just wings, Grey."

"They're not just wings. They're part of you, a huge part. I know what they mean to you. What they represent.

You're God's Warrior, you need your... Wait. You can read my thoughts?"

Michael palmed his chest, gently but firmly pushing him back down. "You still look like shit. You need to rest. Get some of your strength back. We'll talk once you're stronger." He lifted a small cup made out of bark to his lips. "Try to drink just a bit."

Cool water soothed his parched lips, and he didn't resist when Michael adjusted a thin blanket across his shoulders. Questions tumbled through his head, but they seemed to fade into the promise of sleep.

Michael smiled as he tucked a lock of Grey's hair behind his ear. "It's okay. Don't fight it. I'll still be here when you wake up. Promise. Now, sleep."

Panic closed in around his heart. "Won't the fire give us away?"

"Thanks to Lucifer, I was able to ward the structure. We should be fine for a while. And it's damn cold without it."

"Lucifer? How? And what if they come—"

Michael silenced him with a single finger across his lips. "Now's not the time for questions. I've taken care of everything. Shhh..." He smiled. "I'll explain later. Just, rest."

Greyson relented, still staring at Michael until his eyelids drooped. He closed his eyes, telling himself he'd just rest for a minute. Catch his breath. Images played in the darkness—ghostly reflections of him and Michael engaged in battle. Echoes of words shouted in anger, their only intent to inflict the greatest amount of pain possible. A searing cold crushed against his chest, then vanished. Pushed back by a warm, white light that pulsed inside him. The distant lilt of a flute called to him, the song jolting him awake.

He gasped in a quick breath, blinking back the blurriness. The crackle of a fire drew his attention, and he turned, watching Michael adjust the logs, his gaze seemingly fixed on the way the flames danced along the wood. Grey frowned. Now that he didn't feel quite as groggy, he sensed that something was...off.

He inhaled, the answer screaming inside his head. "Why isn't your skin glowing?"

Michael jumped slightly, snorting as he glanced over at Grey. "You're awake." Concern flashed in his eyes as his gaze slid to Greyson's shoulder then back. "Your wounds look a bit better. I'd hoped you'd heal faster, though, I guess we're lucky you're healing at all, considering the bastards used iron. How do you feel?"

"That's not important. Why can't I sense your grace? Even in this place, with it...suppressed like my magic, I should still be able to *feel* it."

Michael didn't answer, just continued to poke at the fire.

Greyson searched his memory, when the dream came rushing back. Guilt and pain tumbled through his gut, threatening to heave what little water he'd managed across the floor. He braced his back against the wall, unable to take his gaze off of Michael. "Oh my God. These images inside my head. They aren't dreams. They're memories."

"Easy. You're still weak."

"Weak! I tried to *kill* you. Half those gashes on your body came from me! Dear God, your wings—"

"I'll heal."

"Physically, maybe. But what about your heart? Damn, what I said..." He took a few shaky breaths. "I can't believe you didn't just leave me there to die."

"Stop it." Michael waited until Grey looked at him again. "It wasn't you. It was the evil they'd put inside you. I know that."

"Still." Greyson scrubbed a hand down his face. "How can you be so calm?"

"You're alive. Not much else matters."

"So your grace? It's just...gone?" He stilled. "Oh, God. Please tell me you didn't fall just so you could come here."

Michael sighed. He placed the stick on the floor then shuffled over to Grey's side. He smiled as he grazed his knuckles along Grey's cheek, toying with the strands of hair by Grey's chin. "Everything's going to be fine."

"It's not inside you. I know it isn't."

"If I'd kept my grace, I never would have made it through the barrier."

A numbing cold settled in Grey's stomach. "So... you did fall."

Michael gave him a small smile. "With any luck, it's only temporary."

"Temporary? Since when is falling temporary?"

"Since I didn't actually have to cast myself out of Heaven. More like a transfer of power. Lucifer has it."

Greyson pinched the bridge of his nose. Surely, he'd heard Michael wrong. "You gave your grace to Lucifer?" He raked a hand through his hair. "Bloody hell, Michael, are you crazy?"

"He gave me some of his, in return. Enough to mask the bit I brought with me without dying when I hit the barriers, though his power has come in handy. It's allowed me to work a few feats of magic here, like warding this shack for the past few hours. Though, even his power is extremely limited."

"He gave…" Greyson snorted. "I guess that explains why you're a bit more colorful in your choice of words since I woke up, but that's hardly the point. What guarantee do you have that he'll give it back?"

"None. But it was the only way." He nudged Grey's shoulder. "Weren't you the one who told me he was still family?"

"Yes, it's just… It's your grace." He blew out an exasperated breath, frowning as he reran Michael's words. "You said you brought a bit with you. What happened to the part you kept? I should still…" Warmth spread through his core, slowly rising to the surface, coloring his skin a pale blue. Grey stared at the glow, more pieces falling into place. He looked up at Michael, tears clogging his throat. "You gave it to me? Why?"

Michael's expression sobered. "You know why."

He shook his head. "You could have found another way to break the curse, to bring me back. Surely Gabriel, or even Lucifer, could have healed me once I'd returned?"

"Even if I'd been able to subdue you, do you really think that's why I gave you my grace? Just to break a curse?"

"Was it to heal me? Because from where I'm sitting your wounds are far worse." He inhaled. "Shit. Without your grace, you can't heal yourself, can you? Damn it, Michael."

"Some increased healing ability is just a fortunate byproduct. There wasn't near enough to do the job properly."

"Then why? The only other reason would be to..." His voice trailed off as the answer rang true in his head. He swallowed against the sudden dryness in this throat, staring at the other man.

His mate.

Michael laughed. "Don't sound so happy about it. You're embarrassing me."

Grey opened his mouth, but nothing made it past the tight feeling in his chest. The room shifted again, but he didn't think it had anything to do with his injuries.

"It's okay. I don't expect you to say anything. Not right now." Michael palmed his jaw, brushing his thumb back and forth along his cheek. "We can talk once we get...back."

Grey frowned. There'd been a slight hesitation in Michael's voice when he'd talked about them returning, as if he wasn't quite telling the truth. Not to mention the fact he'd sounded as if he wasn't sure they should be mates.

He grabbed Michael's arm when the man went to move away. "Just, wait." He shifted his hand down until he'd threaded his fingers through Michael's. "Why do I get the feeling you think things have changed between us? I know I hurt you—"

"I deserved it. Every word." He pushed to his feet and stalked across the room. His back stiffened as he toed the floor before glancing at Grey across his shoulder. "You were right. I did deny you. I was selfish. Nothing you said was a lie, Greyson. And if it hurts, I have no one to blame but myself. What you said was justified."

"Justified?" Grey pressed his hand against the wall, levering up. He ignored Michael's hushed curse, bracing his weight against the stone as he faced his mate. "We're talking about being mates. There's no right or wrong in how you love someone. Did not mating with you hurt? Of course, but that doesn't mean I get to give it back tenfold. And I damn well hit you with everything I had." He did his best to draw himself up. "Are you certain you were truthful before, or was this really all just to end the prophecy?"

A deep flush stained Michael's cheeks as he fisted his hands at his side. He clenched his jaw, striding toward Greyson then trapping Grey between the wall and his chest. The scent of cottonwood surrounded Grey, the telltale lilt of the flute starting to play in his head.

Michael palmed the wall beside Greyson's head, leaning in until his mouth hovered a breath away. "I've made a lot of mistakes in my time, but I've never turned to you out of pity or duty. And I sure as hell didn't start today. So in case you're at all unclear about my intentions... I mated with you because I need you. Because just the thought of spending another day without your touch, your taste, your damn voice in my head, was driving me mad." He brushed his mouth over Grey's then eased back slightly. "I love you, Greyson. That will never change."

The song intensified with every word, each rise and fall of the melody demanding Greyson reciprocate the gesture. Bind Michael to him with the same unforgiving determination. Michael cocked his head to the side, closing his eyes as he hummed the tune playing inside Greyson's head. Grey's breath hitched, and he lifted his hand, drawing his fingers back along Michael's jaw.

He traced Michael's lower lip with his thumb, smiling

at the way Michael's eyes dilated, eclipsing some of the blue. "So soft. So fucking perfect. There's nothing you could ever do to change my mind. You know that, right?"

Uncertainty creased Michael's features. "I'm not the archangel I once was, and there's a chance I might never be that man, again."

"Then I suppose we'll just have to share my magic, instead." He dropped a lingering kiss on his mate's lips. "Archangel. Mortal. Somewhere between. None of that matters because I fell in love with you, Michael. Not what you represent." He eased back enough to glance around the shack. "Not exactly the most romantic place to do this. Or the safest, I suspect."

"And what, exactly, were you planning on doing?"

"You hear the flute. God, why my ancestors chose that godforsaken instrument as a mating call..." He smiled. "Regardless, it's time I silenced it."

Michael's eyes widened, and he stopped Grey with a finger across his lips. "I know what you're thinking, but... not a word until we get out of here. And before you ask— no, it's not because I don't want you to bind yourself to me."

Grey frowned. "Really? Because it certainly seems like that."

"I'm already bound to you. In every way. And the curse has been broken, whether you ever finish the ritual or not. Yes, I fucking need you to say the words as much as you want to say them. But if you complete the ritual now, there's a chance some of my grace might return to me, and you don't have enough to spare."

"The hell I don't. I'm fine. You're the one who needs the added benefits right now. Or are you implying that giving you some of your grace back might undo our connection? Give you a way out?"

"Did you hear anything I said before? Does saying 'I love you' mean something different to fae? I don't want a way out." A hint of a smile teased Michael's lips. "And before you ask, no, not even my father has the power to undo our bond. You're mine, Grey. Forever."

"Then stop being so damn stubborn. You can give me more once you get the rest back from Lucifer."

"If my physical state was all that was at stake, I'd say the words with you, but...there's one last complication I haven't mentioned." He reached into his pocket and removed an ancient coin with strange markings on one side. "You're going to need all of that grace if you're going to get us home."

CHAPTER SEVENTEEN

Michael stared at Greyson, taking a moment to savor the green of his eyes. The way his thumb still caressed Michael's jaw, the gentle touch burning desire low in his core. His cock responded, lengthening against the confines of his jeans. While this was the last place they could ever consider letting their guard down long enough to indulge in physical contact, damn if he didn't want to. Wanted to taste the man's skin. Feel it move beneath his palms as he traced every inch, every hard plane. Look his mate in the eyes as he slowly sank inside him, finally banishing the empty feeling that had plagued his heart since he'd woken alone in his bed that fateful morning.

Greyson's mouth kicked up into a smile. He leaned in, rubbing his erection across Michael's. "Oh yeah. I want all of that and more. I want to suck you dry. Feel you give around me. Hear you shout my name so damn loud the bloody walls shake." He nipped at Michael's lips. "But more than anything, I want to make you mine. So tell me how to get us out of this fucking realm, and I'll make all those fantasies inside your head come true."

Michael groaned as Grey dipped in for a brutal kiss before taking a few determined steps back. The man closed his eyes, fisting his hands at his side as beads of sweat gathered along his brow. The haunting chords of the song seemed to echo around them before slowly fading.

"Shit!" Michael closed the distance, grabbing his mate by the arms. He waited until Grey had taken a few deep breaths before releasing his own. "You still hear the music, don't you?"

Grey chuckled, then opened his eyes. "Who knew one tiny flute could drive a man crazy."

Guilt washed over Michael. "Fuck, Grey, I'm so sorry." He pursed his lips. "I'm just not sure if we should risk—"

"I'll deal with it. I've had some practice." He cursed when Michael looked away, cupping his jaw and guiding his gaze back to Grey's. "I didn't mean that the way it sounded."

Michael sighed. "Doesn't make it any less true. I knew how hard this was for you. Shit, I gave you some of my grace to ease the pain when what I should have done was be the man you needed me to be."

Grey smiled, sliding his hands up Michael's chest then into his hair. "You came all the way to Purgatory. You risked your grace, your life—everything that ever mattered to you. Hell, you went to Lucifer. You think I don't know what that cost you? To ask him, of all people, for help? Having him inside your head is one thing. Actually making a deal with him—one you still have yet to know the true price of—that took real courage. Real sacrifice."

"You might not be so impressed with that fact when we end up spending the foreseeable future watching over Hell while Lucifer takes a vacation, or something equally endearing."

Grey shrugged. "Heaven. Hell. It doesn't matter as long as I've got you." He released his fingers, rolling his shoulders as he appeared to strengthen his resolve. "I can handle the damn flute. Just tell me how we get out of here."

Pride filled Michael's chest. Damn, but he loved the fae.

Grey laughed. "I love you, too. Now stop worrying about anything else but getting us home."

"Fair enough. As for the way back..." He held up the coin. "According to Lucifer, we need to return to where I landed. Then I was supposed to channel what was left of my grace into this coin after placing it on the ground. My brother said it would activate some kind of retrieval spell that would open a portal and send us both back."

"I have to channel your grace into the coin? How the hell do I do that?"

"It's not much different from your magic."

"Which I seem to have no control of here."

"It's part of you. You'll do fine."

"Of course. Channel a power I've never used before while monsters are trying to kill us. All in a realm that prevents that very power from manifesting. Sounds simple."

Michael smiled. "You've had some of my grace with you the entire time, Grey. Trust me. You'll be able to activate the coin when you need to."

"Had some?" He narrowed his eyes. "The beams of

light I was able to use against the demons. That was your grace." He inhaled. "Is that why I was able to resist that amulet for as long as I did?"

"And how I knew where to find you. I heard you call a few times. And once your father filled me in on the whole prophecy thing—"

"So he did know? This whole time? Tharn wasn't lying."

Michael cringed. He hadn't meant to let that slip. "Oberon was trying not to influence your decisions."

"And leaving me completely unaware that the dark fae might come looking for me? That was helping?"

"We can discuss this later. Right now you have to concentrate on playing nice with *your* grace."

"Fine. But don't think I won't be having a very long chat with Oberon." Grey huffed then raked a hand through his hair. "How much farther is this spot?"

"About an hour. Depending on how fast we can travel."

Grey frowned, looking the length of Michael's body. "Shit, you're really hurting, aren't you?"

He gave his mate a warm smile. "I've got you. I'm perfect."

"Michael..." He grazed his fingers parallel to the wounds he'd inflicted, pain shadowing his face. "God, what I did... Not sure I can ever make up for this."

Michael took his hand, holding it over his heart. "You already have. And with any luck, Gabriel or Lucifer will be able to heal whatever my grace can't once we return."

"*If* Lucifer gives it back to you. What if he decides it's the price you have to pay for all he did?"

"Then, I suppose I'll have to be content sharing your magic, as you put it." He raised Grey's hand to his lips then kissed the palm. "As much as I love being an archangel, I love you more. Whatever awaits our return—it was worth the price I'll pay. *You're* worth the price."

Grey's breath hitched, as tears gathered behind his eyes. He closed them, taking a few deep breaths before snorting. "You really need to stop talking like that if I have any hope of not shoving you against this wall and claiming you as mine. And I will. I'll stop fighting this damn flute and bind you to me, risk or not." He locked his gaze on Michael's. "And don't think for one moment I'd be able to go anywhere without consummating our union, first, because..." He moistened his lower lip. "Mating tends to be intense. The need..."

Michael gave Grey's fingers a squeeze before taking a step back. "Get us home and I'm yours. As many times as you need."

"You'd better not have anything planned for the next century, mate." He offered Michael his hand. "Let me help you."

Michael waved him off. "I'm fine." He smiled at Greyson's huff. "Honestly, Grey. I'll let you know if I need any help."

"Right because you're so accustomed to asking for that."

"We'll never make it if you're carrying my ass the entire way. You're still weak."

"At least my wounds aren't still oozing blood. And my wings aren't hanging on by a damn thread."

"Greyson."

"Don't expect me to be happy that I hurt you, whether I was under some bloody curse or not."

Michael merely nodded. He tugged Greyson to him,

slanting his mouth over his in a possessive kiss. Grey tangled his tongue with Michael's, pulling Michael down for one more round before finally parting. He thumbed Michael's chin then motioned to the door.

Michael doused the fire, then scratched out the sigils he'd used to help hide them. His skin prickled as Lucifer's grace burned beneath his flesh. But despite his reservations, he hated to admit that he found his brother's essence strangely comforting.

Greyson arched his brow as Michael's gaze clashed with his, but his mate didn't question the conflicting thoughts he knew were rattling around inside his head. Instead, Grey gave him an encouraging smile, following behind Michael as he opened the door, then stepped out.

A dull gray colored the sky, much the same as when he'd first arrived. He scanned the area, then headed south, doing his best to keep up a steady pace. But weaving his way through the forest took a toll, reopening some of his wounds with a fresh wash of blood across his skin. Fatigue burned his muscles, the edges of his vision dimming slightly.

Greyson tsked behind him, getting as close as he could without touching him. "You're about to pass out."

Michael glanced at his mate over his shoulder, hissing out a breath when he stumbled, tripping onto one knee before straightening. "We're nearly there."

"You need to rest."

"It's not safe. The blood attracts them. We need to push on."

Grey merely sighed, once again dropping back a bit as Michael headed for a brighter patch amidst the trees. A large clearing spread out in front of them as they broke free of the forest. A few dozen corpses littered the ground, their bodies spread out around a huge divot carved into the dirt. The area surrounding the hole had been burned black, a few scattered feathers oddly white against the charred earth.

Greyson gasped, darting up to join Michael. "It looks like a damn meteor hit the ground."

"Just me. Though to be fair, Lucifer warned me it wasn't an easy task."

"Let's just hope the return trip isn't quite as harsh or neither of us might come out the other side intact."

Michael turned to his mate, running his hand along the man's jaw before letting his arm fall back to his side. "Between your magic and my grace, you'll be fine."

"I thought I had to give your power up to open the portal?"

"I said you needed to channel it. It'll still be inside you." He nudged the fae. "Words have meaning, Grey. Every word."

"Jackass." His hint of a smile faded. "So, what protects you if I have your grace?"

Michael shrugged. "Hopefully the bit Lucifer gave me."

Greyson's eyes widened. "Hopefully? You mean you aren't sure, yet you still gave up the one thing that guaranteed you'd make it back alive?"

"I came here to save you. That's what matters."

"Not if it means you'll die in my place. Damn it, Michael." His breath caught before he rounded on Michael, grabbing his good shoulder. "Shit. That's really why you didn't want me to finish the ritual and bond us together, isn't it? You're not sure you'll make it back alive, and you want to spare me the pain of losing my mate. It doesn't have anything to do with not having enough grace to initiate the spell."

Michael sighed, patting Greyson's hand. "We don't have time to discuss this. I sense more creatures closing in around us, and neither of us are up for another round of battles. You need to place the coin in the center of that hole then light it up."

Grey didn't budge when Michael tried to push past him. "Do you really think it will hurt less just because I haven't said the words? That I'm not already bound in a way that will gut me to lose you?"

"You can't blame me for wanting to try. If our positions were reversed, you'd have done the same thing. Now, are we going to stand here arguing, or are we going to get the hell out of here?"

He broke contact, striding purposely toward the charred ground. Greyson cursed then jogged up beside him, looking more than a little pissed. Michael pushed aside the guilt, focusing on covering the last bit of distance. They'd reached the edge of the depression when the trees shook behind them, three men breaking into the clearing. Michael spun, drawing his sword as the creatures tipped back their heads and howled.

He grabbed Greyson, stopping his mate from moving toward the threat. "I'll take care of them. You need to place the coin and try to activate the spell."

"You're too weak. You won't last against three of them."

"Neither of us will live long enough to make it home if you don't open that portal. I'm fine, just...do what you need to do."

Michael charged the men. He didn't know what kind of

monsters hid beneath the flesh exterior, but it didn't matter. He braced for the impact as he swung at the first creature, his sword connecting with some kind of weapon made out of bone. Bits of the shaft chipped away, but it remained intact enough for the bastard to counter Michael's attack. The force of the strike sent Michael reeling back, the sheer strength of simply staying on his feet blurring the scenery.

The men formed a lopsided triangle around him. Michael made small circles, repelling each advance. All he needed to do was buy Greyson enough time to figure out how to tap into his grace. After that...

Michael countered each move, holding his own until he missed a block. The bone club connected with his shoulder, knocking him sideways. He rolled across the ground, groaning when he hit a tree trunk. The rough bark gouged his arm, leaving another cut along his skin. The creatures closed in around him, white teeth gleaming in the dull light.

The closest one laughed, readying his blade when his eyes bulged wide. He stiffened, blood spilling out of his mouth as the tip of a sword burst from his chest, arching the creature backwards. A throaty gurgle rasped free before the guy fell in a bloody heap on the ground.

Greyson turned, killing the next man before the guy had registered the threat. His head landed on the parched dirt first, the bastard's body crumpling behind him. The last creature howled, glancing between them before retreating into the woods. Greyson muttered something under his breath, extending his hand. Michael accepted, falling against his mate as soon as he tried to stand.

Greyson tsked. "You stubborn jackass. So much for asking for help."

Michael moistened his lips, hoping he could talk past the dry feeling in his throat. "I came here to save you."

"So, what? I'm not allowed the same privilege?" He huffed, leading them back toward the site. "I sincerely hope this isn't how the next thousand years is going to play out or that battle we had before will just be the first of many." He grinned at Michael. "Of course, we won't use actual weapons, and the winner gets spanking rights."

Michael chuckled. "I might have to lose a few on purpose."

"Like you'd win every one. You might be an archangel, but I have an entire arsenal of spells at my disposal." He stopped when he reached the spot. "Okay, I think I might be able to channel your grace. I just have to actually hit the coin."

"Remember. It's part of you now. It wants to bend to your wishes."

"Unfortunately, it shares the same stubborn trait you have, so...it's being difficult. Every time I focus on the coin, it veers off at the last second."

"Use your magic to temper it." He held up his hand. "I know. This place. It's hindering your power, but you don't have to wield it. All you need is to let it guide your aim."

Greyson nodded, focusing on the coin when another group of creatures barreled into the clearing. He jerked around, cursing under his breath.

Michael hit him lightly in the shoulder. "Forget them. Channel the grace."

Grey pursed his lips, his gaze centered on the coin again. Michael held his breath, watching the damn creatures close the distance as they raced across the blood-stained earth, weapons drawn, lips pulled back into angry snarls. He gripped the hilt of his sword, mentally counting down to the point where he'd have to engage or risk having Greyson get hurt. Footsteps pounded the earth, the thundering sound echoing around them.

Michael clenched his jaw, knowing they only had a few more seconds before the group reached them. "It's now or never, Grey."

"I think..."

His words rasped into a sharp inhale as a muted blue light swirled across his skin, gathering in his hands before shooting out from his palms. It hit the coin, the force spinning it clockwise as the energy sank below the surface, highlighting the strange markings on the face. There was a moment of eerie silence as everything seemed to freeze, before the light reflected back, filling the clearing with a blinding blue glow.

Howls and shrieks rose above an odd humming sound, but all Michael could focus on was the shimmering pool directly in front of them. It rippled once, as if a stone had dropped and spoiled the crystal clear reflection, then coiled in on itself, the water-like substance creating a funnel. The wind picked up around him, spinning in the same direction as the funnel.

He grabbed Grey's shoulders, locking his gaze on his mate, praying this wasn't the last time he'd look into the man's hazel eyes. "Hold on tight, and whatever you do, don't try to move until we hit the other side. And I mean hit."

Grey leaned in, his mouth next to Michael's. "I love you."

"Whatever happens, I…"

Michael cursed as the words got lost when the wind picked them up and carried them inside the portal. He tried to maintain his hold on Grey, but the force of the rotation yanked them apart. Colored streaks rushed past Michael, isolating him from his mate before the lights gathered in a circle off in the distance. There was a harried feeling of free fall before the circle rushed toward him, burning a path through him. Pain shot through his skull as everything dimmed, nothing but the echoed call of his name following him into the darkness.

CHAPTER EIGHTEEN

"Michael!"

Grey reached for his mate as they got flung apart, both of them still falling within the black void. Streaks of light finally brightened the darkness, pulsing like a heartbeat before racing toward them. Grey crossed his arms in front of him, not quite sure what to expect, when he impacted against something solid. The force bounced him back into the air, dropping him a second time in a dust-filled heap. Pain spread across his torso, creeping up his spine and into his head. A loud ringing sounded in his ears, eventually giving way to what sounded like a version of his name.

"Greyson! Damn it, buddy, open your eyes."

He blinked, groaning as a flash of light ignited a throbbing pain in his skull. He rolled his head, hoping to simply fade when a hand shook his shoulder.

"Grey."

He huffed, trying again. He squinted against the bright images, finally focusing on a face hovering over him.

He arched his brow. "Kei?"

"The fact you posed that as a question doesn't bode well." The mage seemed to give him the once over. "How bad are you hurt?"

As if on cue, every cut and bruise burned to life, shifting the scenery slightly. Greyson bit back a groan, accepting Kei's hand as his friend helped him up, shouldering most of his weight as he swayed just sitting on his ass. He blinked a few times, wondering what the hell had happened, when his memories made him inhale.

He grasped Kei's arm, tugging the mage toward him. "Michael? Where is he?"

Kei frowned, glancing at Gabriel as the man knelt beside them. "We expected him to come through with you, but—"

"He's not here?" Greyson tried to push to his feet only to fall against Gabriel when his legs gave out.

The archangel muttered under his breath, bracing his weight as Kei moved in front. "Easy, Greyson. You're in no shape to move like that. Let me try to heal you."

Grey shook his head, scanning the area, knowing by the familiar shape of the landscape, the hint of cottonwood in the air, that he'd landed close to Michael's sanctuary. "Michael was with me. We both got sucked into that damn portal. He should be here." He gasped when he saw another man standing off to his right, amusement tilting his lips. "You!" Grey shoved away from Gabe, stumbling his way across to the other man. "Did you do this? Is that why you agreed to help Michael? Did you know only one of us would come back?"

Lucifer held up his hands. "Easy there, Prince. This has nothing to do with me. I warned Mikey it was a horrible idea. That the spell was just as liable to kill him as take him where he wanted to go." He tapped a finger on his chin. "Though, obviously he made it there alive." Lucifer bent closer. "And that's definitely Michael's grace I sense in you, but it's not just a bit. He bound himself to you, didn't he, the horny bastard."

"Enough, brother." Gabriel stopped beside Grey, once again bridging Grey's weight when he nearly tripped onto one knee. "Greyson's obviously not well. But he has a valid question. Is this part of the spell?"

Lucifer crossed his arms over his chest. "How the fuck should I know? I've never successfully sent anyone to Purgatory and back. You were standing right here, Gabriel, when I told him that. But the idiot insisted. All righteous about saving his mate. Stopping the damn prophecy." He focused on Grey. "Though, I distinctly told him not to give you *all* of his grace. That definitely complicates things."

Grey frowned. "How?"

Lucifer shook his head in mock frustration. "I swear, you're all getting fucking library cards for Christmas. As I told Michael before he left. The retrieval spell was fueled by grace. I expected him to save some for himself."

"No." Greyson yanked free again, practically falling on Lucifer. "Are you saying he's still there? In Purgatory?"

"It's...possible."

"No."

"Without his grace as a homing beacon, the portal might not have known to grab hold of him. Michael knew that."

"But...why would he give it all to me if he knew he needed it to get back?"

Gabriel sighed. "Completing the bond requires a

certain amount of grace to be shared. Maybe it took everything he had to accomplish that."

Greyson took a few staggering steps back, bumping into Kei. "No. He was there. *In* the portal with me. I saw him, but then these lights appeared between us, and..." He gripped his head against a sudden flare of pain. "He was there."

Kei grabbed him. "Easy, Grey. Let Gabriel heal you so you can think clearly."

"I don't need to think clearly, Kei. I need to know where the hell that portal took my mate. He has to be..."

Kei gave him a slight shake when Grey just stood there, mulling a thought over in his head. "Buddy? You okay?"

"Lucifer's grace."

The fallen angel cleared his throat. "Excuse me?"

Grey stared at the man. Christ, a fallen angel shouldn't be that beautiful, that seemingly perfect. Brown hair, steel-gray eyes, pale skin. It was like looking at a darker version of Michael.

Lucifer chuckled. "Now, you're just making me feel awkward."

Grey stilled. "You heard that, didn't you?"

Lucifer glanced at his brother, nodding toward Greyson. "I think you really need to fix his damn head, bro. The guy's fucking lost it."

"No!" Greyson held up his hand. "I'm not crazy. You can hear my thoughts, can't you?"

"Yeah, so?"

"So, I thought only mates could do that?"

"Whoa." Lucifer waved his hands. "I'm not your mate. I'll *never* be anyone's mate."

"No, but you're connected to mine, right?" Greyson hissed out a breath. "Look, I don't care that you two can chat since that whole deal with Abaddon. I actually think it's a good thing. What I'm getting at is that if you can still hear my thoughts that must mean he's alive. Otherwise our connection would be broken, and you wouldn't be able to read my mind."

Lucifer glanced at Gabriel, looking strangely unsettled. "Hate to be the buzzkill, but that doesn't mean he's not still in Purgatory."

"You said the spell was fueled by grace."

"And this is the head injury talking. We've been over this. Michael gave you all of his."

"But he didn't just have his grace inside him, did he? He had some of yours."

Lucifer chuckled. "You think the portal grabbed on to *my* grace and did what?"

"Sent him somewhere else. Maybe somewhere special to you?"

Kei groaned. "You think Michael's in Hell?"

"Fuck that." Lucifer crossed his arms over his chest. "He's not in Hell. Trust me, I'd feel it. Besides, if Greyson's right—and that's a hell of an if—the spell would toss his ass out at my sanctuary."

Kei frowned. "Isn't that Hell?"

"Really? You think Hell is my sanctuary?"

"Honestly, I didn't know you could go anywhere else." Kei glanced at Gabriel. "Help me out here, Gabe."

Lucifer huffed. "It's not like Gabriel knows where my sanctuary is. And for the record, I wasn't always stuck in Hell, remember?" He shook his head. "Don't look so surprised because I get to have some of the cool toys, too.

There was a time when Dad wasn't pissed at me, so... yeah. I have my own timeshare. Not that I've been there in a few thousand years." He raked his hand through his hair. "This is crazy." He nodded at Greyson. "If he's alive and on Earth, can't you just..." He waved at Greyson's head. "Jedi out where he is? You are mates, right?"

Greyson stepped forward. "I wasn't able to complete my side of things, which means Michael's obviously out cold, or I'd be able to connect with him."

"Just fucking fantastic. Fine. But I swear if any of you ever go there ever again..." He pointed south. "Joshua Tree National Park."

Gabriel arched a brow. "That's surprisingly close to...here."

"Thanks for the feedback, Captain Obvious. Sue me spying on Michael and wanting to be close to my big brother way back when. And I never got the chance to find someplace new after, so..." He rolled his shoulders, looking extremely uncomfortable. "It's glamoured to look like a rock formation. Gabriel will have to zap me there, seeing as I'm pretty much bound to where I'm summoned."

Gabriel gathered them close, placing one hand on Lucifer's shoulder. "Ready?"

An image flashed in Grey's head followed by a bright light. His stomach dropped as the earth shifted beneath his feet, stopping just as quickly as it'd started. The surroundings blurred into focus, nothing but red rock and scrubby trees stretching out toward the horizon.

Lucifer muttered under his breath as he walked over to a large rock face. He palmed the surface, a flash of red fire shooting out across some kind of barrier. The flames flared higher, burning into black before fading, revealing a small stone cottage.

Greyson inhaled as he spotted Michael's limp form lying in front of the door several yards away. "Michael!"

He ran across the short expanse of stone, falling to his knees beside his mate. More welts covered Michael's skin, his wings looking even worse than when they'd been in Purgatory. Grey gripped the archangel's shoulders, gently rolling him over—sliding one hand up to cradle his head. Michael groaned softly but didn't open his eyes.

Kei crouched beside Grey, placing his fingers against Michael's neck. "There's a pulse, but it's weak. Not that it's surprising. Christ, what the hell happened over there? He looks like he took on every damn monster in Purgatory."

"The worst of the injuries came from me." Greyson shook his head. "Now's not the time for that story. He needs his grace back."

Lucifer shrugged. "Sorry, no can do."

"What?" A blue glow swirled to life on Greyson's skin. "I swear—"

"Relax." Lucifer nudged Michael's leg with his foot. "Why does everyone assume the worst?"

"Maybe because you're the Devil?"

Color rose on Lucifer's cheeks as he glared at Grey. "That's a human term, and not one I particularly like. But I can't give Michael his grace back until he's conscious."

"Why?"

"Because it's part of the spell. I don't make the rules, buddy boy."

"Easy, Grey." Kei gave him a small smile. "Gabe can

heal his brother enough to bring him back. Then Lucifer can return his grace."

"No." Grey inhaled, allowing his magic to shimmer along his skin, joining with Michael's grace. "I'll heal him."

"Grey. You need to be healed yourself. You're in no condition to use that amount of energy on anything else, especially healing."

"He would have died for me. I..."

He placed his hands on Michael's chest, not able to voice how much he owed his mate. How much he had to atone for. A soft glow covered Michael's form, slowly fixing some of the symptoms, though it would take far more power than Greyson had to heal the deeper injuries.

Michael groaned, blinking a few times before opening his eyes. He squinted, giving Grey an easy smile. "See? Piece of cake."

Tears gathered behind Grey's eyes, and he didn't care when a few slipped free. "Right. Why was I worried?"

Michael frowned. "You look like shit."

"You sure know just what to say to make a guy feel great about himself. And you look worse, despite my best efforts."

"You healed me?" He laughed. "While I love the gesture, you do realize you have two archangels standing on the sidelines."

"Maybe I just wanted to even the score a bit." He leaned in close. "You knew giving me all your grace meant you probably wouldn't make the trip back. We have so much to...discuss. But first." He motioned to Lucifer.

Lucifer walked over, grinning when Greyson helped Michael to his feet. "Got to hand it to you, Mikey. I really didn't think you'd make it back in one piece." He glanced over Michael's shoulder. "Well, mostly." He held up a knife. "Ready?"

Michael narrowed his eyes, holding out his arm. He winced when Lucifer sliced a line across his flesh. Lucifer grabbed his wrist, his face disappearing amidst a flash of light. Michael stiffened in Grey's arms, sagging against him once the glow dimmed.

Grey tightened his hold. "Well?"

Michael flexed and released his fist, smiling at the light blue hue that rippled along his skin, healing most of the wounds as it wove down his body. "Much better."

"Then why are your wings still...broken?"

Michael sighed. "They're going to take more time." He placed a finger over Grey's lips. "It's fine, Grey. I'll heal." He turned to Lucifer, brow furrowed, eyes narrowed.

Lucifer crossed his arms. "What? Did you really think I'd keep it?"

Michael glanced at his arm, then back. "I'd considered that you might have expected it as compensation."

"Fuck, no. Do you know what it's been like having all of that disgusting purity stuck inside me? I haven't been able to say a mean thing to Gabriel the entire time I've been up here. I feel..." he wiped at his arms, "...dirty." He arched a brow. "But out of curiosity, would you have let me have it?"

"I told you I'd pay any price. Greyson's alive because of you. I'm back... Wait. Where are we? This isn't my sanctuary."

"No, it's mine because you had to be all selfless and give your mate *all* of your grace. I specifically told you to hold on to some, big brother."

"He needed all of it. Hell, I needed to give him all of it, even more. So, the portal flung me here because I still had some of your grace?"

"Saved your sorry ass from getting stuck in Purgatory. You're welcome, by the way. Speaking of which...that grace of mine I gave you, it's still in there. Got a bit of yours..." he tapped his chest, "...right here." He grinned at Michael's sharp intake. "What? You know there's always a price for using the kind of magic we did. Don't blame the messenger, bro. I warned you it was a bad idea, all 'round."

"I could think of worse outcomes. Which reminds me." Michael drew himself up, looking every inch the warrior he'd always been. "Your price."

Lucifer smiled. "Can't a guy just help out his big brother without it being a thing?"

"It's been a long day. So, just tell me what you want."

"You know...this whole, Lucifer is evil thing is getting old. I had a difference of opinion. One that I've more than paid for, I assure you. But, fuck it. Everyone wants me to be the ungrateful asshole, so why not? What I want in exchange for my help is this."

Michael glanced at Grey when Lucifer merely stood there. Grey shrugged. He didn't have a clue what the man meant.

Michael waved at the space between them. "This? What's this?"

"My sanctuary. I want access to it."

"Wait." Gabriel stepped forward. "You want Michael to just, free you? From Hell?"

Lucifer glared at Gabriel. "Did I say that? Pay attention, little brother. I said I wanted access to my sanctuary. He doesn't have to free me for that, just...alter the wards a bit so I can come here."

Gabriel palmed his hips. "And that's different, how, exactly?"

"It's like a one-way express flight as opposed to connecting ones. I just want someplace I can go that's mine. And trust me, Hell isn't that scenic."

"You can't possibly expect Michael to do that? Defy Father—"

"Easy, Gabriel." Michael took a step forward. "It's not defying anything. This is Lucifer's sanctuary. And after all these centuries, I doubt even Father would begrudge him spending some time here. Besides, I'll know every time he travels through the wards."

Lucifer rolled his eyes. "Now, you're just making it feel creepy." He glanced at Gabriel. "I don't need access to this precious realm in order to make deals. Grab me some souls. People give them to me all the time. This..." He motioned to the cabin. "This is so I don't decide to find a way to break the warding, myself." He crossed his arms again. "And don't think for a moment I can't. I've taken my banishment quite well, thus far. Don't expect it to last forever."

Michael walked to the edge of Lucifer's sanctuary, stepping just outside the boundary. He closed his eyes, extending his hands toward the ground. His grace burned bright against his flesh, the blue tinge amidst the white impossible to miss. Grey's chest tightened with pride as he watched his lover, his mate, channel his power.

Not your mate, yet.

The flute picked up the melody, playing the tune over and over until Greyson had to close his eyes in an effort to keep the song at bay. Desire burned hot beneath his flesh, adding to the need pounding in his head. He focused on breathing—pushing the air out through his nose—anything but the relentless battering inside his skull.

A hand grazed his cheek, the soft press of lips finally getting him to open his eyes. Michael stared down at him, brow pulled into a vee, his perfect lips turned into a frown.

He thumbed the edge of Grey's mouth. "The music's in your head, again, isn't it?"

"I'm...dealing."

"You look like you're about to pass out from the strain." He silenced Grey with his thumb. "I can *hear* it, Greyson. Can't imagine how loud it is for you."

"Pretty damn loud. But...we're not done. Tharn—"

"Can wait. No!" Michael pointed his finger at Grey this time. "You've suffered long enough. Gabriel and Kei can stand watch. Give us enough time to fix this. Silence that damn flute for good."

"And that's my cue to leave." Lucifer motioned in the direction they'd come. "I assume you can all see yourselves out. Think I'll stay for a bit..." His gaze found Michael's. "I *can* stay, right? That's what all that mumbling shit was all about?"

Michael nodded. "As per our agreement, you have access to your sanctuary. As long as you stay within the boundary, you'll be fine."

Lucifer arched a brow. "And if, hypothetically, I tried to move beyond said boundary?"

"You get sent back to Hell. And I promise you, it won't be a fun ride."

"It's the little details that make the difference. Fine.

Now, bugger off. All of you. And feel free *not* to summon me again, anytime soon. I've got a reputation to uphold, and you four are far too pure to be seen hanging around with."

The glamour reappeared around Lucifer's cabin the moment they all stepped free of the edge.

Gabriel looked at Michael, glancing to the glamour then back. "Are you sure this was wise?"

Michael sighed. "He was right, Gabriel. He doesn't need to roam the Earth to wield his power. At least here, we know where he is. And I'd rather not piss him off to the point he really does search for a way to break the warding. He's far stronger than we might want to believe. It'd be wise not to give him cause to prove to us just how strong."

"Then I suppose we'll have to see how it plays out. Now..." Gabe moved in beside them. "You said something about standing watch? Someone named Tharn?"

Greyson pushed the melody away as best he could. "Tharn is Belfrey's descendant, and the bastard who took me. He wants to break the protection keeping the dark fae locked in the shadow lands. He left before Michael arrived. I thought he'd be at Michael's sanctuary, but..."

Kei frowned. "We stayed in Michael's cabin the entire time, but... No one came knocking."

"Then he's still loose, and still a threat. We need to—"

"Rest." Michael held up his hand. "Greyson. The prophecy has been averted. Surely we can spend a few hours resting before we attempt to hunt down this Tharn. But just to be safe, I'm sure Kei and Gabriel can stay close by. Alert us if any of the other dark fae decide to make an appearance."

Kei nudged Grey. "You two will ward the room for sound, right?"

"Bastard. Like I haven't had to put up with you and Gabe all the time."

"If you learned to knock before you entered our home, you wouldn't get caught in so many awkward situations."

Greyson swatted at Kei's chest. "Fine. Rest it is, but... at my place. Call me crazy, but being so close to where I made a stupid mistake, not high on my list right now."

Michael sighed. "I was the one who was stupid. And the reason you put yourself in harm's way to begin with. I'm sorry."

"I think following me to Purgatory was an adequate apology. But I won't argue if you let me silence this fucking flute."

"Do you want to take us there, or shall I?"

CHAPTER NINETEEN

Michael stared at his mate, smiling as his magic gathered around them, blurring their surroundings before shifting them back. Only instead of trees and rock, lush foliage lined a meandering pathway, an intricately carved door directly behind them. Michael looked around the glade, finally seeing the beauty he'd missed in it before. How the flowers matched the colors on Greyson's skin, or how he'd incorporated the swirly pattern into the stones lining his porch. Every inch reflected the hidden side of his mate, and it tightened Michael's chest when he realized Grey would never have to hide his true self again. That he could finally feel as if he belonged. Greyson swayed against him, his head connecting with Michael's shoulder.

Michael tsked, slipping his arm around the fae. "You are a stubborn soul, Grey."

"Like you're any better." He groaned, closing his eyes as the soft echo of a flute gathered around them.

"Easy." He glanced up, but Kei and Gabriel were already standing on the pathway.

Kei smiled over his shoulder. "I'll ward the perimeter. And we'll keep an eye out for anything suspicious. Give you two some long overdue privacy." He turned, but then looked back. "And in case you were wondering, Grey, I would have loved you wings and all, from the start. Glad you won't have to hide that again."

They headed off, disappearing around a nearby bend in the path. Crunching footsteps sounded along the breeze, finally fading into the distant chorus of crickets.

Grey groaned again. "You know they'll never let us live this down, don't you? How they were right all along?"

Michael turned Greyson in his arms, backing them up until they hit the solid wooden door. "Maybe it's the fatigue. Or the after-effects of our time in Purgatory. Or that bit of Lucifer's grace still thriving inside me, but I can't seem to muster a single fuck to give right now about how smug Gabriel and Kei will be. Not when I've finally got you right where I want you."

"Pinned to the door?"

"Alone." He lifted one hand, stroking it along Grey's cheek until it settled in his hair. "I'm not sure what I find harder to believe. That I've never been inside your house before, or that I ever thought this was a bad idea."

Grey's gaze softened. "In your defense, I'm not sure I ever invited you. And you weren't the only one with reservations."

"You never tried to deny me."

"I think trying to kill you kind of trumps that."

He gave Grey a wicked grin. "That's right. We never got to really finish that fight. Thinking it might turn out quite differently in here. But first…"

Michael lowered his head as he cupped Grey's face

with his other hand. His grace surged forward, flowing from him into his mate then racing along the fae's body in an ever-increasing wave outwards. Grey's skin gleamed as it dissolved most of his injuries, finally lighting up the swirls on his skin. They glowed in response, accentuating the blue within the white before gradually fading.

Michael eased away just enough to scan Grey's torso. Though most of the burns had healed, a series of scars still crisscrossed his chest, the damage from the amulet not quite erased. He frowned, skimming his fingers over the marks. "These will take time to fully heal. I'm sorry."

Grey palmed Michael's chest, smoothing his hand up until he could tease the strands of hair at the angel's neck. "I don't care about a few scars."

"I do."

Grey sighed, raising Michael's chin with his finger. "You didn't fail me. This isn't your fault, and in the end, we won."

"How did you know—"

"Mates. I can hear all your thoughts, even the ones you're trying to hide. Sense the combination of guilt and arousal coursing through you. A rather unexpected combination, by the way." He grazed his hand back, sinking it into Michael's hair and copying the hold his mate had on him. "But most of all, I feel your love. Which means nothing else matters. So stop thinking, and just love me."

He dragged Michael the scant few inches toward him, slanting his mouth over his. Warm, wet flesh slid along his lips, the pure taste of the man making Greyson moan. Michael stepped into the kiss, pressing every inch of their bodies together as he used his hold to tilt Grey's head back—deepen his possession. The music strummed to life, except this time the song had a peaceful quality to it. A low base filled in the harmony, joining with the flute as it rose and fell, gaining strength as it seemed to echo around him.

Michael nipped at Grey's lip as he eased back, tilting his head before smiling. "It sounds…different. Richer. Less annoying."

He chuckled. "That's because of you. Your grace."

"I like it. It feels more like us, instead of just you."

Grey's mouth gaped open, and it was all Michael could do not to laugh. The fae looked fucking adorable. "Wait. Are you suggesting that I'm the annoying flute part?"

"Well, that was the only part that played before I added my grace to the mix, so it stands to reason…" He grunted when Greyson punched him in the shoulder before pressing against Grey again. "Have I mentioned I love that annoying flute? More than I ever thought possible?"

"To Purgatory and back and you still think some sweet words are going to fix everything."

"Only if they're the right ones." He locked his gaze on Grey's. "You are my sun, my moon, my darkest night."

Grey's mouth opened again, but he didn't say anything, just stared, his heart thrashing against Michael's chest.

Michael brushed his knuckles along Grey's jaw. "Now, either finish the ritual, or zap us into your bedroom because having spent the last several hours feeling my grace thrum inside you without staking my claim has driven me to the edge. Any more delays, and I won't be responsible when your entire kingdom watches me take you against this damn door."

"Were you this bossy before?"

"Greyson."

His mate smiled, dimming the colors around him as his entire face simply lit up. A familiar blue glow surrounded them, and Michael blinked as his back sank into a mattress, the soft brush of cotton caressing his skin.

He focused on his mate, arching a brow as the man hovered over him, Grey's wings like a splash of color amidst the dark wood tones of the room. "While this is the correct destination, I believe I was the one about to ravage you."

"Words have meaning, Michael. And all you said was to bring you here, which I did rather beautifully. I even saved us some time with the whole naked thing." He went to his elbows, his chest brushing against Michael's. "So stop crying foul and kiss me again."

Michael threaded his hands through Grey's hair as the man claimed his mouth, tangling his tongue with his. Warm male spice filled Michael's senses, a hint of cottonwood he suspected was his. He didn't rush his mate, enjoying the brush of Grey's mouth across his when the man finally eased back, kissing a path along Michael's shoulder.

Michael moved his other hand to the edge of Grey's wing, skimming the tips of his fingers along the top, smiling at Grey's harsh intake of breath or how his cock hardened further against Michael's hip. "I love touching you like this. Feeling the thin layer move beneath my fingers. Tracing the swirls of color. Knowing I'll be the only one who ever gets to love the real you."

"I feel the same way. Your wings…" Grey's eyes misted over, but he didn't seem to care. "The fact you were willing to risk them, to risk your grace…"

He crushed his mouth to Michael's in a brutal kiss. A volley of emotions swam though Michael's mind, but there was no denying the overwhelming love his mate felt. The need that bunched his muscles and had him nipping his way down Michael's torso once he'd broken the kiss. Warm, wet flesh skimmed over his chest and along his ribs, Greyson's mouth pausing to tease the sensitive spot next to his hip.

Michael's cock jerked at the simple act, leaving a smear of fluid across Grey's chest as it hit his torso then dropped back to Michael's stomach. He tightened his grip on Greyson, rewarded with a throaty moan from his mate. "Do you know how close I am to reversing our positions? You can only tease me so much."

Grey's smile was nothing short of wicked. "I've barely begun to tease you. And don't think I'd be easy to best. So I suggest you get comfortable. I intend on sucking you dry before I sink inside you."

"Fuck, Grey."

"Soon. Promise. Just…let me indulge. I never thought…"

His voice trailed off, but Michael knew what he hadn't said. He'd never believed he'd get another night with his mate, not after the way Michael had rejected him. And be damned if Michael would take that from the fae.

He let his head press into the pillow as his eyes drifted shut. Greyson took his unspoken surrender as permission to continue, his mouth returning to Michael's hip. Grey nipped at his muscle as it vee'ed into his groin, licking and kissing his way to the base of his cock. His mate nuzzled his shaft, bathing his sac before mouthing his way up to the crown. Michael's cock pulsed at the intimate touch, lifting up again, only to have Greyson hold it in place.

He lapped at the tip, humming at the fluid Michael knew beaded from the slit. "So damn good. I could lick you for hours. Swallow your release over and over and never get enough of you." He sighed, thumbing the underside of the thick head. "Not sure a thousand years will be enough."

Michael clenched his teeth, prying open his eyelids to meet Grey's gaze up his body. "Then we'll start with two and go from there."

Grey froze. "Two?"

"You do remember the part where I'm an archangel, right?" He smiled at Grey's guarded nod. "Which means some of my grace stays within you."

"Are you saying—"

"That your lifespan will match mine, now? Yes." He chuckled. "I hope you weren't exaggerating when you said fae mate for life, because you're in for a very long one."

Grey's lips quirked, a few tears slipping free. "Long, short, all I need is you." He cleared his throat. "Now, I believe I was about to make you pump your release down my throat."

Michael hissed as Greyson sealed his mouth around

Michael's shaft and took it all the way to the back of his throat. Firm pressure surround Michael's length, pooling fire in the base of his spine. Damn, one pass of Greyson's mouth and Michael was ready to empty down his throat.

He stroked Grey's head, occasionally fisting some strands before scratching the man's scalp again. He liked feeling the soft mass brush across his hand as Greyson bobbed up and down his cock, driving Michael to the brink. Each pass threatened to unhinge him as his climax coiled tighter within his core.

Grey eased off for a moment, once again lapping and sucking at his sac. Whispered words breezed across Michael's flesh, followed by a cool sensation around his ass. Greyson grinned up at him, holding up one hand as if foreshadowing his next move, before lowering it. Two fingers circled Michael's hole, teasing the entrance then sinking inside. He moaned, arching into the penetration as Grey set up a steady rhythm, pushing his fingers deep inside Michael's ass then easing them out.

Michael panted out his breath, time blurring into the firm press of Greyson's fingers as they eased Michael's muscles, the mild pinching sensation giving way to intense pleasure. He clenched his jaw, wanting to hold on —make this moment last—give Greyson the kind of loving he deserved, but each stroke made his cock flare to the point he thought he'd go over without Grey's mouth on him. A low chuckle dragged his gaze down to his mate.

"Do you really think I'd let you come without your cock in my mouth? Never." Grey's expression sobered slightly. "And you've always loved me how I deserve. The only thing that's different is knowing this is just the start.

That I'll have an unlimited number of 'next times.' So stop worrying about holding on, and come for me."

Greyson licked the length of Michael's shaft then sucked his cock into his mouth, claiming Michael with pass after pass of devastating pressure. Grey's fingers countered the movement, pressing in as he eased Michael's shaft from between his lips, then retreating as he sank back down. Heat burned beneath his flesh, a light blue glow slowly covering his skin.

Grey looked up again, the corners of his mouth twitching before he seemed to give himself completely over to the act. His wings fluttered behind him, like streaks of light in the air, as he worked Michael's cock, keeping him suspended on the edge. Michael rolled his head across the pillow, his body stuck on the verge of climaxing when Grey hummed.

The tiny vibrations sent Michael over. He fisted his hand in Greyson's hair, the other locking around his wing as he stiffened, his breath lodged in his chest. Dots danced across his vision, a loud roar sounding in his head before Grey pumped his fingers inside again, draining the last of Michael's seed. Pleasure billowed heat around him, and it was all he could do just to breathe in and out through his nose.

The ringing slowly eased from inside his head, his thoughts clearing a bit. He forced open his eyes, locking his gaze on Greyson as the man hovered over him, firm muscles filling Michael's field of view.

His mate grinned, bending down to nuzzle his cheek. "That was definitely worth waiting for."

Michael frowned. "That wasn't the first time you've sucked me off."

"No, but it was the first time as mates…oh, wait. I still have a few words I need to say." His cock nudged Michael's ass, the tip covered in a cool gel. "So let's set the stage."

CHAPTER TWENTY

Greyson stared at Michael, memorizing every detail of his mate's face as he pushed against the man's tight opening, gradually sinking inside his ass. Pleasure creased Michael's brow as he squeezed shut his eyes, a low, throaty moan accompanying Grey's slow glide forward.

Grey stopped once his sac connected with Michael's flesh, already fighting not to finish. He wanted to savor his mate. Catalogue every moment until he could replay their joining over and over again. Until every last doubt was nothing more than a distant memory.

Michael's eyes opened, his gaze catching and holding Grey's. "I'm yours, Grey. For always. No doubts. No regrets. Just you with me. You can take all the time you need, but fast or slow, I'll still belong to you."

Greyson went to his elbows, smiling at the increased brush of skin. The play of Michael's muscles beneath his as he placed his forearms across the archangel's upper chest, allowing his fingers to grip the man's shoulders while his thumbs teased the sides of his neck.

Michael swallowed, the action hampered ever so slightly by Greyson's hold. His mate moaned again, beckoning Grey down to him with nothing more than a look. Greyson claimed the angel's mouth, capturing the raspy sounds he made as Grey set up a steady rhythm, plunging forward then easing back.

Firm pressure encased his shaft, the tight clasp burning a line straight to his balls. His release built slowly, gathering strength until it pulsed at the base of his spine, threatening to spill over with every thrust. Michael pushed his head into the pillow, his eyes fluttering closed as his back arched.

Greyson dropped a kiss on his eyelids, smiling when his mate blinked them back open. "Eyes on me. I want to see those incredible blues as I take you over. Want you to know it's me who holds your heart. Who's going to spend the rest of their life loving you."

A smug grin lifted his lips. "That's not easily forgotten. Nor are you. I never really stood a chance."

Greyson slammed home, smiling at the slight roll of Michael's eyes as a deep flush colored his skin. "If it's any consolation, you had my heart from the moment you said my name back on that godforsaken desert plain. One look, and I was lost."

Michael frowned. "I've always considered that one of my worst days. A failure."

"I've always seen it as one of your best." He slid home again, clenching his jaw from the rush of pleasure. God, he wasn't going to last. "Injured. Outmatched, yet you never surrendered. Never gave up. The way you looked at me…"

Michael chuckled, the sound morphing into a moan as

Greyson claimed him with another hard stroke. "I'd never seen a faery before. Hadn't interacted with them in those early days before they chose to live in a parallel realm. You…" He sighed. "You took my breath away."

"Then let me give it back."

Greyson kissed the man, increasing his thrusts as his climax surged forward, nearly sending him over. He fought to hold it back, needing just a bit more time with his mate before losing control.

Michael nipped at Grey's lip when the parted, anchoring his hands around Greyson's wings. "Just the beginning. You have all the time you need, so stop fighting this, and give yourself to me."

Greyson sighed in defeat, knowing he couldn't stop the rush of heat along his shaft. Couldn't hold off the need to finish a moment longer. He let his forehead bow forward until it rested on Michael's, their heavy breath mixing. His mate tightened his hold, lifting his hips into every thrust, taking Grey even deeper. Each panting exhalation, each clench of Michael's fists around his wings drew Grey deeper until his control snapped, and he sighed in defeat.

"Fuck, yes, Greyson. Now. Hard."

Greyson pounded into his mate, all semblance of rhythm lost. The bed shimmied against the wall, a dull thud accompanying every grind of his hips. He kept moving, chasing the fire burning along his shaft until the room dimmed, and he came.

Michael stiffened beneath him, his mate's release warm and wet against his chest as the man emptied between them, Greyson's name echoing around them. Greyson held still, watching his mate unravel, knowing he'd never tire of loving him. Of seeing him give himself over to Greyson, allowing himself to be vulnerable, even if only for a moment.

The music started off slowly—a distant chord amidst the searing pleasure. Then more notes joined in, finally weaving into the familiar melody that had haunted him since their first coupling. Only this time, it didn't frighten him. Didn't batter against his skull with unrelenting force. It soothed him. Brought him a sense of peace as he stared into Michael's blue eyes.

He shifted slightly, cupping his hands around his mate's face, feeling the truth of this moment all the way to his soul. "You are my sun, my moon, my darkest night."

Michael's breath hitched as a loving smile lifted his mouth. He placed his hands over Grey's, nodding at him to continue.

Tears clogged Grey's throat, but he pressed on. "You are the light that brightens the shadows, the star that guides me home. Always, and in all ways, I am yours."

The flute reached its climax, its last few notes still lingering around them as the song slowly faded, the reality of the situation finally sinking in. He'd mated with Michael. God's Warrior. And it hadn't been a dream.

Michael reached for him, tracing his jaw as if he was seeing Greyson for the first time. "Yours, Grey. For always. I'm only sorry it took me this long to realize that I'm a far better man, better warrior, with you than without."

Grey smiled. "You really need to stop knowing exactly what to say and when. Makes it impossible to ever get the upper hand."

Michael chuckled, then frowned as tremors shook through Grey. He clenched his jaw, gasping when the scenery shifted as Michael flipped them over, his sheer size squishing Grey into the bed.

"Greyson? What's wrong?"

"Nothing."

"You're shaking. So don't tell me it's nothing."

"Just the aftermath of mating. I told you. It's... intense. I..."

Michael's expression eased as he gathered the man in his arms, still poised above him. "Right here. And I'll love you as many times as you need to ease the ache. Prove to you that I'm not going anywhere without you."

Michael bowed his head, his grace shimmering to life around him, only there was no mistaking the blue undertone. He mumbled words Grey couldn't quite make out, a moment before a cool sensation pressed against his ass as their previous release vanished from his skin. Grey arched his brow, but Michael merely smiled.

"As I mentioned before. Mates take on some of the other's traits. And your magic seems to like me as much as you do."

"Then it fucking loves you because I do. Love you, Michael."

He lowered, mimicking the position Greyson had taken just moments ago. "And I you, Greyson of the Fae."

He nudged Grey's ass, moaning as he sank inside. Grey wasn't sure how the man had recovered so damn quickly, not that he was far behind, his cock already hardening between them.

Michael's lips quirked as he nuzzled Grey's nose. "Think of it as a combination of your magic and my grace. It seems to have a 'rejuvenating' effect."

"This reading thoughts thing might not be as cute as I originally thought it was."

"You didn't seem to have any issues when you were inside my mind. But how about I give you something else to concentrate on."

Michael surged forward, stealing every thought from Grey's head except the burning glide of Michael's cock as he joined with him. The way he pressed Grey into the mattress, virtually trapping him there. The raspy sound of Michael's voice as he whispered his love, his devotion. The play of muscles beneath Grey's fingers as they flexed in an effort to drive Michael even deeper.

Greyson mentally told his mate to kiss him, smiling when Michael merely shook his head before slanting his mouth over Grey's. The man's flavor burst on his tongue, the scent of cottonwood swirling around them. Grey ate at his mate's mouth, needing more of him. More skin, more time, more love.

Michael lowered even closer, somehow still moving as his torso pressed against Grey's, every available inch touching. "You have all of me. Now close your eyes, and give me all of you."

Pleasure arced across his flesh as Michael increased his thrusts, the steady motion stealing Grey's breath. He wedged his arms out from between them, burying one in Michael's hair while latching the other around the base of one wing. Michael's movements faltered, his hips making jerky little motions before he growled, his grip on Greyson tightening.

He moved his mouth to Grey's shoulder, sinking his teeth into the firm muscle as he slammed into him, each hard stroke tearing a desperate cry from Grey's lips. This is what he needed. Michael. Raw. Completely untamed.

Grey arched into each thrust, pushing his mate deeper, his release coiling around his sac as every pass hit his prostrate. A muffled moan sounded against his flesh before Michael inhaled, the telltale stiffening of his back a clear indication he was on the verge of spilling into Greyson.

Grey held Michael's head near his shoulder as he brushed his mouth against the man's temple. "Now, Michael."

Michael's back tensed from the strain, then he was coming, hot seed splashing against Greyson's walls. Grey closed his eyes as his orgasm followed Michael's, his release hot and slick across their flesh. Michael kept moving, pumping, until his strength seemed to wane, and he collapsed in a tangle of arms and sweat.

The archangel's heart pounded in time with Grey's, the frantic beat like music to him. He wrapped his arms around Michael's back, content to hold him there for the foreseeable future when his stomach growled.

Michael's body shook as he laughed, the man finally bridging his weight on his elbows enough to meet Grey's gaze. "Something tells me we've neglected your other needs for far too long. When was the last time you ate?"

Grey licked his bottom lip. "I'd say about thirty minutes ago when you came in my mouth."

Desire darkened Michael's eyes, all thoughts of food seemingly forgotten until his stomach rumbled. He frowned, shifting over to the side as he stared at his body. "What is that gnawing ache?"

Grey arched a brow. "You mean hunger? Haven't you had it before?"

"Angels eat, but, it's more for the pleasure of taste than anything else. But this..." He huffed. "It's irritating as hell."

Grey held back a chuckle. "Guess this is one trait that's not as fun as my magic. Luckily for you, I should have some food around. I'll make you a deal. Bathe with me, and I'll cook for you."

Michael hummed, the intensity returning to his gaze. "You. Covered in water. Your cock exploding in my mouth. Yeah, I could get behind that."

"I meant shower, not sex."

He shrugged. "I'm capable of multitasking."

Grey snorted as the man rolled off the bed, offering Grey his hand. He accepted, and they bumped their way from his bedroom into the washroom, hitting more than a few walls on the way as they fought for dominance of each brutal kiss. The water was only lukewarm, but Michael didn't seem to care as he knelt on the floor, teasing Grey until he damn near passed out from his climax. Then his mate pinned him to the wall, daring him to look away as he slid inside him, Grey's legs locked around Michael's back, the man's wings deflecting the spray.

Grey wasn't sure how long they stayed in there, Michael moving just enough to keep them both on the edge. The water had long since cooled by the time Michael grunted through his release, his forehead pressed to Grey's. Even now, the archangel seemed reluctant to venture more than a step away as Greyson refilled their plates with fruit, bread and cheese.

Michael picked up a chunk of pineapple. "I've never

eaten this much at once. Why does everything taste so much better here?"

Grey snorted. "Maybe because you're actually hungry. And it always tastes better when someone else makes it. That's just a simple fact." He turned, grinning when Michael trapped him between his arms and the counter. "I suppose, in all fairness, I'll have to offer you some meat at some point. Gabriel can't seem to get enough."

"If by meat you mean you, then hell yes." He nipped at Greyson's neck. "I doubt I'll ever get enough of you."

Grey chuckled at Michael's choice of words.

The man furrowed his brow. "What?" He leaned in closer when Grey shrugged. "You were thinking about the way I talk. What's wrong with it?"

"Nothing's wrong, it's...let's just say your brother's grace has colored your words a bit." He dragged Michael to him when the archangel looked as if he was going to step back. "I think it's fucking adorable. Wouldn't change it if I could. You...you're perfect, for me, anyway. Just the way you are. And if it's the price for all he did to help you get me back... Michael. Things turned out pretty damn good. Maybe this can be the beginning of something other than anger between you two. Maybe he actually wants to try."

"You always try to see the good in people, don't you?"

"Like it or not, Lucifer's family." He grinned. "And there might be a part of me that would *love* to introduce him to Oberon."

A smile worked Michael's mouth. "I get the feeling you're still unhappy with your father's decision to leave you in the dark, shall we say."

"He's in for a hell of a conversation. Which reminds

me. We still need to discuss that part where you gave me *all* of your grace. Fully knowing you probably wouldn't make it back."

"You know why…"

His words faded beneath a loud banging sound. Grey turned toward the door just as it opened, Kei and Gabriel marching through. They stopped, glancing from Greyson over to Michael then back.

Kei shuffled his feet, looking oddly uncomfortable. "Please tell me you both have pants on behind the counter."

Grey rolled his eyes, muttering some words as a light blue glow hued his skin then faded. "We do, now. Though I don't think we were close to being finished. Why?"

The mage sighed. "There's been a…development. You both need to come with us."

"Development? Where?"

"The keep outside of the royal grounds. It's…" He turned to Gabriel.

The archangel drew himself up. "I believe the dark fae are here."

CHAPTER TWENTY-ONE

"Greyson." Michael snagged Greyson's arm when he moved to push past him, giving his mate a stern look when Grey tugged against his hold. "Before we rush off, we need to go in with a plan."

Grey's mouth pursed into a tight line. "That plan's simple. Kick their asses."

"While I agree some form of battle is likely..." He shifted in front, allowing a trickle of his grace to flow into the other man. "Rushing over there primed for war might not be in your kingdom's best interest. Besides, your father has a great deal of power. I'm not sure even this Tharn person would choose to go up against the King of the Fae and his contingency of well-trained guards. At least, not without a well-developed strategy."

Greyson glanced at Michael's hand then back to his face. "Are you trying to calm me down with your grace?"

"Is it working?"

Grey sighed. "You're right. It's always wise to approach a situation with as much information as you can get." He looked past Michael to his friends. "When you say the dark fae are here, what exactly do you mean?"

"An entourage of warriors just appeared in the glade." Gabriel glanced toward the open door. "Even I felt their dark energy stain the land. They headed directly toward the royal grounds. We thought it best if the four of us investigated together. After Uriel's rampage... I just think it'd be wise not to underestimate any potential opponent. Though, I suppose there's always a chance they're merely here to talk."

Kei snorted. "Right. They kidnap and torture Grey then pop by for a friendly visit."

Gabriel grinned at his mate. "I was trying to be optimistic. You claim I tend to go to extremes."

Kei's gaze softened. "You know I love that about you. And I do appreciate the effort. Though, in this case, I doubt you'd be wrong in assuming the worst."

Greyson turned to Michael. "I warded the portals. They shouldn't have gotten through."

Michael nodded. "I realize that, but in the end, they are fae. Perhaps their common heritage allowed them to bypass the wards."

"Then why wait until now to make a move? They've been banished for millennia."

"You were their best hope." He gave Grey an encouraging smile. "When you vanished—perhaps they decided to attempt a coup regardless. Maybe they're done waiting on prophecies."

"Then it's time for the heir to the throne to give them a proper welcome." Grey's skin sparked to life, glowing bright blue before fading into what appeared to be his royal armor, though there was no missing the fact his wings were still clearly visible. He glanced at Michael, tilting his head as if pondering something before waving his hands.

Michael inhaled as black leather pants replaced his jeans, a matching vest covering his torso. Long guards concealed his forearms, a series of spikes embedded down the sides.

He gazed at his mate as he crossed his arms over his chest. "Was there something wrong with what I was wearing before?"

"You're God's Warrior. Thinking you should look like it."

"You could have chosen my tunic."

"Did the *Terminator* wear a tunic? I think not. You look fucking badass. Trust me." Grey glanced at Gabriel. "You, too."

Gabriel cursed as a similar outfit appeared out of a flash of blue light, the only difference being a small insignia on the vest. Where Michael's was the image of a sword, Gabriel's resembled a horn.

Greyson nodded. "Much better. Kei?"

Kei waved his hands. "You put me in leather pants, and I'll turn you into a toad. Besides, I'll be wearing flames if things turn ugly."

Greyson nodded, motioning them closer. "Ready?"

"Are you sure you don't want to mask your true form?"

"I'm done hiding."

Pride swelled in Michael's chest. "Agreed." Michael grabbed his arm, again. "The last time Oberon's guards phased with both me and Gabriel, he claimed it weakened them."

"They weren't me, were they?"

Michael cursed as the scenery swam, shifting into streaks of blue light before settling. He blinked, groaning inwardly when he realized his mate had taken them straight to the royal keep, materializing in the middle of what looked like a rather heated discussion.

Oberon stopped mid-sentence, turning to stare at them. His eyes widened, his focus falling on his son. The king cocked his head to the side, as if deciding on what to say, when someone cursed behind him.

Michael shifted his gaze, landing on a man several yards off. He resembled the two dark fae he'd seen in Purgatory, his slate-gray eyes openly assessing Michael. Similar black wings fluttered in the air behind the faery, a blood-stained sword hanging on his hip.

Heat burned just beneath the surface of the other man's skin, and Michael didn't stop a hint of his grace from coloring his flesh. His wings snapped with annoyance, sending a small jolt of pain through his chest. A dozen more dark fae stood behind the man, all with the same stoic expression.

The guy snorted, performing a sweeping bow. "Ah, Greyson. I'd wondered where you'd scurried off to. No longer hiding who you truly are, I see."

Greyson held his head high, seemingly oblivious or uninterested in the hushed gasps that rose from the gathering of fae. "Tharn. I told you I wouldn't turn to the shadows. You should have listened to me. Maybe then, some of your companions would have been spared."

Tharn shrugged. "Monsters. Demons. A means to an end, really. You actually did me a favor by killing them." His focus slid to Michael. "Though it wasn't really you behind the carnage, now, was it?" He laughed, the sound like metal grating across rock. "I have to hand it to you. An angel rescuing you from Purgatory. *That*, I didn't see coming." He paced to his right, appearing completely at ease. "I did try to discover your mystery man's identity." He rolled his eyes. "You would think that Sezil could remember one tiny location. But sadly, he sent me on some wild chase. By the time I decided it wasn't worth my effort and returned..." He waved at the surrounding glen. "You were long gone. Back to the faery realm."

His expression hardened. "I had hoped you were still lost in Purgatory somewhere, but it appears you have some very powerful friends." He nodded at Michael. "I didn't catch your name."

Greyson stepped forward, mentally telling his mate not to answer. "What do you want? The prophecy has been averted, and you know I'll never willingly open the barriers between our world and the shadow lands. You've lost."

Tharn held up his hand, shaking his finger at them. "You see, that's where you're wrong. True, it would have been much easier to have had you break the warding for me—fulfil the prophecy and end any chance of you ever sitting on the throne when that dark energy destroyed anything worth keeping, leaving you an empty husk." He grinned. "Much like the fate of your sister, Sirena, as I understand it."

"You son of a bitch—"

Michael palmed the small of Greyson's spine. "Easy, Grey."

Tharn laughed. "But I won't need you when I'm king."

Greyson glanced at Oberon, giving his father a nod before facing Tharn. "You have no claim to the throne."

"Don't I?" He ripped open his shirt, baring his chest. Crossed swords had been burned into his flesh, a decorative shield etched behind them. "Do you know what this is?"

"Just because you bear the mark of Belfrey's crest doesn't make you in line for the throne. I'm afraid the man hasn't ruled in this kingdom for millennia."

"It matters not. As a descendant of his, I demand the Right of Ascension."

Greyson stilled, his gaze once again flying to his father's. Thoughts tumbled through his mind, too fast for Michael to latch onto. He inched closer, keeping his hand on Greyson's back, when Oberon moved to the edge of the stone path lining the keep.

He seemed unnaturally calm. "In order to be granted the Right of Ascension, you must prove your heritage. That…" he waved at Tharn's chest, "…is hardly proof that Belfrey's blood runs through your veins."

Tharn squared his shoulders, wisps of red light arcing across his skin. "Then open the barriers and ask his people."

"I'm afraid that would be…unwise."

"Are you so afraid of my power, old man, that you would cower behind excuses? Is the great Oberon scared to face me in battle? How can you be fit to rule your kingdom if you're not willing to bleed in order to save it?"

"Enough!" Greyson's voice echoed across the glade, drawing everyone's attention. He glanced back at Michael, then marched forward to stand beside his father. "The Right of Ascension doesn't allow you to challenge the king." He held up his hand at Tharn's glare. "You must challenge his heir. If you win, only then can you claim the throne and end Oberon's rule."

Michael froze as Greyson's words washed over him. He stared at his mate, a mixture of fear and pride tightening his chest. He'd only just gotten Grey back. Watching him fight to save his kingdom... Grey looked at him over his shoulder. He smiled then winked, once against focusing on Tharn.

Tharn cocked his brow, looking far too smug. *"You* want to face *me* in a challenge? You?"

"What's wrong, Tharn? Afraid you can't best me if I'm not bound to a chair by iron chains?"

"I fear no one, least of all you." He drew his sword, pointing it toward Greyson in a formal declaration. "Then I challenge you, Prince Greyson of the Fae, to a duel to the death. The winner claims the throne."

Michael's grace flared in protest to the words. If Tharn thought he'd merely stand there and watch any harm befall his mate...

Gabriel's hand closed over his wrist. "Easy. Your mate is more than skilled. Let him decide how to handle this. It *is* his kingdom, and he will be king one day."

Michael reined in his power, meeting Grey's gaze across the glade. His mate nodded, mentally telling him he had this.

Greyson stepped off the platform, closing half the distance between him and Tharn. "I accept your challenge, but let's make one thing clear. Unlike your ancestors, we aren't a barbaric race. We don't fight to the death. The challenge is over when one of us yields."

"Isn't death the ultimate form of that?"

"That is the law. Do you accept?"

"And if I choose to kill you when I have the opportunity, which I suspect won't be long from now?"

"Then your victory will be forfeit, and your chance at the throne along with it."

Tharn snorted. "Very well. But mark my words. *That* will be the first law I change. If you can't win, you're not fit to live." The fae turned, removing his cloak and handing it to his companion.

Michael took the opportunity to dart to Greyson's side. He stepped in front of his mate, waiting until Greyson made eye contact. "What the hell do you think you're doing? I just got you back. You're still sporting scars from that amulet. You're in no condition to fight, Greyson."

Grey palmed his cheek, giving him an easy smile that flipped Michael's stomach and tightened his chest. "I'm Prince of the Fae. I have to answer his challenge. You know that."

"The man is mad. He abducted you and tried to force you to join them. Surely that means something in all of this."

"Whether his request is just or not, it makes no difference." Greyson silenced Michael's protest with a gentle finger across his lips. "Tharn has a point. If I'm not willing to prove I'm fit to rule, I won't have the respect of my people when it comes my time to sit on the throne. If I walk away—or hide behind some words scribbled upon an ancient script—then everything I endured in Purgatory was for nothing."

Michael clenched his jaw, feeling the muscle in his temple flex as he tried to contain his anger. "You know he won't simply allow you to yield."

"He won't have to. I intend on winning." He frowned. "Do you have that little faith in me?"

"Of course not. You can take him and his men. A thousand times over. It's just…"

Greyson leaned in, dropping a quick kiss on his lips. "I love you, too."

Michael huffed. "He'll cheat. Find a way to use his dark arts. Ward yourself. And if I get even an inkling he's going to use that magic to kill you outright…"

"Have I told you you're damn sexy when you go all archangel on me?" He gave Michael a light swat in the shoulder. "I'll be fine."

Michael nodded, stepping aside as Greyson moved forward. "Grey."

His mate stopped, glancing back at him.

Michael motioned toward Tharn. "Kick his ass so fucking hard he'll have to cough up your boots.

CHAPTER TWENTY-TWO

Greyson nodded at Michael, watching his mate make his way back to where Kei and Gabriel waited on the edge of the keep. Despite the reservations that had roiled off Michael in waves, Grey sensed his mate's unwavering faith. His pride. And that was all Greyson needed.

He rolled his shoulders, clearing his mind. Michael was right. Greyson couldn't trust Tharn to keep this challenge strictly swordplay. The dark fae would resort to his magic—quickly—if Grey's hunch was right. And once he did, it allowed Greyson to respond in kind. A hint of white light warmed his chest before settling just beneath the surface.

Tharn glared at him, shifting his gaze between Michael and him. "You know, there was more than just magic inside you when last we met. I sense that same light, only stronger. Please tell me you didn't actually mate with an angel." He laughed. "Dear God, you did. It's written all over your face." He readied himself. "Answer me this? Do you think you'll go to Heaven when you die, now, because of him?"

Grey shrugged. "Perhaps. But one thing I do know—I'm pretty sure I can send your soul to Hell. Ready?"

He didn't wait, launching his attack as soon as Tharn nodded. Tharn parried his sequence, initiating one of his own once he'd knocked Grey slightly sideways. Greyson blocked each swing, mentally cataloguing each strike. While the dark fae displayed excellent sword skills, Grey suspected men like Tharn depended on their strength to overpower an opponent. All Greyson had to do was bide his time until the man tired and opened himself up.

Tharn shuffled back, eyeing Greyson as he circled to his left. "Not bad. You've actually practiced. Perhaps even fought a few battles. I'm impressed. You would have made an excellent slave for us. There's still time if you'd like."

"If you'd like to yield already, be my guest."

Tharn laughed. "Oh my dear boy, we're just getting warmed up."

The fae lunged at Greyson, his blade nothing more than a silver blur as it cut clean arcs through the air. Grey blocked the first few blows, rolling across the ground when Tharn suddenly changed direction mid-stroke, nearly catching Greyson's wing.

He gained his feet, keeping his sword at the ready. Seemed his assumption had been correct. Grey had sensed the small burst of dark energy a moment before the other man's blade had altered course. Though Grey had to hand it to Tharn. He'd been extremely discreet. Enough that Greyson wouldn't be able to use his magic in return.

Greyson heard Michael curse in his mind. Obviously his mate had felt the surge of power as well. Grey looked for an opening, then struck, knocking Tharn back. The dark fae growled, giving Grey a slight shove with his energy before striking again. Grey managed to raise his sword in time, deflecting the swing then landing a kick to the man's chest.

Tharn tumbled backwards, rolling twice before pushing to his feet. He made a show of dusting off his armor, giving Grey a stunning smile. "Well played. I didn't expect you to be this skilled. If only I'd been giving it my all."

The man attacked, using a series of moves that left Grey's muscles aching from the punishing strikes. Sparks bounced across the grass as the blades connected, the metal edges grinding against each other. Grey parried one of the swings, cursing when Tharn took to the air just enough to avoid the blow.

Tharn arched a brow. "Something tells me you've never used your wings as a means of defense. Guess you were too busy hiding what you really were. Pity. It might have made the difference in this fight."

He launched at Grey, feet skimming above the ground, the hum of his wings beating through the air sounding around them. Grey dove out of the way, somehow blocking the man's next strike before catching a slice along his arm. He batted at the fae, jumping back. He managed to gain just enough altitude avoid the next blow, before stumbling a few steps across the glade. Blood welled along the laceration, the telltale burn of iron making him hiss out his next breath. Another curse sounded in his head, Michael's tone far more menacing that it'd been before.

Greyson glared at Tharn. "You have an iron blade?"

Tharn drew himself up, casually flicking Grey's blood off his sword. "Do you not use a weapon you know will have an effect on your enemy?"

"Fae are not my enemy. Even in instances of self-defense, I don't want to kill my own kind. My blade is made of silver. Designed to kill those monsters you seem to enjoy making deals with."

"Then you're a fool. Anyone who challenges you is your enemy. That's how you stay on top. How you gain power and respect."

"You don't want respect, Tharn. You want to rule with fear. With hatred. That's not the makings of a good king. Or a sustainable kingdom. Why do you think we've lasted this long? We don't make enemies when we can make friends. Alliances. It's what separates us from the monsters."

Tharn laughed. "I think you've been spending too much time in the human world. Hanging around with fire mages and angels. They've poisoned your brain. Yield to me, and I'll help you grow into the man you truly should be. You're one of us, Greyson. Prophecy or not, our blood runs through your veins. The wings, the markings—join us and we can make the faery realm great again. Reclaim our position in the universe. Crush the humans who have no respect for nature. For life. If you feel any fondness for them, you can keep them as pets. But stop living in your father's shadow and embrace mine."

Greyson shook his head. "My father is a far greater man, a better leader, than you could ever hope to be. I'm not living in his shadow. I'm standing beside him in the light." He readied his sword. "Make your move."

"You could have lived like an emperor. Instead, you'll grovel at my feet."

Tharn rose into the sky, diving toward Greyson. Grey launched himself backwards into the air, angling right as Tharn bared down on him. The dark fae banked toward him, cursing when Greyson folded his wings, dropping onto his feet. He rolled with the force, once again taking to the skies as Tharn dipped toward him for another pass.

Their swords connected, the impact spinning Grey around. He managed to land a strike across the edge of Tharn's left wing, slicing a thin line as the fae soared past him. The man grunted, gliding to the ground before turning. A deep crimson colored his skin a moment before the red light exploded outwards, rushing toward Greyson. He held out his hands, creating a light blue shield around him. The dark energy hissed as it impacted the barrier, curling around the bubble before slowly fading.

Grey lowered his arms, Michael's grace still shimmering along his skin, as he faced his opponent. "It's against the rules to use your magic as a weapon. But since you initiated the first strike…"

Greyson raised his hands, again, drawing his power to the surface. Brilliant blue light filled the glade, streaks of white softening the color. The energy gathered strength, whipping grass and leaves into the air as clouds billowed into towering masses above his head.

Tharn answered in kind, red glowing all around him as the clouds darkened, creating shadowed pockets along the ground. He threw back his head as he held his arms out wide then snapped both forward, channeling all his energy at Grey. The red streak hit his barriers, angling skyward as the warding held, the blue color finally bleeding into the red.

Tharn frowned, trying again when Grey countered the man's attack, sending a wall of light toward him. Tharn erected his own barrier, the criss-crossing red bars like a giant net spread out before him. The strands crackled when Grey's energy collided with the ward, tendrils of smoke curling up toward the sky. They fanned outward, cloaking the glen in a thick layer of gray.

Greyson readied himself, knowing Tharn would use the smoke to hide his next attack. Grey scanned the area, listening for the telltale hum of the other man's wings, just as a fluttering noise sounded behind him. He turned, using his sword to block Tharn's strike as the man materialized out of the fog. The metal clashed together, knocking Tharn off his path. He stumbled across the ground, tripping onto one knee as he appeared to lose his balance.

Greyson moved toward him, channeling his energy into the ground as he recited a spell. Light flared from the plants surround the glen, a collection of vines shooting out across the grass. They wrapped around Tharn's arms and legs, pulling tight and pinning him to the ground. The fae gasped, muttering words Grey didn't recognize in what he assumed was an attempt to counter his spell.

The vines shook but held as Greyson closed the distance, knocking Tharn's sword away. He pointed the tip of his blade at the man's neck, resisting the urge to scratch a line across his throat. He arched a brow, using more of his energy to clear the air. A series of gasps rose from the crowd, Grey just wasn't sure who was more surprised—his people or Tharn's.

"It's over." Grey held his ground. "You've lost."

"Then do what's right and ensure I don't have the chance to rise again. Strike back when you least expect it."

"I won't kill you. Why let you off so easily when you can spend the next five hundred years reliving this moment? Knowing I was the one who showed you mercy."

Greyson stepped back, slicing through the vines holding the man down. "Tharn of the Dark Fae. As heir to the throne, I hereby banish you and your followers from this realm. Any attempt to return, or inflict harm on the people under Oberon's protection, shall be deemed treason against the crown and shall be punishable by death." He bent low. "Now get the hell out of my kingdom, and never come back."

He spun, moving quickly away from the man before he changed his mind and erased the threat as Tharn had suggested. But doing so would make him no better than the dark fae, and he'd be damned if he allowed the man's hatred to infect him. He stopped once he'd gotten several yards away, turning back to face his opponent.

Tharn rose, brushing bits of vine off his armor. He lifted his hands, clapping them together in mock celebration. "Well played. That bit with the vines—you do know your spells. Though, they're far more limited than mine. There's just something about dark energy—it overpowers the light."

"I'm not interested in your power. You issued a challenge, and you lost. Now leave."

Oberon stepped forward, remaining off to Greyson's right and still looking far too calm. "It would be wise to listen to the future King of the Fae, before I decide to block the entrance to the shadow lands in such a way your kin can never return."

Tharn cocked his head to the side. "Something tells me you'll never welcome them back, anyway, so...I've got nothing to lose."

He gathered his magic, the air crackling around them as a crimson ball materialized in his hands. He aimed it at Oberon, releasing it in a fiery haze. Oberon raised a barrier, deflecting the energy out to the sides, forcing Greyson to shield himself from the backlash as flames danced around him. He saw another blast hit his father's wards, a few fingers of red light getting through.

Greyson reacted, lowering his barrier in order to channel his magic beyond his father, stopping Tharn's energy from hitting the crowd gathered in the keep. The two lights collided, exploding the dark magic toward the sky. Greyson muttered a quick spell, tying the warding off so it remained in place when movement caught his eye. He twisted just as another ball headed toward him, too close for him to do more that brace against the inevitable hit. The light rushed at him, prickling the hairs on his arms before suddenly bursting into a thousand fractured shards. Sparks erupted in an ever-increasing circle, curling around the edge of a white light before vanishing amidst an angelic glow.

Grey inhaled, staring at Michael as he stood in front of them, wings stretched to either side, his skin burning so brightly Grey had to shield his eyes against the glare. A hint of blue wove through the light, a testament to their unique bond.

"Damn it." Tharn stomped a few feet closer, pointing at Michael. "You're starting to become a real fucking pain in my ass, angel. First, you somehow get yourself transported to Purgatory—a feat I honestly thought even Lucifer couldn't achieve—then you block my strike." He crossed his arms over his chest. "There was enough power in that ball to destroy ten angels, yet, there you are—still standing. Your damn skin glowing like a beacon straight from Heaven. Who, exactly, are you?"

His mate locked his gaze on Tharn, the shine on his flesh increasing. "They call me Michael."

CHAPTER TWENTY-THREE

Michael stood there, his grace barely contained beneath his flesh, as Tharn's eyes widened. The bastard gave him a long, slow sweep before shaking his head.

"Your name is Michael?" Tharn looked past Michael at Greyson. "His name is Michael? You're mated to an archangel?"

"So, you've heard of me."

Tharn snapped his focus back to Michael. "Heard of you?" He whistled. "They tell me you're God's Warrior. His deadliest weapon. I'm told that it was fear of you and your brothers, in particular, that compelled my faery kin to make a pact with your God. Protect the mortal realm and forsake my ancestors because they didn't share His faith in humanity."

"Earth was never yours to claim."

"You're the reason my people dwell in the shadows."

"Belfrey was the cause of your ancestor's exile, not Heaven."

"None of that matters. This isn't your fight. This has

nothing to do with your precious human world. It's a matter within the faery realm. You have no authority here, or are you breaking that treaty? Claiming this realm as Heaven's property?"

"You mistake my intent, Tharn. I don't stand before you as an ambassador of Heaven. I'm here as the mate of the Prince of the Fae. That gives me the right to defend him and his people." Michael reined in his power. "The crown has shown you mercy. I suggest you accept it and leave."

"I'm not done, yet."

Tharn launched another attack, hurtling several bursts of energy at Michael. He released his hold on his grace, erecting a massive wall of light across the glade. The spheres smashed against his barrier, hissing from the contact before breaking apart. More smoke billowed around them, blocking out Tharn's warriors. Michael shifted his warding to join Greyson's and protect his mate's people, when Tharn appeared in front of him, sword cutting through the air. Michael drew his weapon, catching enough of Tharn's blade to deflect the strike aimed at his chest. Instead, it sliced a line down his arm before he was able to toss Tharn back with a burst of his power. Pain teased the edge of his consciousness as the laceration began to burn, small tendrils of heat rising from the cut.

Tharn laughed, picking himself up off the ground, even as Michael's friends moved to stand behind him, Greyson placing himself directly at Michael's side. The dark fae pointed to Michael, amusement tilting his lips. "Oh, this is just too good. An angel affected by iron. Don't you see? Your connection weakens you. *He* weakens you."

Michael glanced at the wound, noting the charred edges. The red welts along each side. Greyson inhaled sharply beside him. He moved closer, but Michael shook his head, giving his mate a reassuring smile.

He met Tharn's gaze, absently wiping the blood off his skin. "That's where you're wrong. While I might have a few new…traits as a result of our pairing, Greyson's soul is far stronger than mine. He's my greatest asset. The unwavering light that banishes my doubts. He's the reason you'll lose."

He took a step forward, channeling his grace. Clouds gathered overhead as the wind picked up around them, whirling dirt and leaves through the air. Lightning flashed in the distance as rain pelted the ground, creating a fine mist that wove through the glade, casting a warm, white glow across the land.

Michael pointed at Tharn, his and Greyson's energies burning bright across his skin. "Tharn of the Dark Fae. You have been banished from this land."

More lightning forked across the sky, impacting the ground not far from where they were gathered. Thunder rumbled through the clouds, shaking the earth beneath them.

He motioned back the way they'd come. "Leave now, or I swear I will rain the wrath of Heaven upon you and your followers."

Tharn's men looked around the glen, eyes wide, brows creased. Indecision hunched their shoulders as they all took one step back.

"Stay your ground!" Tharn stood firm, his magic fanning out around him in an eerie black smear against the green background. "He's but one angel."

"I'm not alone."

"Neither am I."

"You don't have enough warriors to win this fight."

Tharn tipped back his head and laughed again. "Do you really think this small contingency of men is all I brought with me?"

He spread out his arms, increasing the darkness behind him until it blanketed the entire glade. Dozens of warriors stepped out of the shadows, eyes gleaming red, their combined power saturating the air—making it hard to breathe.

Tharn grinned, focusing on Michael. "Are you so sure you can take all of us? Before this erupts into a bloody war? Because the backlash from this much dark energy engaged in battle will level this entire glen. There'll be no safe havens left. What price are you willing to pay to see your mate sit upon the throne? That's assuming there's anyone left for him to rule."

Greyson nudged Michael's arm. "He's right." He kept his voice low, just enough to carry between the four of them. "If they all attack us using their magic—the clashing of dark and light will destroy my realm."

"I'm done dealing with subordinates." Tharn pointed at Oberon. "Oberon, King of the Fae. Either surrender to me, or I will see your kingdom burned to the ground."

The man in question merely glanced at his son. "You decided the ultimate fate of this meeting, Tharn, when you challenged my son. As per faery law, it's his to finish as he sees fit. Any interference on my part would violate that law, and grant you the Right of Ascension." The man's earthly glow shimmered around him and his kin. "I have complete faith that Greyson will do what's needed. Even if it seems…contradictory at first."

"Then the prince has one minute to decide the fate of his kingdom. And I think we both know I'm not bluffing."

Greyson glanced at Michael. "I can't give in to Tharn's demands, but…it's not just my life at risk."

"It's not defeating Tharn that worries me. Gabriel, Kei and I can deal with his forces. But it will take a great deal of power. I'm not sure how much damage will result. I know not all faery gifts are the same, which means some aren't capable of phasing the way you do. Are you strong enough to get your people clear? Take them to a distant part of the glade?"

"The only safe place is another realm. Their dark energy will stain the land. Poison the air. Even if we win, there's a good chance my world will become uninhabitable."

"They can go back to the humans."

"With the portals warded, it'll be slow going. I can't transport that many at a time. I never thought about a threat from within…"

"Within what?" Michael grabbed his mate. "Greyson."

He lifted his gaze to meet Michael's. "Contradictory."

"I don't understand."

"My father. He was trying to give me a message." Grey shook his head. "It doesn't matter." He placed his hands on Michael's vest. "Do you trust me?"

"With my soul."

"Then I think I have an idea. But…I'll need the three of you to keep their energy contained. Prevent it from spilling over into the rest of the glen. When I call you, we'll need to get them into the sacred garden."

"This doesn't sound like a safe plan. Is it at least better than your idea to summon my brother? Lock Abaddon in a book?"

"Need I remind you, both of those worked?"

Michael huffed. "One day, we're going to talk about these crazy schemes of yours."

"Like the one where I got you to give me one night?"

"Just like that." Michael placed his fist across his chest. "I'll do all I can to keep your kingdom safe."

"*Our* kingdom. I'll call you. Remember, the garden."

Michael snagged Greyson's arm. "I love you."

"Your minute is up, Prince." Red sparks crackled around Tharn. "Bow to me, or watch your kingdom die."

Greyson turned to face Tharn. "I told you before. I'll die before I surrender to the likes of you. If it's a battle you want, then step forward, but I promise, it's the last you'll see of this realm."

Tharn grinned. "As you wish. Just remember—the blood of your people is on your hands."

Michael moved in front of Greyson, glancing back at his mate. "Go. We'll contain their power as much as possible."

Grey nodded, appearing a moment later in front of his father, his head bent low in conversation. Oberon arched his brow, glancing at them before nodding. He waved his hands, tied off his barriers, then vanished with his son.

Michael readied himself, sword in one hand, his grace strumming just beneath his skin. The hint of blue coloring his flesh helped him focus. He'd meant what he'd said. Greyson was, by far, his greatest strength. Though, he'd have to be cautious of his new limitations, as he had no doubt Tharn would try to capitalize on them. The laceration along Michael's arm burned in agreement as a suffocating silence descended on the glade, as if both sides were simply waiting for the perfect moment to strike.

Shadows creeped along the ground, like fingers stretching toward them. Michael released some of his grace, pushing the dark energy back toward Tharn's forces. Gabriel followed suit, flames flickering within his orange light.

Tharn looked behind him, giving his men a curt nod before brandishing his sword. "For Belfrey!"

He attacked, a blast of darkness exploding in all directions. Michael countered with a surge of white light, keeping the black essence from shooting past them. It arced upward, coiling in the air just beneath the clouds, streaking them a bloody shade of red.

He held firm, wanting to engage—to use his grace to level Tharn's warriors—but it meant lowering the barrier. And it would only take a small amount of darkness to poison the royal grounds and beyond. To fail.

Another wave hit his wards as more of Tharn's men channeled their power. The impact knocked him back, leaving two grooves in the ground as he slid across the wet grass, leaning into the pressure to hold his position. Red flames danced along his barrier, searching for any form of weakness.

Michael growled, drawing more of his power to the surface. His light gleamed white against the blackness, once again chasing away the shadows. A loud scream sounded nearby, followed by a sword slicing toward him. He dove out of the way, allowing his grace to feed the wards as he turned to face the new threat. Tharn appeared amidst the gray smoke, skin glowing red, his sword pulsing with crimson light.

The fae snarled, then charged, no hint of fear in the firm line of his back or the tight press of his lips. He swung at Michael's head, altering each blow as Michael blocked the sequence, landing a strike across Tharn's biceps when he overshot one hit.

The fae hissed, glancing at the blood dripping down his arm. "Not bad. But how long can you fight and still maintain your barrier?"

He charged again, gaining ground as Michael divided his efforts between maintaining the ward and deflecting Tharn's strikes. He didn't need to best the man, just keep the bastard and his men from breeching the glade's protection.

Fatigue burned his muscles when Tharn launched into the air, swooping down at Michael. He pushed off, but only managed a few moments of flight before crashing to the ground. Pain thrummed through his wings, the glamour he'd created to hide the broken limbs fading.

Tharn landed nearby. "An angel who can't fly. How poetic."

Michael drew himself up. "I don't need wings to best you."

"But they'd sure as shit help, wouldn't they?"

He took off, circling around before aiming at Michael. He readied his sword, aware Tharn's added maneuverability gave the dark fae an edge, when a blast of fire knocked the man out of the sky. He hit hard, smoke curling up from his body. Michael spun. Kei stood several feet off, flames licking skyward from his palms. Blood stained one of his shoulders, more cuts along his ribs.

The mage grinned. "Didn't think you'd get all the payback, did you? Bastard hurt my friend."

"You're injured."

"Gabe can fix me once this is over."

"Shouldn't you be beside him? So he can harness his grace?"

Kei's mouth kicked up farther. "We're...improving. Let's just hope Greyson's nearly done. We won't last too much longer without actually engaging them."

Kei turned when a group of warriors appeared behind him. He muttered some words, sending a strange blue wave across the ground. The men froze, seemingly stuck in place.

Kei glanced back at Michael. "Grey's not the only one with a few spells. You worry about the dark magic. I'll hold these soldiers back."

He disappeared into the smoke, his fire lighting up the gray mass. Michael cursed. If anything happened to Kei because of him...

"Now. Michael. The garden."

Greyson's voice echoed in his head, pain lacing his words. Urgency prickled his skin as he turned, staring at Tharn as he picked himself up. Perhaps if Michael grabbed Tharn, the rest would follow. He took a step when the air thrummed around him.

Oberon appeared beside him, fatigue creasing his brow. "I can get Tharn's forces there, but the toll... I won't be able to help."

"I won't let anything happen to Greyson. You have my word."

The elder fae nodded, sweeping his hands in the air. A green glow slowly covered the glade, stretching out past the gathering of Tharn's men. Tharn turned toward his warriors, barking out orders, but the words were crushed beneath the hum of Oberon's magic as its light grew in intensity, finally blocking out the rest of the glen.

The scenery shifted, blurring into a wash of colors before jerking back. Michael tripped onto one knee from the sudden jarring motion, the hard dirt biting into his flesh. He glanced up, eyes wide. Tharn's contingency now stood within the sacred garden, their numbers scattered amidst the foliage. Oberon was stretched across the grass beside him, eyes closed, a dim glow sinking back beneath his flesh.

He reached for the man when a red ball whirled past his head, impacting some trees behind him. The bark hissed, the brown color bleeding into black as the leaves withered and fell, nothing but dead brittle branches swaying in the light breeze. He searched the grounds, locking his gaze on Tharn as the man staggered to a halt beside a stone bench, another red sphere hovering above his palm.

He motioned to the surroundings. "A garden? That's your final play? You think some sacred trees are going to stop us?"

"Not trees, exactly, Tharn."

Michael snapped his gaze up as Greyson's voice echoed through the garden. His mate stood directly behind them on a raised platform, his skin glowing a light blue color.

Tharn glared at him. "Are you done running? Ready to fight with your angel, or have you brought us here to surrender? Save what you can of your glade."

"On the contrary. I'm giving you one last chance to surrender. Leave now, or face your punishment."

"I see you choose death." Tharn readied his blade, his magic whipping wildly around him.

Grey pointed at Tharn. "Then you leave me no choice."

He turned and raised his hands, his magic flaring brightly behind him, making his silhouette ghost-like against the glare. The collection of vines on the far side of him shook as Grey's magic wove through the thorny stems, lighting them up in the same patterns that swirled across his flesh. The ground rumbled beneath them, chunks of dirt erupting into the air. Dark clouds gathered overhead and lightning forked across the sky.

Grey started chanting, his voice a lilting tone above the rolls of thunder. The vines began spinning, slowly unraveling until they exposed a metal gate. Greyson pointed his palms at the iron bars, unleashing a stream of blue light. It stuck the center, exploding into red shards as the gate creaked then opened. A water-like film covered the entrance, distorting the images beyond. Though there was no mistaking the long, thorn-covered passage that extended beyond the barrier, two dark silhouettes standing at the far end.

Grey glanced back over his shoulder then channeled his magic against the barrier, sending ripples out across the surface. They gathered strength increasing in size until they began coiling in on themselves. The motion created a funnel, drawing leaves and twigs off the garden floor into the vortex. A familiar symbol burned red within the abyss then faded to black.

"No!" Tharn tried to back away, the gusting wind already dragging his men toward the opening. "This can't be! The prophecy wasn't fulfilled. You don't have the power."

Greyson's body glowed, his hair whipping about his head as he braced himself against the strong wind. "That's where you're wrong, Tharn. The power was always inside me. I just had to choose to use it." His flesh glowed brighter. "You want to see your kin again so much, you can join them."

An ungodly howl roared through the garden, shaking the trees as rain struck the ground. The wind picked up, dragging the first row of warriors into the funnel. They thrashed against the churning current then disappeared beneath the surface.

More quickly followed as the pull increased, uprooting a few small trees and sucking them into the hole. Michael stuck his blade in the ground then grabbed Oberon, tugging him close. He used the elder fae's sword to wedge the man in place, keep him from being dragged into the abyss. Tharn fought against the punishing force, sliding feet first across the grass when his sword snapped in half. He clawed at the dirt, halting his movement for several moments. A noise sounded beyond the whirling mass, and Michael knew the dark fae were trying to break through.

Tharn kicked at the stones beneath his feet, screaming when his lost his hold and flew toward the entrance. He slammed against the edge of the gate, wedging his foot on the iron bars enough to launch forward. One fist closed around Greyson's shirt, tripping Grey forward as the wind grabbed ahold of both of them. Tharn sank halfway below the surface, still taking Greyson with him. Grey extended his arm, using his magic to anchor him to a tree. The trunk creaked, but held as Grey continued to power the vortex.

"Greyson!"

Michael let go of his hilt, allowing the strong eddies to fling him forward. He twisted in the air, using his massive wingspan to veer him off to one side. He landed to the right of Grey, one foot locked on the top of the gate, the other near the bottom. He reached for his mate, grabbing the man's sword from his belt. He raised his arm, slicing the blade through the air. It cut through Grey's shirt where it bulged out from Tharn's hand, severing their connection. Tharn held still for one more heartbeat, then disappeared beneath the watery surface. Michael levered off the gate, taking Greyson to the ground as he tackled the man.

Grey shoved at him. "I need to shut it before they come through."

Michael rolled to his feet, yanking Greyson up. He aimed his light at the gate again, this time using his power to close it and recoil the thorns. Shouts echoed from beyond the barrier, slowly fading into silence as the vines clamped shut, any trace of Greyson's magic winking out.

Grey sagged against Michael, his head lolling against Michael's chest. Michael shouldered the man's weight, helping him back to the stone bench. He lowered him onto the seat, brushing his hair back from his face. Sweat and dirt caked his skin, dark smudges lining his eyes.

Michael shook his head. "That was your plan? To unlock the gate to the shadow lands and suck Tharn's army inside?"

Grey chuckled. "It sounded far better in my head."

"Most plans do." He smiled as Gabriel and Kei joined them. "How did you know your father could transport that many dark fae here?"

"Are you kidding? He's not the king for nothing. Though he'll probably be out for a week."

Michael glanced at the vines. "Did you mean what you said? You have the ability to open that barrier whenever you choose?"

"It wasn't the prophecy that gave me the power, Michael. Tharn simply tried to abuse it. Use it for evil. Wasn't it Gabriel who said that it's a choice to stay in the light?"

Gabriel laughed. "I'm glad at least one person listens to me."

Kei swatted the man in the chest. "I listen."

"The same way you promised to stay close. Is that how you got those gashes across your body?"

Kei's expression softened. "I knew you could heal me. And if the darkness had gotten through..."

"Thanks to both of you, it didn't." Michael twisted and cupped Greyson's chin, waiting until his mate gazed up at him. "Don't scare me like that again, mate."

Grey grinned. "Can't let Gabriel and Kei have all the fun adventures." He kissed Michael's palm. "But I could do with a break. For a few days. I'll just see my father—"

Gabriel placed a hand on Grey's shoulder. "We'll take Oberon back to his chambers. I think you two look even worse than when you got back from Purgatory. Go. Rest. I remember how intense those first few days are after bonding. We'll alert you if you're needed."

Michael stood, giving his brother a gracious nod. "Thank you. Now, which way..."

His voice keened into a gasp as the air thrummed, blurring into light blue before setting. They were back in Greyson's cabin, Grey pinned between him and the counter. He glanced down, not surprised to see bare skin amidst the wood furnishings.

He arched an eyebrow. "You aren't strong enough to waste your power like that. We could have walked."

"Seems I was more than strong enough, and walking would have taken far too long." He wrapped his arms around Michael's neck. "Now, I recall promising to feed you. I'm betting you've never had breakfast in bed before."

"It appears I'm in for a number of firsts."

He locked his hand behind Grey's head, stealing a long, lingering kiss. Greyson grinned, chuckling when Michael cursed as the world shifted once more and he landed on the bed, Grey straddled across him.

Michael arched his brow. "I thought we were having breakfast in bed?"

Greyson shrugged. "Technically, we're in bed."

"You don't look like it's food you want."

"I was kind of hoping that maybe you were hungry for something else."

Michael grinned, channeling his grace then flipping them over. He stared down at his mate, skimming one hand over the swirls along his skin. "Always. But I believe it's my turn."

"It was your turn in the shower. It's definitely my turn."

Michael dipped down, dropping a kiss on the edge of Grey's mouth. "And to think you only asked for one night."

Greyson's mouth kicked up into a huge smile. "Looks like my plan worked perfectly."

"Did that include the detour to Purgatory? Nearly having your kingdom wiped out by the dark fae?"

"That was just a bonus. Think of the stories we can tell a thousand years from now." Grey palmed his cheeks, his hazel eyes wide. "I know I asked you to make the last night worth remembering for a millennium, but...how about another go at it? Think you can make this one even more memorable?"

Michael chuckled. "That sounds like a challenge, Grey. I am God's Warrior. Can't back down. So I suggest you get comfortable. This night's going to last a lifetime."

EXCERPT ~ LUCIFER

"I'm sorry. But I can't bow before them, Father." Lucifer rolled his shoulders, snapping his wings in a show of defiance. "I won't."

The field where they were gathered grew silent, nothing but the odd whisper of the breeze along his feathers sounding above the eerie quiet. He didn't move, didn't flinch as clouds slowly gathered overhead, the white color bleeding into black. A few hushed voices finally rose around him as the wind picked up, stumbling him a few steps closer to his father before Lucifer had the strength to push back—halt his movements. Thunder boomed above them, a flicker of lightning charging the air.

A shadow fell in beside his—smaller. More delicate. He didn't have to turn around to sense her presence. He felt her heartbeat echo in his head. Smelled the sweet essence of her skin surround him. He wasn't sure why she affected him the way she did. Why he wanted to gather her in his arms—love her in the same fashion as the very creatures his father wanted him to honor. To kneel before.

His brother stepped out from the line of angels standing on the other side of the clearing, Michael's gaze falling on Lucifer. Michael had been the first to bow—to swear his service to their father's new creations—not that it surprised Lucifer. Michael had always been the good son. The one to follow commands without question. Lucifer wouldn't have expected any less of the angel.

Michael sighed. "You must yield, brother. I beg of you."

Lucifer lifted his chin. He didn't like going against his family. Seeing disappointment gleam in Michael's eyes. Lucifer had always looked up to his older brother. Had idolized him and had always wanted to be close to him. He'd even gone so far as to establish his sanctuary close to Michael's. Standing there, on opposite sides, made Lucifer want to acquiesce.

He glanced at his father. "I've done everything you've ever asked of me. I've fought your battles. I've made everything you hold dear sacred to me. And not once have I questioned your orders. But this... I won't bow to a race that will never love you the way I do. Please don't ask me to."

Michael's expression fell before he looked away, shoulders hunched, eyes closed. Lucifer frowned, moving forward, when pain blossomed in his chest. His breath hitched, held prisoner by the crushing force in his chest. Stones bit into his knees as he lurched forward, the scenery dimming around him.

A small hand landed on his arm. He managed to catch a glimpse of the green in her eyes before a blinding white light blanketed the area. Lucifer covered his eyes with his arm, shouting Michael's name when the ground vanished beneath him. There was a moment of silence, then the air rushed past him, crushing his cries for help. He opened his wings, doing his best to slow his descent, as the earth raced upwards. He braced for impact, inhaling sharply when he passed through the surface, still falling amidst the darkness. Heat arced across his skin, momentarily lighting up the surroundings. He clenched his jaw as the surface rushed toward him, slamming into him.

Pain splintered through his body, the taste of blood and dirt heavy on his tongue. He focused on breathing, groaning against the fiery sensation in his ribs until he was able to open his eyes. Shadows spread out around him, the only light coming from a flicker of flames far off in the distance. Sulfur saturated the air, the pungent aroma making his stomach heave.

He pushed onto his hands and knees, gasping in several searing breaths. Even the air burned, the taste of smoke making him cough. He waited until the retching stopped, ignoring how his limbs shook when he tried to bridge his weight. His once white wings had turned a bloody shade of red, some of the feathers littering the stone surface around him. He glanced to his left and his heart stopped cold.

She was lying on the ground not far from him, eyes closed, lips pursed into a grimace. Her wings stretched out to either side, the golden feathers nothing more than blackened ash against the gray stone. Blood covered most of her creamy skin, a small pool collecting beneath her.

"No. Not her. Please."

Lucifer crawled over to her, staring at her limp body

before brushing back her pale hair from her face. Her eyes squeezed shut, then opened, most of the spark he'd always admired gone. She dampened her lips, crying out as she tried to move her head to look at him.

He shushed her. "Just, lie still. Let me heal you."

She shook her head, somehow managing to grab his hands as he placed them on her chest. "No, Lucifer. You can't. It's too late."

"Don't say that. I still have my power, I feel it, I..." He swallowed past the lump in his throat. "Please, don't leave me, Grace. I can live through anything if I have you with me. You're all I need."

She gave him a stunning smile, lifting one hand to touch his face. "It won't be forever. You'll find me, again. I know it. And when you do, we can be together for as long as you'll love me."

"I already love you that much." He gave her a gentle shake when she closed her eyes. "Grace!"

Lucifer shook his head. He wouldn't fail her. Not now, when she'd stood beside him—loved him enough to defy her birthright. He drew on the power still strumming inside him. A golden glow surrounded him, the color quickly fading into red as he tried to heal her broken body. But despite the surge of energy he pumped into her fragile form, the light faded from her eyes. She whispered her love one last time, before her head lolled to the side, and her eyes drifted shut.

Another flash of white light knocked Lucifer back on his ass. He covered his face, again, waiting for the glow to fade before blinking away the fuzziness. Nothing but a ghostly outline of her body remained, a single, golden feather resting on the rock.

Lucifer picked it up, holding it against his chest as a numbing cold bled through his body. He tipped back his head, staring at the endless darkness above him. "Why? Why did you have to hurt her? I'm the one you're mad at. Punish me!"

He waited, but only his own ragged breathing sounded around him.

"Father!"

Panic quickened his heart as the absolute silence suffocated the area. Was this really how it ended?

"Michael. Hear me." Lucifer reached out for the connection he'd always shared with his brothers, focusing on Michael. If he could reach anyone, it would be him.

A hazy image formed in Lucifer's head—Michael on his knees, hands fisted on the patch of dirt where Lucifer had been standing just moments before. Tears glistened in the angel's eyes, before he closed them.

The picture faded into black, all sense of his brother vanishing with it. Emptiness filled Lucifer's chest, burning as surely as the fires in the distance. He let his head bow forward, staring at the desolate stone as the reality of his fate sank in. He'd been cast out. Exiled to some kind of barren wasteland. And Grace had paid the price. Had suffered for being close to him. For loving him.

Lucifer pushed to his feet, the feather still clutched in his hand. This wasn't over. Not until he'd found a way to make his father's beloved creations suffer the same loss. Until he'd buried his love for life—for everything—so far inside him, nothing and no one could ever resurrect it, again. Until the very Earth crumbled around him.

Present Day…

"Lucifer."

Lucifer groaned inwardly, closing his eyes as Michael's voice echoed inside his mind. While he generally enjoyed being a thorn in Michael's psyche, now wasn't the time. *"Christ, Mikey, if I'd known you'd use this connection to check up on me every fucking time I ventured to my sanctuary, I never would have made it in the first place. It's bad enough you can 'sense' me moving through the wards."*

A hesitant sigh sounded from his brother, followed by a long, slow breath. *"I'm not checking up on you. Not, really."*

Lucifer laughed. *"So, you're inside my head because you wanted to chat? And to think I was still planning on kicking your ass the next time we met."*

"Must you make it so hard? Every time?"

"Try telling me the truth, and maybe I'll be more reasonable."

"I'm not lying. I didn't call out to you as a means of spying on you. I just wanted…"

Lucifer stilled at the desperate quality in Michael's voice. He hadn't heard that tone since his big brother had pleaded with him to bow before humanity—that last peaceful moment before Lucifer had been cast out.

Lucifer straightened, ignoring the indignant huff of the woman sleeping beside him. He didn't often bring humans to his sanctuary, but tonight was different. He'd wanted to escape—to pretend for a few precious hours that he wasn't an outcast. That somewhere, someone missed him—felt the same empty hollow in the pit of their stomach, as if a piece was missing.

He glanced at the woman. She resembled Grace—same

golden shade of hair, with delicate features and pale skin. But that's where the similarities ended. And he knew, he could parade an endless number of women through his door, each one a better replica than the one before, but none of them would be *her*—that her soul was forever lost to him.

"Lucifer?"

He released a weary breath. *"I'm still here. Can't really go anywhere, can I?"* He chuckled. *"Okay, you've got my attention. Why did you ring me up if you're not trying pinpoint my exact location?"*

Silence stretched between them until Michael grunted. *"I told Grey this was a bad idea. That there was just too much... shit between us. But you know how Fae are—forever optimistic, especially where family is concerned."*

"You've lost me, brother. What has your mate got to do with you chattering away inside my head?"

"Grey thinks we should...talk more. About regular stuff. Try to bridge this gap between us."

Lucifer chuckled. *"Your faery prince thinks we should be besties? How quaint."*

"He didn't...seriously, Lucifer? Must you mock everything and everyone?"

"Need I remind you that until Gabriel's fire mage decided to summon my ass from the fiery depths of Hell, in a desperate attempt to stop Abbadon from torching all of humanity, I hadn't seen any of you since... Well, since the night Dad tossed me out. Which was on this very night, a few thousand years ago, if you're keeping track."

"Fuck... Tonight's the anniversary?" He sighed. *"I didn't..."*

"Whatever. Though, I'm glad that bit of grace I left you has

loosened that stick you used to have shoved up your ass. Or maybe Greyson did that. Tell me, how is mated life treating you?"

Lucifer's stomach clenched as the words rolled off his tongue. What the Hell was he doing? The last thing he needed was to be reminded of what he'd really lost that night so long ago—*who'd* he'd lost.

Michael's sharp intake of breath drew his attention. *"Are you...okay?"*

"I thought you wanted to talk about regular things?"

"I do, it's just...even for you, you sound...off." Michael murmured something Lucifer couldn't make out. *"It's the anniversary, isn't it? I should have realized..."*

"It's been a couple of millennia. I think the initial shock is over."

But the pain of losing Grace—the part of his soul he knew he'd never find, again, even if his father ever forgave him. If Lucifer was ever welcomed back home—that never lessened. Never stop poking at him. It was the one festering wound he couldn't heal.

"You say that, but...all those echoed thoughts in your head I'm picking up on... I don't believe you. I think it's still as fresh as it always was. And I think it will be until you get back what you lost."

"No one can give me back what I lost, Michael. Not even Father."

"That's not true. There's always a way back home."

"Is that why you think I'm upset? Because I can't go home? Christ, I don't think any of you ever truly knew me."

"But...what else is there?"

"As if you don't know."

"Know what?"

There was no mistaking the tightness in Michael's

voice. The edge of fear that hadn't been there before.

Lucifer huffed. *"You really don't know?"*

"I'll say it, again. Know what? Dad cast you into Hell. What else is there to know?"

"How about the part where I wasn't alone?"

He swung his legs over the edge of the bed then pushed to his feet, opening the small iron chest on the table beside the bed. A single golden feather rested against the red velvet interior.

He picked it up, cradling it gently in the palm of his hand. *"Why did she have to pay for my choice? Explain that to me, big brother!"*

"She?" His breathing kicked up. *"I don't understand. Who are you talking about?"*

Lucifer groaned. He needed to derail this conversation. Now. *"It doesn't matter. No one can change what happened, and I have to spend eternity knowing she died because I wasn't strong enough to save her."* He scrubbed a hand down his face. *"I'm tired. And I'd rather spend the rest of this cursed night with the lovely lady sleeping in my bed, so…if we're done here."*

"Lucifer. Please. Talk to me. Who died? Who fell with you?"

He chuckled. *"If you really want to know, why don't you go ask dear-ole Dad. I'm sure he'd love to chat. Say hi to Greyson for me. We'll talk, again."*

Lucifer cut off the connection, building a barrier even his father wouldn't be able to break. Then, he leaned against the wall, staring out the window at the starlit sky. Grace would have loved it here—the rocks. The moonlight. The endless silence. But he hadn't gotten the chance to bring her. Just another regret to add to the list.

He glanced at the feather, raking his hand through his hair as he watched a shooting star light up the sky, a ghostly image of her wavering in the distance. His mind playing tricks on him as it did every year on this night. And if she seemed just a bit more real this time, it was only his imagination. She was lost, and despite her parting words, he'd never find her, again.

ABOUT THE AUTHOR

Author, single mother, slave to chaos—she's a jack-of-all-trades who's constantly looking for her ever elusive clone.

Subscribe to her newsletter to get the latest scoop on new and upcoming releases as well as exclusive free reads.

https://www.subscribepage.com/krisnorris

Kris loves connecting with fellow book enthusiasts. You can follow her on these social media platforms...

krisnorris.ca
contactme@krisnorris.ca

facebook.com/kris.norris.731

twitter.com/kris_norris

instagram.com/girlnovelist

amazon.com/author/krisnorris